Colliding with the Coffee Shop Owner

Angel's Peak

Ellie Masters

Master of Romantic Suspense

JEM Publishing

DEDICATION

This book is dedicated to my one and only—my amazing and wonderful husband.

Without your care and support, my writing would not have made it this far.

You pushed me when I needed to be pushed.

You supported me when I felt discouraged.

You believed in me when I didn't believe in myself.

If it weren't for you, this book never would have come to life.

ALSO BY ELLIE MASTERS

The LIGHTER SIDE

Ellie Masters is the lighter side of the Jet & Ellie Masters writing duo! You will find Contemporary Romance, Military Romance, Romantic Suspense, Billionaire Romance, and Rock Star Romance in Ellie's Works.

YOU CAN FIND ELLIE'S BOOKS HERE:

ELLIEMASTERS.COM/BOOKS

Shop Ellie Masters Romantic Suspense and Steamy Contemporary Romance by series.

Angel Fire Rock Romance

Guardian HRS: Alpha Team

Guardian HRS: Bravo Team

Guardian HRS: Charlie Team

Guardian HRS: Delta Team

Cerberus Personal Security

The LaRouge Triplets

The One I Want Series

Angel's Peak Series

Billionaire Boy's Club

The Lovers

Changing Roles

Rescuing Jinx

Rescuing Maria

Bravo Team

Rescuing Angie

Rescuing Isabelle

Rescuing Carmen

Rescuing Rosalie

Rescuing Kaye

Cara's Protector

Rescuing Barbi

Charlie Team

Rescuing Rebel

Rescuing Stitch

Rescuing Mia

Jenna's Protector

Rescuing Sophia

Rescuing Malia

Rescuing Ally (Part 1)

Rescuing Ally (Part 2)

Delta Team

Rescuing Ember

Rescuing Aria

STANDALONES IN THE GUARDIAN HOSTAGE RESCUE SERIES YOU CAN READ ANYTIME

Military Romance

Guardian Personal Protection Specialists

Sybil's Protector

Lyra's Protector

Angel's Peak Series

Steamy Instalove Small Town

EACH BOOK IN THIS SERIES CAN BE READ AS A STANDALONE AND IS ABOUT A DIFFERENT COUPLE WITH AN HEA.

SNOWED IN WITH THE MOUNTAIN DOCTOR

Rescued by the Mountain Guide

Stranded with the Resort Owner

Matched with the Small-Town Chef

Trapped with the Forest Ranger

Snowbound with the Vineyard Owner

Reunited with the Hometown Hero

Colliding with the Coffee Shop Owner

Falling for the Firefighter

Wrecked with the Reclusive Author

Tangled with the Single Dad

Whirlwinded by the Helicopter Pilot

Sheltered by the Veterinarian

Bound by the Sheriff

The One I Want Series

(Small Town, Military Heroes)

By Jet & Ellie Masters

EACH BOOK IN THIS SERIES CAN BE READ AS A STANDALONE AND IS ABOUT A DIFFERENT COUPLE WITH AN HEA.

Saving Abby

Saving Ariel

Saving Brie

Saving Cate

Saving Dani

Saving Jen

The LaRouge Triplets

Asher

Brody

Cage

Billionaire Romance
Billionaire Boys Club

Hawke

Richard

Contemporary Romance

Cocky Captain

Romantic Suspense

EACH BOOK IS A STANDALONE NOVEL.

The Starling

The Swan

~AND~

Science Fiction

Ellie Masters writing as L.A. Warren

Vendel Rising: a Science Fiction Serialized Novel

To My Readers

This book is a work of fiction. It does not exist in the real world and should not be construed as reality. As in most romantic fiction, I've taken liberties. I've compressed the romance into a sliver of time. I've allowed these characters to develop strong bonds of trust over a matter of days.

This does not happen in real life where you, my amazing readers, live. Take more time in your romance and learn who you're giving a piece of your heart to. I urge you to move with caution. Always protect yourself.

Angel's Peak

Grab the First Book in The Guardian Hostage Rescue Specialists Series for Free

https://elliemasters.com/RescuingMelissa

Angel's Peak

Chapter 1

THE GRINDER HUMS TO LIFE, SHATTERING THE PRE-dawn silence as I measure beans for the first batch of the day. Outside, Angel's Peak is still dark, the mountain silhouette barely visible against the navy sky. Inside Mountain Brew, copper pendant lights cast a warm glow across polished wood counters and gleaming espresso machines—my sanctuary, my promise, my next potential financial disaster.

I inhale deeply, letting the rich aroma of freshly ground coffee center me. Five a.m. has become my favorite time of day, these quiet moments before the world intrudes, when it's just me and the perfect chemistry of coffee.

The grinder stops, and I tap the grounds into the portafilter, tamping with precision. Thirty pounds of pressure, perfectly level. In coffee, as in life, precision matters. One mistake and everything turns bitter.

I should know...

Steam hisses as I stretch milk for the first latte of the day—mine. The microfoam swirls into the espresso, creating a perfect rosetta pattern without even trying. My hands remember even when my mind wanders.

And wander it does. Two years in Angel's Peak, and I'm still waiting for the other shoe to drop. For someone to walk through that door and say, "Hey, aren't you that girl from the BrewTech scandal?"

So far, it hasn't happened.

I take my latte to the front window, watching as the first hints of pink touch the mountain peaks. Angel's Peak is nothing like San Francisco. No fog. No tech bros talking loudly about disrupting industries they know nothing about. No ex-boyfriends stealing your life's work and then framing you for corporate espionage.

Just mountains, clean air, and people who don't Google everyone they meet.

A sharp rap on the front door startles me from my reverie. I check my watch—five forty-five, fifteen minutes before official opening. Through the glass, Marie from High Country Farms is bundled against the morning chill, breath fogging in the air. She balances a crate of produce on her hip, waving with her free hand.

I unlock the door, letting in a gust of mountain air along with Marie's cheerful energy.

"Morning, Lily. Thought I'd catch you early." She sets the crate on the nearest table, unwinding a knitted scarf from her neck. "The greenhouse is producing like crazy this week. Brought you some extra mint for those chocolate mochas everyone's been raving about."

"You're a lifesaver," I say, inspecting the vibrant green leaves. "The last batch was gone by Tuesday."

Marie's family has farmed in Angel's Peak for three generations. When I first opened Mountain Brew, she was one of the few locals who immediately offered support, insisting I use her herbs and produce rather than ordering from distributors.

"How's business?" She asks, her expression softening with concern.

I busy myself transferring the mint to a storage container. "Oh, you know. Surviving."

"That bad, huh?"

"Just the usual seasonal dip. It'll pick up once the summer tourists arrive." I force brightness into my voice, not wanting to admit how dire things actually are.

Marie places a weathered hand on mine, stilling my movements. "Lily, half the town knows you got that rent increase notice. Ruth's been on a rampage at The PickAxe about 'corporate vultures swooping in on our small businesses.'"

I suppress a sigh. Of course, everyone knows. In Angel's Peak, privacy is more theoretical than actual.

"Thirty percent is robbery," she continues, indignation coloring her tone. "Have you talked to Lucas Reid about it? He owns half the commercial property in town, maybe he could—"

"I'll figure it out," I interrupt, more sharply than intended. "I always do."

Marie studies me for a moment, then nods. "Well, consider this delivery on the house. Call it my investment in keeping the best coffee shop in Colorado running."

"Marie, I can't—"

"You can and you will." Her tone brooks no argument. "Besides, my kale is growing faster than I can harvest it. You're doing me a favor taking it off my hands."

I know it's not true, but I accept the kindness for what it is. In the city, such gestures would come with expectations. Here, they're simply the mountain way—neighbors helping neighbors through hard times.

"At least let me pay you in caffeine," I offer, already moving to the espresso machine.

Marie smiles, settling onto a stool. "Now that's an offer I won't refuse. Got any of those cinnamon scones from Margie's?"

As I prepare Marie's cappuccino and warm a scone, I mentally adjust my ledger. The savings from the free produce delivery won't make a dent in the rent increase, but every little bit helps. I need to increase business by at least forty percent to absorb the new costs, in a town with a permanent population of just over a few thousand.

"You know what you need?" Marie asks, breaking off a piece of scone. "Some fresh tourist blood. New faces with disposable income."

"Tourist season doesn't hit for another month."

"I wasn't talking about the usual hikers and skiers." She leans forward conspiratorially, her eyes glinting with mischief. "Word is, The Haven's got some tech bigwig staying in the Aspen Cabin for a month. Eleanor was telling everyone at bingo night."

I roll my eyes. "Of course she was. Eleanor lives for that kind of thing."

Marie laughs, setting her mug down. "You know how she is—town gossip, town matchmaker, master meddler. Anyone under fifty is 'one of the young ones' to her, and it's her personal mission to see us all paired off like some Hallmark movie."

"Don't remind me," I groan, thinking of Eleanor's not-so-subtle attempts to pry into my love life last week at the farmer's market.

Marie grins. "Well, don't look at me to save you if she tries to corner you again. Speaking of meddling, I've got seedlings waiting. Thanks for the breakfast!"

She checks her watch, stands abruptly, and is gone in a flurry of activity, leaving the scent of earth and greenery in her wake. I tuck the herbs away and continue my opening routine, trying not to dwell on financial worries.

The door chimes six-fifteen on the dot. Right on schedule.

Eleanor Morgan stands in the doorway, silver braids

crowned atop her head, wrapped in a hand-knit sweater the color of huckleberries. At eighty-two, she moves with more energy than people half her age, arriving each morning for her "medicine," as she calls it.

"Morning, Eleanor." I'm already preparing her usual— dark roast, a splash of cream, served in the blue pottery mug her grandson, Hunter, made for her.

"You're looking particularly grim this morning, Lily." Eleanor settles onto her regular stool at the counter, sharp eyes missing nothing. "Numbers still not adding up?"

My hands falter momentarily on the coffee carafe. "The transition between seasons is always rough. Once summer tourism picks up..."

"If you'd let me invest—"

"No." The word comes out harder than intended. I soften my tone. "But thank you. I need to do this on my own."

Eleanor accepts her mug with a knowing smile. "Stubborn as a mountain goat. Speaking of new blood, have you heard about our newest visitor?"

"Should I have?" I turn to the display case, arranging fresh pastries from Margie's Bakery.

"Lucas Reid rented out the Aspen Cabin to some tech fellow from California. Handsome, from what I hear. Single, too."

A familiar weight settles in my stomach at the words "tech" and "California" in the same sentence. "I'm sure he'll be *very* happy with his mountain retreat."

"Hmm." Eleanor sips her coffee, eyes twinkling over the rim. "Don't dismiss him before you meet him. Not everyone from your old world is the enemy."

My old world. As if California and tech were some distant planet I escaped, rather than the life I built and lost. The words sting more than they should, but that's Eleanor for you —always prodding, always reading between the lines.

"I'm not looking for complications, Eleanor. The shop takes all my time." My voice is firm, but I know nothing I say will stop her from pushing. Subtlety isn't in Eleanor's vocabulary.

She gives me a knowing look, the kind that drives me mad because it means she already has a plan forming in that scheming, matchmaking brain of hers. The fact that she's privy to my past only makes her meddling sharper.

Eleanor is the sole person in this town who knows the truth about me—my connections to California tech, to a world so far removed from this quiet mountain life. And to her credit, it's one of the few things she's managed to keep to herself, which is saying something. But I also know she can't resist spinning everything into a tidy story with a happily-ever-after.

"Oh, of course, the shop." She smiles, far too sweetly. "But even hard-working girls need some excitement now and then."

I glare at her, but she just keeps on sipping her coffee, those twinkling eyes of hers filled with the promise of yet another one of her meddlesome schemes.

"You just made my point for me." Eleanor's gnarled fingers tap the counter. "All work makes for thin living, dear."

I bustle around the counter, wiping already clean surfaces. "The only relationship I'm focused on is the one between me and financial solvency."

"Well, at least you haven't lost your sense of humor." Eleanor drains her mug and slides it across the counter for a refill. "Ruth says he's staying a month. Working on some hush-hush project."

"Perfect. Just what Angel's Peak needs—another tech bro using the mountains as his personal think tank before returning to his real life."

"Your aura's darkening by the second, Lily Brock."

I force a smile. "Just thinking about the books. The quarterly taxes are due, and—"

"And you'll figure it out, like you always do." Eleanor rises, leaving a generous tip beneath her mug as always. "Don't forget the mixer at The Haven tonight. You need to get out more."

"I'll try." We both know it's a lie.

Eleanor pauses at the door. "Oh, and Lily? Open that heart of yours a crack. The mountain air is good for healing old wounds."

The bell chimes her exit, and I'm alone again with the quietly hissing machines and my thoughts.

As morning progresses, the shop fills with the regular rhythm of locals. Mayor Reynolds arrives precisely at seven-thirty.

"Morning, Lily." He greets me with the practiced warmth of a career politician. "Double Americano, please. Council meeting at eight."

"Trouble in paradise?" I ask, pulling his espresso shots.

He sighs, rubbing his temple. "Lucas Reid is pushing for expanded parking near The Haven. The environmental committee is pushing back. And somewhere in the middle, I have to find a compromise that won't alienate half the town."

"Sounds like politics as usual." I slide his drink across the counter.

"The price of progress." He takes a grateful sip. "Speaking of which, how's business?"

My smile stiffens. "Holding steady."

Mayor Reynolds's expression grows serious. "I heard about the rent increase. If there's anything the town council can do—"

"I appreciate the concern," I cut him off politely, "but I've got it under control."

He studies me for a moment, then nods. "Well, if you

change your mind, my door's always open. Angel's Peak needs its best coffee shop."

After he leaves, I allow myself a moment of doubt. Perhaps I should accept help. Perhaps Eleanor's investment offer or the mayor's assistance could solve everything. But accepting help means owing something—becoming vulnerable again, dependent on others' goodwill.

I've been down that road before. Never again.

The morning brings a steady trickle of customers. The Johnsons share a cranberry muffin and hold hands across the table. Paul Ramsey from The Haven's maintenance team grabs coffee for the entire staff. Sheriff Donovan stops by to discuss the upcoming summer festival security.

At nine forty-five, the bell chimes again, and Hannah Lewis enters, her auburn hair piled messily atop her head, arms laden with books.

"Oh, thank god, you're still here," she says dramatically, dropping her library tote onto the counter with a heavy thud. "I need caffeine like I need oxygen right now."

I smile, already preparing her usual chai latte with an extra shot of espresso—what she calls her "librarian's little helper."

"Rough morning at the book repository?" I ask, steaming the spiced milk.

"Liam has a cold, so I was up half the night. Then Mrs. Winters came in first thing wanting to argue about the 'inappropriate content' in the young adult section." Hannah rolls her eyes. "Apparently, teenagers shouldn't know that kissing exists."

I slide her drink across the counter. "The usual censorship crusade?"

"Every spring like clockwork." She inhales the steam appreciatively. "You are a miracle worker, Lily Brock."

Hannah settles at the corner table by the window—her usual spot—and begins arranging books around her drink. I bring over a blueberry scone, knowing she'll have forgotten to eat breakfast.

"On the house," I say, placing it beside her.

She looks up with a grateful smile. "You're an angel. Oh! Speaking of angels, did you hear about our mysterious visitor?"

I suppress a sigh. "The tech guy from California? You're the third person to mention him this morning."

"Small towns," Hannah shrugs, offering a knowing smile. "Though I have to say, the speculation is reaching fever pitch. Eleanor is convinced he's some eligible bachelor sent by the universe specifically for you."

"Me?" I arch a brow. "What about you? Eleanor needs a hobby that isn't matchmaking."

Hannah laughs, shaking her head. "Oh, Eleanor tried with me. You know how she is. But I got her off my back when I told her I was still grieving."

I glance at her, surprised. "And that worked?"

Her smile turns a little wry. "It's Eleanor. She means well, but even she knows better than to push too hard on that one. I figure I'll ride the 'grieving widow' excuse for as long as I can —it's a good way to buy time. Besides..." She leans forward, her eyes twinkling. "It keeps her energy focused on someone else. Like you."

"Oh, great. So I'm just a convenient distraction?"

"Pretty much," Hannah teases. "But seriously, do you know who this guy is? I looked him up last night, and Lily..." She pauses, lowering her voice dramatically. "He's *kind of* a big deal in the tech world. The encryption software that half the banking industry uses? That's his. He's not just some guy with a laptop and a start-up—he's *the* guy."

I blink, just barely managing to keep my expression neutral. The name rings a faint bell, though it's distant, buried in all the memories I try not to revisit.

"So... what, he's got a fancy résumé and a lot of money. What's he doing here in the middle of nowhere?"

Hannah smirks, sitting back in her chair. "Hiding, obviously. People like that don't just come to places like this unless they're running from something."

I know that better than anyone.

The words are casual, but they feel like a jab. I know she didn't mean them unkindly, but my gut tightens anyway. My grip on the handle of my coffee cup tightens, too, and I force myself to loosen it before I speak.

"Well, whatever he's running from isn't my problem. I'm not interested."

My stomach tightens. Of course. Max Lawson is a big deal. Another tech wunderkind with a golden touch is exactly what I *don't* need.

"Fascinating," I manage, keeping my voice neutral. "I'm sure he'll enjoy his mountain solitude before returning to his very important life."

Hannah gives me a knowing look. "Your tech allergy is showing again."

"I don't have a tech allergy."

"Lily, you still use a flip phone and refuse to get a smartphone. Not to mention, you still don't have a website up and running."

"I prefer analog." I busy myself wiping down the already spotless counter. "Anyway, what's with the book avalanche today?"

Sensing my desire to change the subject, Hannah gestures to the stack. "Summer reading program planning. I'm trying to develop something that will get kids excited about books instead of screens."

For the next twenty minutes, we discuss ideas for the library's summer programs. Hannah's passion for literacy is infectious, and I find myself relaxing into the conversation.

This is what I love about Angel's Peak—people who genuinely care about the community and its connections.

When Hannah eventually packs up to head to the library, she pauses at the door, her bag slung over her shoulder. She hesitates, giving me a pointed look. "You know, not all tech people are evil corporate monsters."

"I never said they were," I reply dryly, though I know better.

They most definitely are.

Her expression softens, and her tone shifts, gentler now, almost pleading. "You didn't have to. Maybe... maybe give this Max person a chance if you run into him? He might surprise you."

I narrow my eyes at her, suppressing a smirk. "Your Eleanor is showing."

Hannah freezes, then groans, pressing her hand to her forehead. "Oh, lord, you're right. Sorry! Just—I don't know, blame the small-town air. It's contagious."

"It's definitely something," I deadpan.

She grins sheepishly, the tips of her ears going a little pink. "Alright, I'll stop. But still... just think about it, okay?"

I roll my eyes. "I'll think about it the way you think about all of Eleanor's suggestions."

Hannah grins as she pushes the door open. "Touché. See you later, Lily."

With that, she's gone, leaving me alone in the shop with the faint sound of the bell above the door still echoing. I shake my head. Eleanor's influence really is everywhere.

After she leaves, I clear her table, finding the generous tip she always leaves despite my protests. Tucked under the saucer is a note: *"PS: He's really hot. I checked his photo online. Just saying."*

I crumple the note with a laugh that feels more genuine

than I expected. Leave it to Hannah to try brightening my day with inappropriate reconnaissance.

Three hours pass in the comforting rhythm of morning service. The town slowly wakes. Doctor Mc'Dreamy, Cole Blake, swaggers in, picking up caffeine infusions for him and his new wife, a trauma doctor from Denver. The usual rotation of locals, who form the backbone of my business, filter in and wander out just like clockwork.

Not enough of them, though. The ledger doesn't lie. Without the summer surge, Mountain Brew is barely staying afloat. Two years of careful rebuilding could vanish in one bad season.

The morning rush—such as it is—tapers off by ten, leaving me time to prepare for my afternoon specialty showcase. My signature cinnamon lattes, made with house-made syrup, have developed into something of a cult following. Not enough to save the business, but enough to give me hope.

Before starting the afternoon preparations, I pull out the letter that arrived yesterday, smoothing the creases where I crushed it in my initial anger. The landlord's message is clear: rent increasing by thirty percent, effective next month.

Take it or leave it.

I reach for my ledger, flipping through the carefully maintained pages. The numbers haven't changed since yesterday. Or the day before. The conclusion remains the same. I can't afford this increase, given the current revenue the shop generates.

Shoving the letter back under the counter, I focus on what I can control.

Creativity. Quality. Experience.

The things that set Mountain Brew apart.

I arrange the specialty drinks on a silver tray—four perfect mini lattes in glass cups, each with different latte art and flavor variations. The display case has become a small tradition, drawing in curious customers and often leading to multiple sales—a tiny bit of theater in my otherwise practical shop.

The bell chimes just as I lift the tray. Probably Darlene from The PickAxe, who often stops by before her shift.

My head is down, concentrating on keeping the tray balanced. The first warning is the scent—expensive cologne with notes of bergamot and something woodsy. Not a local.

Then it happens.

A solid wall of human collides with me. The tray tilts... and physics takes over.

Angel's Peak

CHAPTER 2

HOT LIQUID SPLASHES ACROSS MY HANDS, SOAKS MY apron, and splatters onto the floor. My stomach lurches as the glass in my hand shatters, swearing loudly as coffee arcs magnificently across the room—and worst of all, directly onto a sleek silver laptop perched in the arms of some stranger.

"What the—!" A deep, angry voice growls over the chaos.

My head snaps up, already braced for impact, and suddenly my world narrows to the most startling blue eyes I've ever seen. Ocean blue. Glittering blue. The kind of blue so shocking and vivid it makes you forget things—sensible things—like what you're doing or why your stomach is flipping inconveniently like a hooked fish.

Their owner doesn't look any more thrilled than I am. Coffee drips from his liquid-slicked laptop, a device I can tell at a glance costs more than my monthly mortgage, the screen already fizzled into black. His jaw clenches as he stares at the damage, a sharp muscle ticking in the corner, and when his gaze finally snaps to me, it's incredulous. Furious. Like I just obliterated his life's work—and honestly, maybe I did.

He's tall, well over six feet, with dark hair that's artfully mussed in the kind of way you'd see in men's luxury magazines —half tousled, half deliberate. His black wool trench coat shifts sharply over broad shoulders; his designer jeans and polished leather boots scream a man who doesn't belong in my small-town coffee shop. Which he doesn't. Yet here he is, standing so close I can feel the crisp winter chill clinging to him.

The universe really does hate me.

"Watch where you're going," he snaps, blue flames flashing in his eyes like some kind of storm god.

"Me?" The word is sharp, defensive—a flimsy shield against the strange, unwanted heat curling through me. "You walked straight into me." I gesture to the floor where the shattered mug and puddles of sticky liquid have turned into the scene of a coffee homicide. My hands are shaking slightly now, but I keep going. "I was carrying a full tray. Which was clearly visible—and is now clearly destroyed."

He arches a cynical eyebrow. "I was on a call." He holds up his phone in his free hand, the screen still lit. The other cradles the laptop like a wounded soldier.

"In a coffee shop doorway." My blood simmers as I cross my arms. "Which is, you know, for *walking through*, not loitering in."

His jaw tightens. "Who's the owner here?"

My lips part to shoot back another retort, but it dies when I see his eyes flicker to the name embroidered on my apron. Damn this small-town branding.

"I am," I admit, tipping my chin up. "Lily Brock. Mountain Brew's owner, barista, accountant, and apparently, janitor. Nice to meet you." Without another word, I grab a towel from behind the counter and toss it to him.

He catches it with a flick of his wrist, his long fingers securing the towel with ridiculous precision—then fumbles with it for a half-second, like the entire act of mopping up coffee is beneath him. But my traitorous stomach chooses that moment to loop and twist in a way it absolutely shouldn't. I shouldn't be noticing his hands. Or his coat. Or the way he's looking at me like he can't decide if I'm a disaster or a puzzle.

"Your laptop might be salvageable if you power it down and dry it immediately," I tell him, my tone clipped—anything to distract myself from how his voice made my toes curl when he barked at me.

He hesitates for a beat, then carefully sets the laptop on a nearby table, about as gently as you'd set a baby bird. His brow furrows as he dabs at the soaked edges with the towel.

"Do you have rice?" he asks, his voice calmer now—smoother. Too smooth. It's the kind of voice that could make you forget what you're mad about if you're not careful. Luckily, I'm still mad.

"In the kitchen," I say curtly. "Give me a minute."

I spin on my heel and head to the back room, grateful for the momentary reprieve—from the disaster, yes, but also from him. Alone, I take a breath, trying to ignore the way my pulse is still racing, fast and shallow. This isn't normal. I should be annoyed—livid, even—but the only thing I can think about is how ridiculously attractive he is and how infuriating that is. My stomach flutters, and I grip the edge of the counter, glaring down at the container of rice like it's my worst enemy.

Pull it together, Lily. He's just another entitled tech jerk with a God complex.

When I return, container in hand, he's removed the laptop battery and set its components neatly across the table, methodically patting them dry. His fingers are sure and steady, working with practiced precision. Deft. Calculating.

Every movement breathes competence, and that only makes him more insufferable. This should not be attractive.

"Here," I say briskly, plunking the rice down beside him.

"Submerge it completely. Battery separated. Leave it for at least 24 hours."

He looks up at me, surprise flickering through those vivid blue eyes. "You know your tech emergency protocols."

"I know coffee damage control," I lie easily—because what other explanation could I give for knowing what to do? There's no way I'm telling him about my past.

He huffs out a low sound that's almost a laugh, though there's no humor in it. "This laptop contains six months of work." His voice is tight with restrained frustration, tense and measured like a man trying very hard not to lose it.

"Hopefully, you have backup protocols," I say, crossing my arms again. It's petty, sure, but no one walks into my coffee shop and speaks to me like that.

His gaze flickers to mine, irritation sparking for just a beat before, unexpectedly, the corner of his mouth twitches with the hint of something else—humor, maybe? Or resignation? For the first time, his blue eyes soften, just slightly, and it catches me completely off guard.

"Fair point," he finally says.

And against my better judgment, my insides do another damn backward flip.

He arranges the laptop parts in the rice while I mop up the mess, acutely aware of the space between us, of every subtle movement he makes and the irritating way he seems entirely too composed for someone who just watched his entire digital life nearly go up in smoke—or rather, coffee.

The clean, masculine scent of his cologne teases my senses, layered with cinnamon and the burnt coffee disaster I'll be smelling for hours. It's both distracting and annoying that I even notice.

I salvage what I can of the destroyed display. Four specialty drinks wasted, shattered glass everywhere, and sticky puddles across the counter and floor. Not to mention my nerves, which are trying to process the lingering weight of those ridiculously blue eyes whenever they flicker in my direction.

"I'm sorry about your...display," he says eventually, gesturing toward it with restrained civility. His tone is measured, almost detached, and it makes his apology feel too polished to actually land. "I'll pay for the damages."

"It's fine," I reply shortly. It's *not* fine—the drinks were expensive to make, the mess will take forever to clean up, and my business runs on razor-thin margins. But I don't want his money, don't want *anything* from him.

"I insist." A glint of leather catches my attention as he pulls out a wallet. Of course it's leather. He extracts several bills without even glancing at them, laying them on the counter with an efficiency that screams *routine*.

When I glance at the stack—five crisp hundred-dollar bills —I blink, stunned by both the absurdity and audacity of it. "Seriously? You're giving me five hundred dollars for four drinks?"

"To cover the drinks, the inconvenience..." He gestures vaguely to the mess I'm scrubbing up. "And your time."

"Why not just pull out your black Amex and call it even?" I mutter as I toss a drenched napkin into the trash.

He smirks faintly, entirely too amused. "It's in my other wallet."

I scowl at him while he seals the rice container, carefully cradling it under one arm. Every move he makes is so precise, so confident that it'd be hard to imagine him rattled—if he weren't infuriating me so thoroughly.

"You know your laptop might still have a chance," I say pointedly as he adjusts the strap of his bespoke messenger bag. "If you leave it powered off and let the rice work its magic for twenty-four hours."

He arches an eyebrow, curious. "You mean leave it... here?"

I blink at him. "Yeah, in the container. I'll keep an eye on it."

A light flickers in his gaze, amusement mingled with something sharper. "I appreciate the offer, but no thanks. Nothing personal, Lily—" His smile turns almost apologetic as he focuses those blue eyes on my apron again, like he's locking my name into memory, "—but I don't trust *anyone* with this laptop. My work stays with me."

"Of course it does," I mutter under my breath, a bitter edge slipping through despite myself. His gaze sharpens, catching it, but I don't bother pretending it was anything other than exactly what it sounded like.

"What was that?" His tone isn't defensive, just curious in that maddening way of his, like he's filing the moment away for later analysis.

I straighten, crossing my arms. "Nothing. Just thinking it must be exhausting."

"Excuse me?" His brow furrows, but there's an almost playful tilt to his mouth, like he's daring me to elaborate.

I glance at him, my irritation and fascination battling it out in real time. "Being the smartest guy in the room all the time."

For the first time, his composure falters—just a little. He blinks, clearly not expecting that. "Who says I am?"

"Oh, please." I gesture toward him broadly: the suit, the laptop, the smooth confidence. "You walk in here like you've got the most important brain in a fifty-mile radius. You ooze it."

"I'll take that as a compliment," he says dryly, smirking like I just proved his point.

"Don't," I say flatly. "You might be the smartest *man* in the room, but..." I tap the side of my head, dishing out a hint of the self I buried years ago—just for a fleeting second. "You're not the smartest person."

That wipes the smirk off his face. He tilts his head slightly, studying me with renewed interest like I just surprised him. I hate how gratifying that tiny moment feels.

He recovers quickly. "Fair enough," he concedes, his tone lighter now, but there's something in his gaze that makes my chest tighten. He's cataloging me, dissecting me—like I'm a puzzle just out of reach.

"Has anyone ever told you that you're wasted in a small-town coffee shop?" he asks suddenly.

The words hit so fast and sharp it takes me a second to process them. My stomach twists as the molten anger rises up again—this time laced with something deeper.

"Has anyone ever told you that your urban superiority complex is showing?" I snap back, the words coming out sharper than I intended.

He doesn't flinch, though. Instead, a faint, almost genuine smile tugs at the corner of his mouth. "Point taken," he says, nodding slightly. "But I wasn't trying to insult you. There's just... something about you. The way you handle problems— fast, precise." He gestures to the mopped floor and the salvaged display. "This isn't where you learned to think like that."

I grit my teeth, trying to ignore the nerve he's brushing up against. Memories flare, unbidden: hours bent over code. A whiteboard so crowded with theories and flowcharts we were practically writing on the walls. Late nights ticking down to impossible deadlines, and the drive—the *need*—to build some-thing that mattered.

But that life's gone. Dead. Burned like the coffee splattered all over the floor.

"I run a coffee shop," I say coolly, pulling my walls firmly back into place. "Problem-solving comes with the territory."

He gives me that look again, like he doesn't believe me but can't prove otherwise.

"When do you open?" he asks, switching gears so suddenly it's jarring.

"Why?" I ask warily.

"Because, I might want to get an early start on my day." he says plainly.

I roll my eyes. "Six a.m."

His lips twitch again. "I'll see you then."

He slings the messenger bag over his shoulder and moves toward the door, but just as he reaches it, he pauses, glancing back over his shoulder at me. The deliberate pace of his movement sends a flicker of irritation skittering up my spine.

"What now?" I snap, annoyed at the heat crawling into my chest under the weight of his gaze.

For a moment, he doesn't answer—just watches me with the same analytical intensity as before, a slight, thoughtful tilt to his head. Then, finally, he says, "Nothing. Just... interesting."

"Is that supposed to mean something?"

But he's already gone, the bell jangling faintly over the door.

I glare at the rice container on the counter, his voice still trailing after me. *Wasted in a small-town coffee shop.* What the hell does he know? He's got no idea who I was, or what I left behind.

But as much as I want to stay mad, I also want to know what other infuriating things he might say tomorrow.

I lean against the counter, exhaling slowly. My hands still tingle where they brushed against him during the collision. My heart beats too quickly, a physical reaction I haven't felt in two years. Not fear—something more primal. Recognition, maybe. Danger sensing danger.

The bell chimes again, and I straighten quickly, composing my features. Darlene bursts in, her PickAxe apron already tied around her waist.

"Was that him?" she asks without preamble, eyes bright with curiosity. "The California tech guy?"

"News travels fast," I mutter, turning to the espresso machine.

"Small town," Darlene says with a shrug. "Plus, I saw him walking out. Quite the specimen." She fans herself dramatically. "Those eyes! Like the alpine lakes in summer."

"If you say so." I concentrate on making her usual double espresso.

"Oh, don't play cool with me, Lily Brock. I saw your face when I walked in." Darlene leans against the counter, studying me with the keen observation that makes her the town's unofficial information hub. "You looked like someone who just touched a live wire."

"I looked like someone who just had four specialty lattes destroyed and glass shattered all over her floor," I correct, sliding her espresso across the counter.

Darlene's gaze drops to the money still sitting untouched. "Generous tipper, at least."

"It's not a tip. It's payment for damages." I finally pick up the bills, tucking them into the register. "And it's too much."

"Keep it. Consider it karmic balance for your rent situation." She sips her espresso, watching me over the rim. "Half the town's talking about it, you know. Ruth's organizing what she calls a 'community economic support initiative.'"

"A what?"

"A fundraiser," Darlene clarifies. "To help cover the increase until you can get on your feet."

Mortification washes over me. "Absolutely not. I don't need charity."

"It's not charity, it's community." Darlene's expression softens. "Angel's Peak needs Mountain Brew, Lily. You've created something special here."

The sincere compliment catches me off guard. "I appreciate the sentiment, but I'll figure this out on my own."

Darlene studies me for a long moment. "You know, accepting help doesn't make you weak. It makes you part of something."

Before I can respond, she glances at her watch and curses. "Gotta run. Ruth will have my head if I'm late again." She downs the rest of her espresso. "Think about it, though. And maybe think about that California guy too—could be good for business to have a tech mogul as a regular."

After she leaves, I find myself alone with the aftermath of the morning's chaos. The shop smells of coffee and cinnamon, with faint notes of expensive cologne lingering in the air. The rice container sits on the table where Max left it, an unexpected reminder of the collision that felt more significant than it should have.

I never should have moved to this town to start fresh, because clearly the universe wasn't done punishing me yet. And something tells me Max Lawson is just the beginning of my problems.

Angel's Peak

CHAPTER 3

THE MORNING RUSH—IF YOU CAN CALL EIGHT customers in two hours a rush—keeps me busy enough to almost forget yesterday's disaster.

Almost.

The memory of intense blue eyes and the lingering scent of bergamot cologne proves surprisingly difficult to shake.

I arrive at Mountain Brew at my usual pre-dawn hour, letting myself in through the back entrance. The quiet of the empty shop has always been comforting, a blank canvas waiting for the day's rhythm to unfold. The air smells faintly of yesterday's espresso and the sharp, clean bite of roasted beans I prepped last night.

Normally, the stillness soothes me. Today, however, my eyes keep darting toward the front door, my pulse jumping at every imagined creak of the hinges, wondering if he'll return.

Not that I care. If anything, it would be a relief never to see Max Lawson again.

Eleanor arrives on time at six fifteen, bundled in her over-sized scarf, muttering about the morning chill. She beelines for the counter like a woman crossing a desert for water, her hand already outstretched for the steaming dark roast I slide her way —black, no sugar, as medicinal to her as penicillin.

Usually, she lingers for a full five minutes, sipping and dropping hints about the latest goings-on in Angel's Peak. This morning, she hesitates instead of flitting out the door.

"So…" Her gaze narrows over the rim of her cup. "Are we going to talk about Coffee-Gate?"

"Coffee-Gate?" I pretend to wipe down the already spotless counter.

Her brows shoot up. "Don't play innocent with me, Lily Brock. Half this town knows Max Lawson showed up yesterday, and you dumped coffee all over him. Darlene said there were *sparks*."

I laugh, rolling my eyes. "You are entirely too much of a romantic. There were no sparks, Eleanor. Just a misunderstanding over coffee."

She tilts her head, studying me like a puzzle she's determined to solve. "Funny, because Darlene swears you were flushed when he left, and she doesn't miss a thing."

The bell above the door jingles before I have to answer. Mayor Reynolds himself steps in, right on cue, wrapped in his olive trench coat against the lingering morning chill. His usual —double Americano, extra hot—waits on the counter before he's halfway across the shop. He smiles in that polite, distracted way of a man already planning his day, drops a few bills in the tip jar, and heads back out.

The next wave rolls in not long after.

George and Martha Washington shuffle in together, snow still clinging to George's boots. Martha orders her spiced chai with oat milk; he gets his black coffee with one sugar, no stir, because he swears the sugar dissolves better on its own.

I don't need to ask anyone what they want. After two years, I've got the town's caffeine quirks memorized as well as my own heartbeat.

Late morning, Dr. Cole Blake stops by for his cappuccino with exactly one shake of cinnamon and no foam spilling over the lip of the cup. Mrs. Winters collects her lavender latte with a drizzle of honey, while Margie and Harold from the bakery—both barely awake despite running their own morning business—grumble for iced mochas even though it's barely twenty degrees outside.

Sheriff Donovan strides in at a quarter to eight, his uniform pressed, badge gleaming, gun riding easy at his hip— the very picture of small-town authority.

"Morning, Lily." His weathered face creases into a smile. "The usual, please."

"One step ahead of you, Sheriff." I'm already preparing his black coffee, adding the single pump of vanilla he pretends not to want.

The corner of his mouth twitches when I slide his drink across the counter.

He settles at the counter, removing his hat and placing it beside him. "Heard you had some excitement yesterday. Tech fellow spilled coffee all over himself?"

I suppress a sigh. Of course, the story has already made the rounds, though with notable inaccuracies. "Other way around. I spilled coffee on his laptop."

"Ah. That explains why Darlene's version had you heroically saving expensive equipment with quick thinking and rice." He accepts his coffee with a nod of thanks. "Town gossip —better than any police scanner for spreading information, worse than any witness statement for accuracy."

"I wouldn't call anything about the interaction heroic," I mutter, wiping down the already spotless counter.

Eleanor is still perched on her stool, sipping her coffee like she has nowhere else to be. Which means she's waiting for me to crack.

I busy myself with the grinder. "You can stop staring. There's nothing to tell."

"Mm-hmm." She leans in, voice dropping to a conspiratorial whisper. "And I'm the Queen of England."

Sheriff Donovan studies me with the shrewd assessment of someone who's spent decades reading people. "Lucas says this Lawson fellow is some big shot from California. Security software or something."

"So I've heard." I busy myself with the pastry case, arranging muffins that don't need arranging.

"Might be good for business, having a tech celebrity hanging around." He sips his coffee thoughtfully. "Though I imagine that depends on whether he comes back after you baptized his computer with coffee."

Despite myself, I laugh. "Not my finest customer service moment."

"We all have off days." Sheriff Donovan stands, dropping a five-dollar bill in the tip jar. "Speaking of which, need me to have a word with your landlord about that rent increase? Might be able to apply a little official persuasion."

I shake my head, touched by the offer but determined to handle my problems on my own. "I appreciate it, Sheriff, but I've got it under control."

"Offer stands." He settles his hat back on his head. "Oh, and Lily? Word of advice from someone who's seen his share of strangers coming through Angel's Peak—not everyone with money and education is out to cause trouble. Sometimes they're just looking for the same thing as the rest of us."

"And what's that?"

His eyes crinkle at the corners. "A decent cup of coffee and a place that feels like it matters." With that cryptic comment, he heads out.

The morning drifts in with the usual parade of locals. I'm arranging a fresh display of mini cinnamon lattes—replacing the casualties from yesterday's collision. It's all so predictable, my little bubble of peace.

Until the bell chimes.

My hands still mid-air, cinnamon dust whispering down like a spell half-cast.

He's back.

Not just back—*transformed.*

Gone is the rumpled, irritated tech bro from yesterday. In his place: sleek control draped in a charcoal cashmere sweater that clings to shoulders built for hard labor—or maybe just *harder things.* The kind of shoulders you want to lean into, except you'd absolutely never do something so impractical.

His dark hair is artfully tousled again, but this time, it's intentional. The kind of tousled that invites fingers, whispers promises you have no business exploring. A brand-new laptop is tucked under one arm, sleek and silver, like a postscript on the way he commands the space.

"Good morning." His voice warms the air instantly, low and deliberate, like a secret murmured against your skin.

Heat flickers straight through me. Not because of him, of course. The espresso machine, maybe. Or the cinnamon. *Definitely not him.*

I quickly straighten, smoothing my palms over my apron like it's armor. But it's not—it's thin cotton and absolutely no protection from the way he's watching me. My pulse taps in my throat despite my complete lack of interest in the way his mouth curves slightly. Okay, maybe not *complete.*

"Your electronic patient didn't make it?"

"I performed emergency surgery," he says, each word slow and measured, the barest crook tipping his lips—a smile with a knife's edge. "But the prognosis wasn't good."

I press my mouth into a thin line, trying not to let the heat rising in my cheeks betray me. "Coffee and circuitry make poor companions."

His gaze sharpens, taking me in with careful precision. He doesn't just *look*—he observes. I don't like the way it makes my insides knot, like he's peeling back layers I've worked too hard to build.

Silence blooms, swelling in the warm, cinnamon-thick air. The espresso machine exhales a slow, sensual hiss, and the hum of conversation fades into a static nothing under the weight of him.

"I owe you an apology," he says, taking a step closer.

Too close. Close enough, I feel the heat rolling off him, the subtle shift in air every time he moves. Like he's breaking into my space, not with force, but something worse—*effortless ease*.

"Oh? For what specifically?" I ask evenly.

"For being... abrupt yesterday. Borderline rude," he says, his tone quieter now. He pauses, watching me with unapologetic intent, soaking in every reaction like he's calibrating himself to me.

"Borderline?" I arch a brow and cross my arms.

"My apologies for being an insensitive ass," he says smoothly, a flicker of something self-aware collecting in his smile.

This time, I let my own mouth curve. "Collision physics tends to bring out the worst in people."

I busy myself setting a tiny cup back on the refreshed display, but his gaze follows the motion, lingers on my cinnamon-dusted knuckles like I've suddenly found a way to fascinate him. And when his eyes drift up, landing on my mouth, my lips inexplicably part before I can stop them.

His voice drops an inch lower. "Still. I should have watched where I was going."

I manage a nod, an acknowledgment without surrender, tamping down the sudden warmth curling beneath my ribs. "How can I help you today, Mr. Lawson?" My tone sharpens slightly around his name, as if to remind myself to keep the boundary intact. "Another coffee to sacrifice to the laptop gods?"

"Actually..."

His eyes sweep deliberately over the room—not a casual glance, but slow and intentional, like he's mentally mapping every detail. The mismatched vintage chairs, local artwork climbing the exposed brick walls. The copper pendant lights glowing over the wooden tables. When his gaze locks back onto me, the air feels thinner, the room smaller. Or maybe just warmer.

"I'm looking for a workspace," he says finally, his tone even but threaded with just the right amount of charm to disarm someone not paying attention. "Minimal distractions. Excellent coffee." He pauses, his mouth tensing slightly in distaste. "The Haven is too..."

"Busting with wealthy tourists taking selfies with overpriced lattes?" I supply, one brow lifting.

That earns me a real smile—no trace of sarcasm, no restraint. It's devastating, the kind that ripples under your skin, low and decisive, and it takes everything in me not to flinch under its weight.

"Exactly," he says, his eyes sparking with something that makes my chest stupidly tight. "I was told your coffee was the best in three counties."

My lips twitch in response. "Whoever said that isn't wrong."

"Confidence." His gaze sharpens again, but this time, an unmistakable hint of admiration flickers there, heating the space between us. "I like that."

Stop. Just stop. He doesn't get to look at me like that.

He glances toward the corner booth tucked beneath one of the big windows—the one with the view of Main Street stretching into the deep greens and whites of the mountains beyond. My booth. My refuge.

"May I?" he asks, gesturing to it with a subtle nod.

I stiffen. It's just a booth. It's not a piece of my soul—but it feels like one. Letting him sit there is as personal as handing over keys to my house, and for the life of me, I can't figure out why.

"That's my booth,"

Angel's Peak

CHAPTER 4

Max's lips tilt into a slow, devastating smirk. "Your booth?" Then, his voice dips, softer but sharper, threaded with that maddening confidence that makes my pulse jump against my will. "What if I promised to keep it warm for you?"

The air between us tightens, like a string stretched too far. My mind trips over the words, imagining them twisted into something they shouldn't be. Something dangerous. Something that ignites all the wrong kinds of sparks. And from the faint curl at the corner of his mouth, I know he knows exactly how they landed.

"It's a free country," I manage, my tone laced with forced indifference, turning away before my expression betrays me. "What can I get you?"

"What do you recommend?" he asks, his words deliberate, like they're designed to linger.

I glance back over my shoulder, already irritated—half at him, half at myself—and find those piercing blue eyes waiting, unwavering. He holds my gaze like it's the most natural thing in the world while the space around him bends, everything else fading to a soft blur.

Most people order coffee and move on. But not him. Of course not. He waits, gaze steady, as if the answer I give is some sort of test.

I let the silence stretch just long enough to regain a sliver of control. "Depends. Purist or adventurer?"

He leans subtly against the counter, close but not touching, reducing the space until I can feel him there. It's electric, magnetic, impossible to ignore. "In coffee? A purist," he says, the corners of his mouth threatening something between a smirk and a smile. "In life? I'd like to think I'm an adventurer."

Somehow, the air gets even heavier, hotter, his voice dripping with double meanings I refuse to acknowledge. Refuse.

The flutter in my chest betrays me anyway—it drops lower, sinks deeper, like an anchor far too close to uncharted waters.

I clear my throat. "Let's start with a single-origin Ethiopian, pour-over. Blueberry and chocolate notes come forward as it cools."

The small smile shifts into something slower, rawer. "Sold." The single word lands rough, his gaze holding mine for a beat too long, and it sounds like he's agreeing to something larger than coffee.

The cinnamon clings sweet in the air between us, thick and clouded, wrapping tighter around the tension already coiling in my chest. The espresso machine exhales softly, a steady hum that seems to sync with the deep breath I don't realize I needed to take until he breaks the stillness.

And for a beat—a long, charged moment neither of us moves. Even the buzz of conversation from the morning crowd fades, leaving only us.

No. Not us. There is no us. There's just him. Standing

across from me like he's been dropped here on purpose, upsetting every carefully crafted defense I've worked years to build.

So I move. Quickly. Breaking the moment with a sharp inhale as I pivot to the pour-over station. The motions should center me—grinding the coffee, measuring the beans, carefully fitting the filter into place—but each deliberate shift only makes me more hyperaware of him. The weight of his presence presses with the force of a winter storm, unrelenting and impossible to block out.

Then, the scrape of a chair leg cuts across the room, a grating sound that seems to hit every nerve under my skin. I glance back toward the corner, where my booth now houses him. The sight of him settling into the cushioned seat—lanky but controlled, hands smoothing easily across the polished table—feels almost like an invasion. His laptop bag drops with a quiet thud. He owns it now. The view of Main Street. The mountains. The booth. My booth.

I bite down on the urge to tell him to move and turn back to the steady pour of water over grounds, steam curling upward between us like a barely drawn curtain.

"You really know your coffee."

His voice catches me off guard, close, cutting through the low hum of the machine and my own focused movements. Too close. He's not sitting anymore—I don't know when he got up, but now he's there, leaning just slightly against the counter, his tone low and intent.

I glance up. And sure enough, he's watching. No. Not watching. Studying. It's like he's taking me apart piece by piece. Not in the scalding, once-over way some men look at you. No. His focus is pinpointed. Like every movement, every pause I take is some equation he's determined to solve.

"It's my job," I say abruptly, trying to sound casual as my pulse thuds hard at his attention.

He tilts his head, a faint, knowing glint in his eyes. "No."

The way he says it, soft but certain, makes my stomach twist tight. He lets the word hang in the air, heavy with things left unsaid, before adding, slower now, "It's your passion."

I turn back to my pour, hoping the familiar ritual cools the heat that his words ignite far too easily. But it doesn't work. Nothing about this man fits into tidy compartments. Not his presumption, not his gaze—not even the unsettling accuracy of his observation.

Passion. I almost flinch. The last thing I need is some stranger—even an insufferably attractive one—peeking into the cracks of a part of me I've buried for a reason.

"It's coffee," I reply finally, keeping my voice steady, even. Flat. "It's both."

I risk a glance his way, expecting his challenge to falter. But no. If anything, his eyes burn brighter, like he's fueling up on the sparring.

"Coffee isn't enough to give you that spark," he says, soft but firm. "There's something more."

I stare at him, hands fisting the edge of the counter before I can think better of it. "You think you know me because I make a good cup of coffee?"

"No," he says, his tone too unshakable, like he's not challenging me, just stating facts. "I think I don't know you at all. And that, Lily..." His voice dips just enough to scrape against something buried deep and raw. "Is what makes you interesting."

The water burns my fingertips as it overflows, jarring me back into reality. My jaw clenches as I set the kettle down hard and finish the pour without looking at him. I can feel his eyes on me—reading, catching far too much.

When I finally meet his gaze again, I push the finished coffee toward him. "Here's your pour-over, Max," I say curtly, the steel back in my voice, though the echo of my quickened heartbeat betrays me.

He watches me for a moment longer. Then, with a slight dip of his head, he takes the coffee and moves back to the booth—my booth. Or at least, it was.

And as much as his presence grates on my nerves, the worst part is realizing how much quieter the counter feels without him pressed against it.

"Let it bloom before your first sip." I call out.

His focus shifts from me to the cup, a flicker of interest in his expression. "Bloom?" He draws the word out slowly, like it's something that deserves to be tasted even before the coffee.

I lean against the counter, keeping my tone even as I explain. "Develop. The flavors change as it cools. If you rush, you miss out."

His gaze snaps back to me, the cup momentarily forgotten, and I regret the words as soon as they leave my mouth. His head tilts slightly, and that faint, knowing smile curls his lips again.

"I see." He nods as if my advice is some profound philosophy. "Patience, then."

For some reason, the word hits harder than it should, as if it's not just about the coffee. As if it's for me.

He curls his fingers around the ceramic mug, but doesn't lift it, clearly obeying my instruction. The small gesture sends a dart of heat through my chest, sharper than it has any right to be, and when his eyes meet mine again, I know I've lingered too long.

"Thank you, Lily," he says, my name low and deliberate, sliding from his tongue like it belongs solely to him.

The sound of it catches low in my stomach, curling there, unwanted but impossible to ignore. I turn my back and retreat behind the safety of my counter before I do something reckless, like keep standing there, letting him look at me the way he's already doing.

I pretend to busy myself wiping down surfaces that are

already spotless. The routine is meant to calm me, but somehow I feel even more exposed. Every nerve in my body is tuned to him, tracking his movements without glancing his way.

But I can feel him. Leaning back in my booth. One hand wrapped around the cup, but still not drinking, like he's drawing this moment out on purpose. Like he's following my instruction to see what I'll say—or what I'll do.

From the corner of my eye, I catch him watching me. Not the distracted glance of someone whose mind is somewhere else, but something far more deliberate. Deep. He's not just watching—he's studying. Mapping.

His focus shifts with me, the kind of attention that pulls strings beneath your skin without permission. It's not casual curiosity. No, this is measured. Calculated. Dangerous.

The heat of his gaze follows me everywhere: the way I shift my weight when I lean over the counter to grab a towel, the absent flick of my wrist when I tidy the espresso machine, the nervous habit of tucking my hair behind my ear. It's like every movement I make feeds whatever equation he's solving in his head.

I scowl at myself. He's just a guy. A customer. Nothing more. Yet somehow, he's managed to crawl beneath my skin in less than 24 hours, making me irritable, restless, and far too aware of him.

"Good coffee," he says suddenly, his voice cutting through the music in the shop. It takes me a second to realize he's speaking to me—not to his phone, not someone on the other side of a screen, but me.

I glance up, caught off guard. He's holding the cup now but hasn't lifted it—still waiting, still patiently following my instructions. But there's something in his expression that makes it impossible to dismiss. Like he's not just talking about coffee, even though he hasn't tasted it yet.

"You haven't had it," I point out, crossing my arms and leaning back slightly to regain some semblance of control.

"That's not what I meant." His lips curve again, but this time the smile reaches his eyes, softening the austere angles of his face in a way that's almost devastating. And completely uncalled for.

The words hold steady in my chest, untethered from whatever meaning they're actually supposed to have, and I don't dare dig deeper because I know he'll have an answer ready.

"I hope it lives up to the hype," I say instead, fighting for tone territory between sharp and disinterested.

"I'm sure it will," he replies, not breaking the steady, burning contact of his gaze.

Another customer—a regular named Pete—walks in, and I nearly break out into applause for the rare intrusion. Pete greets me with a wave, but it feels too casual, too far removed from the tension radiating between me and Max, who's sitting entirely too still, entirely too aware of the break in our bubble.

"Be right with you, Pete." I retreat to the register, only half-conscious of Pete's cheery small talk while I punch in his regular order. The tension pulls taut again as Pete moves on, glancing curiously around the space but mercifully planting himself at the opposite end of the café with his coffee.

When I glance back toward the booth, Max has finally lifted the cup to his mouth. The smallest of sips, slow and savoring.

The moment feels heavier than it should. Why? Because of the way his eyes flicker up over the rim, catching mine mid-sip? Or the way he sets the mug down like it's the only thing in the world worthy of attention right now?

"Good coffee," he says again, this time with finality. And something else. His voice carries a weight, a quiet kind of authority that makes me hate how much I care about his opinion.

I busy myself rinsing out a pitcher, but my mind keeps circling the moment like a bird over prey. Too much tension. Too much heat. He feels like a spark in dry tinder, an inevitable wildfire waiting for one careless breath.

A soft chime breaks the moment—his phone lights up on the table. He doesn't glance at it right away, but then it buzzes again. His expression tightens by a fraction, and the shift in his energy makes my stomach drop.

Something changes in his face. The sharp confidence—the deliberate focus on me—fades, replaced by something colder. The glint in his eyes dulls as his jaw tightens, and he taps his phone screen to silence it.

He exhales roughly, muttering under his breath, "Not now."

"What's wrong?" The words are out before I can stop them.

His gaze lifts sharply, locking onto me from across the space, and for a moment, the weight of it pins me. My heart stumbles in reaction, suppressing the wild urge to step toward him.

"Nothing," he says, smooth but clipped.

But I know that's a lie.

And the look he gives me before turning back to his laptop says that maybe, just maybe, whatever's creeping into his world will burn its way into mine.

Angel's Peak

CHAPTER 5

THE REST OF THE MORNING BRINGS A STEADY stream of customers—the mid-week rush hour that keeps me moving between the espresso machine, register, and pastry case without a moment to breathe. I fall into the familiar rhythm, each drink a practiced sequence of movements, each customer interaction a well-rehearsed dance. The noise, the pace, the quick back-and-forth with locals—it's all comfortable.

Automatic.

And yet, nothing about today feels normal.

Through it all, I'm hyperaware of Max's presence in the corner booth. Occasionally, I catch him watching me over the top of his laptop, his gaze thoughtful, assessing. It's not the kind of distracted staring of someone who's zoning out.

No, it feels far too intentional.

And worse, the look isn't impatient or displeased—two things I'd expect from some big-shot tech guy stuck in a small-town café. Instead, it's laced with quiet curiosity, like he's figuring out how all the pieces of me fit together. The idea of him puzzling me out sends an unwelcome shiver down my spine.

I don't have time to dwell, though, because they arrive.

Mrs. Winters and her knitting circle sweep through the door punctually at 10:30, nearly taking down a younger couple trying to leave as they charge in a flurry of hand-knit shawls and cheery greetings. They're my favorite handful of chaos, and their weekly appearance is as reliable as the sunrise.

"The usual for everyone?" I call across the counter before they even have a chance to sit.

"Martha's watching her caffeine," Mrs. Winters announces, shooting a meaningful glance at the smaller woman fumbling with her oversized tote of yarn. "Doctor's orders. Something herbal for her."

I tuck my tongue between my teeth to hide my smile when Martha, sulking from beneath her vibrant purple hat, mutters, "If I can't have caffeine, I'm at least having sugar."

"I'll get you something herbal that you'll love," I promise. "Chamomile lavender. And if sweetness is the goal, maybe one of the shortbread cookies to go with it?"

Martha brightens slightly at that. "Cookies," she says, like the word itself is a lifeline. "Yes, please."

I dive into their usual chaos without complaint, juggling one extra-hot chai tea latte, one half-caf mocha with almond milk, and one vanilla cappuccino, all covered in just the right dusting of cinnamon. The tea steeps, the espresso brews, and my hands move with clockwork precision as conversation swirls loud and lively around me.

When I glance up, Max has stopped typing.

Briefly, the knitting ladies' order pulls his attention—his gaze sharp and focused as he tracks the ballet of simultaneous drink preparations. There's no hint of mockery in his observation, only interest, as though he's taking in the choreography of my movements the same way he evaluates everything else. But then, inevitably, the knitting circle notices him.

"You're new," Mrs. Winters calls across the café without hesitation, aiming her voice like a bullhorn. Max, entirely unprepared, leans back slightly in his seat, caught mid-thought. His eyes flick to her as if he's bracing for whatever's coming next.

"Yes, ma'am," he answers politely, inclining his head.

"You're the tech fellow staying at The Haven, aren't you?" Mrs. Winters presses, taking his startled acknowledgment as a license to dig deeper.

"Seems that I am," Max responds, a faint smile pulling at his lips. If he's irritated by her over-familiarity, he hides it well. There's even an amused glint in his eyes, like he's waiting to see where this is going.

"How do you find our Lily's coffee? Better than those fancy city shops, I'd wager."

I freeze. The espresso machine wheezes behind me, and for a split second, I consider fleeing into the kitchen and pretending none of this is happening.

But Max takes it in stride. "Significantly better," he says, his voice smooth, warm. He glances in my direction, then, eyes catching mine briefly before he looks back at Mrs. Winters. "There's care in every step."

Mrs. Winters beams, utterly charmed as if Max just handed her a basket of roses. "Told you," she announces proudly to the group. "Our Lily's a treasure. Studied coffee science, didn't you, Lily?"

I stiffen, managing to keep a neutral expression as I focus on finishing Martha's tea. I've never been good at being the center of attention, especially when Mrs. Winters decides to highlight bits of my background. "Just years of practice," I deflect, keeping my tone light.

"Don't sell yourself short," Martha says, the shameless

busybody chiming in. "Eleanor said you've got some kind of degree in coffee chemistry."

I can feel Max's interest sharpen from across the room, his gaze pinning me as effectively as if he'd spoken. This is exactly the kind of conversation I didn't want him to overhear.

"Just a few courses," I say smoothly. "Nothing special." The lie slips easily from my lips, ingrained after years of burying the truth. My past doesn't belong here—especially not with him.

"Well, we're proud of you," Mrs. Winters says when I deposit their drinks. She pats my arm like a proud grandmother. "Not many people around here with your kind of expertise."

I retreat to the counter as quickly as possible, feeling Max's gaze burn into my back the entire way. I don't dare look at him, but the weight of his curiosity wraps around me like a living thing.

For the next hour, I pretend he doesn't exist—and fail spectacularly. Every time I catch the flex of his fingers on the keyboard or the slow shift of his shoulders as he stretches, he pulls my attention like gravity. Worse, I know he notices. I can feel it in the way the space between us feels warmer, tighter, whenever I glance in his direction.

And then his phone rings.

"Lawson," he says, answering with practiced efficiency. The tone of his voice snaps something into the air—a sharpness that commands attention, even from across the room.

He pushes to his feet and moves toward the window, the sun cutting a sharp outline against him. All that lean strength wrapped in charcoal cashmere. All that certainty.

"Yes, I've reviewed the beta issues," he says, pacing slowly. His tone deepens, resonant but sharp, reaching into spaces it has no right to reach. "The security protocols are my primary concern. No, I won't compromise on that."

I can't stop watching him. The deliberate pace, the precise movements of his hand as it gestures lightly—it's like he's bending the world around him with nothing more than words. It makes every inch of my skin feel hot and tight. Too much.

"Three weeks," he says, turning slightly, the sunlight casting heat across his expression. His jaw tightens, and even from here, I can see the furrow of his brow as he listens. "No. We're not chasing competitors. We do this right, or we don't do it at all."

It's not just what he says—it's the way he says it. The quiet command threaded through every word. The unshakable calm that tells you he's used to getting exactly what he wants. The particular timbre of his voice does dangerous things to my pulse.

When he returns to his seat, the relaxed man savoring coffee is gone. What's left is sharper, more dangerous—a wolf slipping back into its skin but still carrying the scent of the hunt.

He sits, the sweater stretching over his chest as he leans to adjust the laptop. My eyes betray me, tracking the way his forearm flexes, the way his fingers curl around the edge of the table like he could crush it if he wanted.

Heat blooms low, sudden and insistent, chasing up my spine and settling just beneath my ribs. My hands fuss with a stack of mugs that don't need straightening, anything to keep from staring at the man who just turned a simple phone call into something I felt in my bones.

His jaw is still hard from whatever decision he just enforced, but when he glances at me, some of the tension softens. I freeze under the intensity of it, wondering—not for the first time—what it would feel like to have that focus, that unshakable command, directed entirely on me.

It's ridiculous. I've dated confident men before, but

there's something about him—about that calm certainty, the way he moves like he owns every square inch of space he steps into—that makes the air in here feel heavier.

Thicker.

Because a part of me knows he's the kind of man who doesn't just break walls. He tears them down piece by piece, then dares you to thank him for it.

And God help me, a part of me wants to know what it would feel like to have that focus, that command, turned entirely on me.

I don't want to date him… I want to be consumed *by* him.

As if the thought drags him to me, his head lifts. That same sharp, unblinking intensity from the call locks onto me, pinning me mid-fuss with the mugs. It's a touch without contact—warm, deliberate, and impossible to ignore.

"Careful, Lily." His voice is low, smooth, still carrying that edge of authority. "You keep looking at me like that, and I'll start to think you want my attention." A pause, a slow curve of his mouth. "If you're going to stare, you might as well pull up a chair."

Heat rushes to my cheeks. "Sorry," I murmur, the word slipping out before I can stop it, softer than I mean it to be. "I didn't realize—"

One brow lifts, his gaze holding mine a fraction too long, making the apology feel like more than an exchange of manners.

The bell above the door chimes, snapping the connection.

Ruth Fletcher bustles in, her salt-and-pepper hair pulled back in a practical ponytail, leather jacket creaking as she moves.

Angel's Peak

CHAPTER 6

"LILY BROCK, LIGHT OF MY MORNING." RUTH's voice fills the shop with its customary vigor. "Darlene's running late, and I need a caffeine infusion before I tackle inventory alone."

"Coming right up. The usual?"

"You know it. Double shot, minimal nonsense." Her sharp eyes scan the shop, landing immediately on Max. "Well, well. The famous new arrival has found our coffee sanctuary."

Max looks up, wariness crossing his features. "Good morning."

"Ruth Fletcher. I own The PickAxe." Ruth approaches his table with the confidence of someone who has owned Angel's Peak's only bar since Prohibition. "You must be Max Lawson."

He stands, offering his hand. "Word travels fast in small towns."

"Faster than your internet connection, I'd wager." Ruth shakes his hand firmly. "Lucas mentioned you'd taken the Aspen Cabin. How are you finding our little mountain haven?"

"It's... peaceful." His eyes flick to me, lingering just long enough to warm my skin. "With unexpected quality in unexpected places."

Ruth's gaze bounces between us, missing nothing. "I see you've met our Lily. Best coffee artist this side of the Rockies. You should see what she can do with microfoam."

I nearly drop the portafilter. "Your espresso is coming right up, Ruth."

"No rush, darling." Ruth settles herself at Max's table without invitation. "So, Mr. Lawson, what brings a tech genius to our humble mountain town? Besides the obvious escape from Silicon Valley vultures?"

His posture stiffens almost imperceptibly. "Work. And the vultures, as you say, are everywhere—not just in California." His gaze slides back to me, slow and deliberate. "Though... some things here are worth the distraction."

The portafilter feels suddenly heavier in my hand. Heat crawls up my neck, pooling low, my pulse tapping out a quick, traitorous rhythm. I duck my head, pretending to fuss with the tamp, but my hands aren't steady, and Ruth's sharp eyes don't miss a thing.

"True, true, but they can't circle as effectively through our mountain passes." Ruth winks. "We protect our own here."

I deliver Ruth's espresso, hoping to rescue Max from her interrogation. Not out of kindness—purely to prevent Ruth from extracting information about my past along with his.

"Lily, have you formally met Max? He's the founder of Nexus Systems. That security app that everyone's talking about?"

The name clicks into place, and my stomach drops. Nexus Systems. The rising star of cybersecurity, with a revolutionary approach to personal data protection. I'd gone out of my way not to read about them after leaving the tech world, but even I couldn't escape hearing the name.

"We've met." My tone is deliberately neutral. "We had a coffee collision yesterday."

"Literal collision," Max adds, mouth curving into a half-smile that feels personal. "My laptop was a casualty."

Ruth's eyes gleam. "Sparks flew, did they?"

"Only from short-circuiting electronics," I mutter, avoiding the fact that the air between us is sparking plenty right now.

His gaze holds mine for a beat too long, like he's imagining a different kind of collision entirely.

"Well, consider this your proper introduction then." Ruth gestures between us like a matchmaker from a Victorian novel. "Lily Brock, coffee sorceress, meet Max Lawson, tech wizard. You two have more in common than you might think."

If only she knew how wrong she was. Or how dangerous it would be if she were right.

"Ruth, don't you have inventory waiting?" I prompt, my voice lighter than I feel.

"Always trying to get rid of me." Ruth rises, taking her espresso. "Max, you should stop by The PickAxe sometime. First drink's on the house for newcomers."

"I might take you up on that," Max says, but his attention is on me, not Ruth. His eyes skim over my face as though he's searching for something beneath the surface—and finding more than I'm ready to admit.

Before leaving, Ruth catches my eye, tilting her head subtly toward Max with a questioning look. I respond with a nearly imperceptible shake of my head. Ruth's matchmaking tendencies are legendary in Angel's Peak, second only to Eleanor Morgan's, and the last thing I need is her deciding Max and I are somehow destined for each other.

The bell over the door swings shut behind Ruth, leaving the shop in a hush broken only by the faint hiss of the espresso machine. I busy myself wiping down already-clean equipment.

Max doesn't go back to his laptop. He leans back in the booth instead, one arm stretched across the bench, eyes fixed on me like I'm far more interesting than whatever meeting or code might be waiting for him.

The weight of that gaze pins me in place. My fingers tighten on the tamper, pressing harder than necessary into the coffee grounds.

"What?" I ask, too quickly.

"Just wondering," he says, voice low, unhurried, "how many layers I'd have to peel back before I figured you out."

Heat flares under my skin. I turn toward the espresso machine, pretending it demands my full attention, but my pulse is a drumbeat in my ears.

"I'd hate for you to waste your time," I say over my shoulder, forcing my tone light. "There's nothing to figure out. Nothing special here."

"Hmm." The sound is thoughtful, not dismissive. "I don't believe that for a second."

I glance back despite myself. He's watching me like a man who's just spotted a locked door and decided opening it is now his favorite problem to solve.

"So," Max says after a moment, his gaze still fixed on me. "Coffee sorceress?"

"Local hyperbole."

"And me, apparently a tech wizard." He types something on his laptop without looking away for long. "Though wizards generally don't lose their wands to caffeine damage."

Despite myself, I smile. "Technology is more fragile than magic."

"Depends on the technology." His eyes lift, catching mine, heat flickering there. "And the magic."

The moment stretches, taut and electric, until I force myself to turn away, retreating to the safety of beans, grinders, and measured pours.

The afternoon slips into a lull, the shop empty except for Max and his growing collection of empty mugs. I take the opportunity to prep for tomorrow's rush—measuring beans into tins, portioning syrups, wiping down counters.

"I've been meaning to ask," Max says, breaking the comfortable silence. "What's the story behind the name? Mountain Brew is simple, but it fits perfectly."

I glance up, surprised by his interest. "Nothing elaborate. The mountain gives me peace. The brew gives me purpose. It seemed natural to combine them."

"Elegant in its simplicity." He leans back, stretching slightly, sweater pulling across his chest. "Most business names try too hard. Nexus Systems included."

"Let me guess—you wanted something that conveyed connection and technological power?"

He laughs, the sound unexpectedly warm. "Guilty as charged. My marketing team insisted Max's Security Stuff lacked gravitas."

The admission is disarming, cracking his polished CEO veneer just enough to let something more human—and more dangerous—slip through.

I set a new cup on his table—a vanilla-cardamom flat white with an intricate fern traced in the foam. As I pull my hand back, his fingers brush mine, warm and sure. The contact lingers, deliberate. His gaze drops briefly to the silver ring on my index finger, its weathered band etched with faint, intricate markings.

"Interesting piece," he says, thumb grazing the side before I can retreat. "It means something to you."

I swallow. "It's... old. Family thing."

His eyes lift, studying me like he's adding this to some private file. Then, as if sensing I need the heat to cool just a fraction, he leans back, voice easy. "So. What's next in your coffee alchemy?"

The bell chimes, and Darlene bursts in, cheeks flushed from the chill air.

"There you are." She beelines for the counter, her PickAxe apron knotted at her waist. "Ruth said you were entertaining Angel's Peak's most eligible new bachelor."

I close my eyes briefly, summoning patience.

"Ruth says he's gorgeous." Her stage whisper is pitched perfectly to carry to the corner booth. "Those shoulders—and don't get me started on the blue eyes."

Max's fingers move over the keyboard with the corner of his mouth twitching like he's fighting a smile.

"Can I get you something, or are you just here to torment me?" I ask, keeping my voice low.

"Both." Darlene grins, shamelessly. "Double espresso to go. Oh—and Ruth wants to know if Max is coming to the mixer at The PickAxe on Friday."

"Why don't you ask him yourself? He's sitting right there."

"Because I'm being subtle."

I snort. "You wouldn't know subtle if it hit you with a truck."

"Fine." She pivots toward him, leaning on the counter like she's about to auction him off. "Hey, handsome. You're coming to The PickAxe Friday night. We've got live music, decent whiskey, and the best-looking women in three counties."

Max looks up, brows lifted, expression caught between amusement and alarm. "I, uh, hadn't planned on it."

"Well, plan on it now." Darlene winks like she's just sealed a deal. "Lily will be there too, won't you, Lily?"

"I most certainly will not," I say firmly, sliding her espresso across the counter.

"Spoilsport." She downs half in a gulp. "Fine, but you're

missing out. Doc Blake is playing, and you know he does that thing with the guitar that makes all the ladies swoon."

"I'll survive the disappointment."

After paying, she leans in, this time dropping her voice to something just shy of conspiratorial. "Seriously, though. You should come. Get out of this shop and have some fun for once."

"I have plenty of fun," I protest, weak even to my own ears.

"Inventory and ledgers don't count as fun." Her gaze flicks toward Max, then back to me, eyes glinting. "And neither does pretending you're not interested in tall, dark, and techy over there."

"I'm not—"

"Save it." She pats my hand with mock sympathy. "I've seen the way you look at him when you think no one's watching. Pure chemistry. And I don't mean the coffee kind."

Across the room, Max's head tilts slightly, that almost-smile playing at his mouth again. He doesn't comment, but the subtle flush along his neck says he caught every word.

With a final smirk, Darlene sails out, leaving the shop quiet except for the steady tap of his fingers on the keys and the rush of my pulse in my ears.

For the next hour, we play our parts. He works in his corner with that maddening, unhurried focus, while I scrub counters that don't need it. Every time I turn, I swear I catch him watching—glances that land heavy enough to make my breath catch before he goes back to his screen.

I finally give up pretending I'm not aware of him and pull a clean mug from the shelf. The air fills with the warm bite of espresso and the bittersweet drift of chocolate as I work the steam wand, layering flavors until it's exactly the way I like it. Not too sweet. A little bite beneath the velvet.

When I slide it onto his table, the rich swirl of mocha still curling in the foam, he glances up.

"Mocha breve," I tell him, stepping back before I can get caught in those eyes for too long. "Half-and-half instead of milk. Strong enough to keep you awake, smooth enough you won't regret it."

His hand wraps around the mug, but his gaze doesn't follow. It lingers—slow, deliberate—until heat creeps up my neck. "So this is how you win people over?"

"Just being hospitable," I say, tucking a strand of hair behind my ear. "I like the challenge—finding the exact blend that makes someone want to come back."

A ghost of a smile tugs at his mouth. "Guess I'll have to keep coming back until you figure mine out. That is... if you don't mind me occupying this table all day." He leans back, still watching me. "For what it's worth, I'm getting more done here than I have in weeks. Something about this place makes it easy to work."

"Then consider this an open invitation," I tell him, my voice warmer than I intend. "That spot's yours for as long as you're in Angel's Peak."

His mouth curves, slow and deliberate. "Then I'll be here from the moment the lights go on... until the lights go out." His gaze lingers, a spark that makes the last part feel heavier.

Angel's Peak

Chapter 7

The afternoon stretches into evening, shadows creeping into the corners of the shop, softening edges until everything feels... closer. Warmer. The rush of earlier is long gone. Now there's just me, the low hum of the espresso machine winding down, and Max—steady and solid in the corner booth.

It irritates me how aware I've become of his presence. How much space he seems to take up without ever crossing a line. He hasn't said a word in hours, completely engrossed in whatever he's typing, but every now and then, I catch his gaze drifting—watching me from beneath those dark lashes—and I swear the oxygen in the room shifts.

I expected him to be the arrogant type. Entitled. Dismissive. Most people like him barrel into a small-town coffee shop like mine, expecting instant service and somehow siphoning all the air from the room.

Max Lawson is different.

There's something measured about him, like every glance and every word is deliberate. A pointed kind of stillness that makes you hyperaware of how much chaos you live in by comparison.

I tell myself the quiet is good. That I'm grateful for the slow hour. But the truth is, it's maddening. Because every time I force myself to focus on wiping down the counter—every time I shift mugs, rearrange supplies, try *desperately* to pretend he's just another customer.

That there's nothing brewing between us.

And worse, I feel the way that heat reaches lower, simmering in my stomach like embers waiting for a gust of wind.

The evening deepens, the sky outside cooling into gold and gray. A wintery breeze drifts in every time the door chimes, reminding me that closing time is close, edging toward inevitable.

A scattering of customers wander in and out, their steps muted as they hurry back into their lives. But Max doesn't leave. His focus stays pinned to his laptop—but not entirely. Because somehow, in the moments my attention slips toward him, his gaze always finds mine.

Always deliberate. A slow, purposeful pull at the edges of whatever tightrope I pretend I'm walking.

At closing, Max finally powers down. The faint click of his equipment disengaging feels personal somehow, like the final notes of a quiet symphony only I'd been hearing. He packs up his sleek black cases with his usual precision—every cable rolled methodically, every small movement fluent. Confidence pours off him in waves, understated but unrelenting.

Nothing rattles this man.

"Thank you for the workspace." His voice draws my gaze like a magnet, pulling my focus from where I'm sanitizing the espresso machine. He stands now, tall and steady, one hand flicking at his sleeve, the other slinging his bag over his shoulder. The room isn't nearly big enough between us. "And the excellent coffee."

"Will you be back tomorrow?"

The question escapes before I can reel it in. It lands softer than I meant it to, strangely open, too heavy to hang between strangers. His gaze meets mine—for longer than necessary—and then, wickedly, he smiles.

"Definitely." The word slides off his tongue, rich with layered meaning. He pauses, gaze dipping to my lips before returning to my eyes, and something tightens low in my stomach. "If that's all right with you."

"It's fine," I manage, fighting to keep my reply even. "I mean, of course."

"I'll see you tomorrow, Lily." One corner of his mouth lifts—not a full smile, just enough to disarm me entirely. He lingers by the door, hand curling loosely around the frame, what should be a casual gesture laden with tension instead. The sharp glow of the evening sun through the window catches on the edge of him—his jawline, the rise of his chest beneath the charcoal sweater—and he looks more at ease here than anyone should have a right to.

"And Lily," he says, his voice lowering just enough to make standing still a challenge. "For what it's worth..."

"What's that?" I tilt my head, impatient despite myself. Or maybe impatient because of him.

He studies me, eyes lingering in a way that carries weight, like he knows things I haven't said yet. Then he lets his lips curve, the faintest shift that shouldn't feel as devastating as it does.

"Ruth's right about one thing," he murmurs, his tone honeyed now. "You are something of a sorceress with coffee."

The way he says it vibrates through me like a low hum, warm and unsettling, and I'm too stunned to respond. He takes one last lingering look before he slips out the door, words hanging in the space he leaves behind.

I stand at the counter, gripping a dishrag like it's a lifeline, watching the door shut softly behind him.

After he leaves, I move through my closing routine on autopilot, my mind replaying our interactions with irritating persistence. The way he watches me work. The unexpected humor beneath his professional exterior. The unmistakable tension that seems to vibrate in the air between us.

Every muscle in my body feels strung too tight, like I've been pacing the edge of some dangerous current waiting to be swept off my feet.

I'm wiping down the counter when the door opens again. Darlene slips in, flipping the sign back to CLOSED behind her.

"I knew it," she exclaims. "You're blushing."

"I'm not blushing. It's just warm in here." I throw the cleaning cloth at her. "What are you doing back?"

"Forgot my card," she says cheerily, plucking it from beneath the register. "But actually," she says, her tone dripping with mischief as she leans smugly against the counter, "I was hoping to see your face after Mr. Tall and Tech finally left. And, honey, it tells me everything I need to know."

"There's nothing to tell," I say flatly, scrubbing aggressively at a non-existent stain on the counter.

"Mmm-hmm." She hops onto a stool, crossing her arms like she's about to set up shop the entire evening. "So, how long has Mr. Silicon Valley been making those puppy dog eyes at you?"

"He doesn't make—this is his second day here."

"Second day?" Her eyebrows shoot up. "Girl, the electricity between you two could power the whole town. Ruth says he couldn't take his eyes off you the entire time she was here."

I pretend to count something in the register, my stomach twisting uncomfortably. "Ruth needs better hobbies. And so do you."

"Honey, in Angel's Peak, you are *our* hobby." Her expression softens. "Look, I know you've got your reasons for keeping to yourself. God knows I've tried for two years to get you to open up about whatever sent you running to our little mountain town."

I tense, but she continues, her voice gentler than usual.

"I'm not asking for your secrets. Just saying that maybe—just maybe—it wouldn't be the end of the world to let someone new into that fortress you've built."

"He's here for a month, Darlene. Then he goes back to his real life."

"A month can be a lifetime." She slides off the stool. "Or at least enough time to remember what it feels like to be alive."

After she leaves, I stand in the empty shop, her words echoing uncomfortably in my mind. The problem isn't that Max will leave in a month. The problem is that for the first time in two years, I've met someone who makes me wish he wouldn't.

Angel's Peak

CHAPTER 8

BY THE THIRD DAY, MAX HAS ESTABLISHED A pattern. He arrives at seven, orders the coffee, whatever I recommend, and works steadily until closing.

Always the corner booth. My booth.

Always focused, but with moments of distraction when his gaze drifts to the counter or me.

I tell myself his presence is good for business—one guaranteed customer during the slow hours.

What I don't admit is how the atmosphere in Mountain Brew changes when he's there, charged with a current that makes every movement feel deliberate, every glance weighted.

On the fifth day, I'm restocking beans when Audrey Tristan and Hunter Morgan enter, bringing with them a blast of chilly mountain air. They're holding hands, Hunter's build making Audrey look diminutive beside him.

"The feared food critic graces us with her presence." I smile at Audrey. "I thought you were in New York until next month."

"Surprise visit. The magazine's letting me work remotely more often." Audrey's smile is radiant as she glances up at

Hunter. Their happiness is both beautiful and a sharp reminder of what I've walled myself off from.

"The usual for both of you?"

"You know it." Hunter's eyes drift to the corner booth, recognition dawning. "Is that—"

Audrey follows his gaze, her food critic instincts visibly activating. "Max Lawson." Her voice drops to a whisper. "Hunter, that's the Nexus Systems founder I showed you in that tech feature last month."

I tense, preparing for the invasion of Max's privacy. But Hunter, bless him, simply nods acknowledgment. "His security software helped the restaurant upgrade our systems last year. Good stuff."

Max looks up, clearly recognizing he's being discussed. I expect him to be annoyed, but instead, he closes his laptop and stands.

"You must be Chef Morgan. Lucas Reid mentioned you're heading up the new farm-to-table program at Timberline."

Hunter seems surprised to be recognized in turn. "That's right. This is my wife, Audrey Tristan-Morgan. She's the real celebrity—her culinary reviews have launched more successful restaurants than my cooking."

Max stands to meet them, grip firm, expression easy. "I read your piece on sustainable tech in commercial kitchens. Smart use of what already exists."

Audrey brightens. "Thanks. We're rolling some of those protocols into Hunter's new kitchen at Timberline."

I deliver their drinks—steam ribboning up, citrus oil shining on the cappuccino foam—and watch the exchange with a knot of confusion. Max handles the attention smoothly, but tension gathers at the corners of his eyes, a practiced calm stretched too tight.

"We won't keep you from your work," Hunter adds, sensing... something. "Just wanted to say your security protocols made a real difference for small businesses like ours."

"I'm glad to hear it." Max's mouth lifts; the smile stops short of his eyes. "That's what we built it for."

They drift to a window table. Max returns to the booth, opens his laptop, and doesn't touch the keys. Distance shadows his face.

I pull a chilled bottle of tonic, twist an orange peel, and pack a double shot. Bubbles rise, amber and bright, as espresso meets ice. The glass sweats in my palm while I cross the floor.

I set it down within his reach. Espresso tonic—citrus, clean, a reset. "Try this."

His gaze snaps to mine when I set the mug in front of him, something flickering in those cool blue eyes—a surprise that deepens into warmth, like I've given him more than coffee. His fingers wrap slowly around the mug, his knuckles brushing against the smooth clay, condensation from the steam beading along the curve of his hand.

It's a casual enough gesture, but my stupid heart stumbles on the way his hand tightens around it, like he's anchoring himself with the small comfort I didn't know I'd meant to give.

He inhales, the faint tangle of cinnamon, piloncillo, and orange peel blending in the charged silence between us. Then, he takes a slow sip, deeper than I expect, his long throat working it down. The tension in his brow eases slightly. Another sip—longer this time—and the faint line in his jaw softens too, just a fraction.

"You okay?" The question escapes before I'm ready, barely above a whisper but heavy with meaning I wish I'd kept hidden.

His gaze shifts past me, toward the window, the pale light softening the harsh set of his jaw. "Just... work," he says, but the pause carries weight.

There's something more.

"Looks more like brooding." I lean a hip against the table before I can stop myself, the closeness threading a dangerous pulse through my veins.

One corner of his mouth tips into the suggestion of a grin. "Is there a difference?"

"Thinking is productive," I counter, narrowing my eyes. "Brooding is just marinating in your own stress juices."

That does it. A laugh breaks free from his mouth, unpolished and real, the kind that sends unexpected warmth pooling low in my belly. I watch as one hand drags through the perfectly disordered strands of his hair, mussing it just enough to make him look... touchable. The laugh eases him, loosening something I hadn't realized had been knotted in my chest.

"Fine," he says, his voice rich with amusement. "I'll try to simmer in a smarter marinade."

I should move. Take the cue, step away, leave him alone with his pondering. I should wipe tables, count beans, do *anything* but keep standing there, caught in the gravity pull that thickens the quiet around us.

Instead, my mouth betrays me. "Do your systems actually help towns like ours?" The honesty in the question is unexpected even to me. "Not just the big guys."

His posture shifts, like I've caught him off guard. His shoulders settle slightly, losing some of the tension I hadn't realized I'd been tracking. When he speaks, his voice is steady, certain, the timbre of it dropping a little deeper.

"That's the point. Big clients can afford whole teams. Places like this..." His finger taps lightly against the mug, the soft chime of ceramic and glass filling the quiet between us. "They're exposed. One breach can take out payroll. Bookings. Havoc for months. We build guardrails that small businesses can afford."

The quiet conviction in his voice is unexpected, catching me off guard the same way my question did to him.

It's not rehearsed.

It's something deeper. More personal.

The more he speaks, the more I feel trapped in the orbit of him—steady and warm and far more present than I'd pegged him to be when he first walked through my door.

Warmth presses under my ribs, splintering into something inconvenient and sharp. "That's... more decent than I gave you credit for."

His mouth tilts into an easier smile now—softer, reaching his eyes. "Careful. You'll ruin my tech bro reputation."

I narrow my eyes, but a traitorous grin pulls at the edge of my lips despite myself. The fact that he clocks my bias and meets it with humor is infuriating. And appealing.

I take a calculated step back—not far, but enough. The citrus from the café de olla lingers in the air, and Max takes another drink like it's something he needed—not just coffee, but whatever intention I put behind it.

"Good?" I nod at the glass, keeping my focus there instead of on him. Pretending that's all I care about.

"Sharp. Clean." He lifts the mug slightly, appraising it, but his eyes stay on mine, pinning me there with something I don't have the will to name. "Exactly what I needed."

The pattern holds all week. Max settles into Mountain Brew like he belongs—part espresso machine, part mountain view. People start to clock him, but they respect the invisible perimeter around the corner booth.

I start building drinks for him the way a luthier tunes a violin—tiny shifts, listening for resonance. A lavender honey latte on Monday. Maple-cinnamon cortado Tuesday. Wednesday, smoked sea-salt mocha. He always pauses, always tastes like it matters. The way his shoulders loosen when the balance hits is a problem I pretend not to notice.

Purely professional interest. The clean satisfaction of craft appreciated.

Not the prickle across my skin when he steps through the door. Not the way I time my routes—reaching past him for sugar, clearing his empty demitasse with the same hand that "accidentally" brushes his knuckles, offering a fresh cup the moment the current one cools.

Definitely not the weight of his gaze when he thinks I'm focused on the register.

Friday, Noah swings in alone near the end of the day for a quick coffee, sheriff's jacket unzipped, spring dust on his boots. I hand over the cup; he leans in, concern tucked behind casual.

"Everything okay with your new regular?"

"Max? Just a customer." The words come out smooth, practiced.

"Good, just checking in on you." The warning follows me into closing.

The sign is flipped to CLOSED, the room settling into soft clinks and low steam as I wipe tables. Max stays put, last man standing.

The room settles into the comfortable quiet of closing. The espresso machine lets out one last, drawn-out sigh, as though it's just as tired as I am. The walls exhale too, soft clinks of mugs echoing in the space as I wipe tables, stray dishes finding their way to the sink.

All the while, Max stays where he's been all day—booth occupied, laptop dark, but his frame just as steady and present as ever. A sharp contrast to the ghost of customers past.

"I can head out if you need to lock up." His words break the quiet, a low hum that carries far too much weight in the stillness.

"No rush," I say without thinking, glancing at him before

catching frozen mid-wipe. His hand rests on his trackpad, his head tilted faintly. "Sidework left."

So he stays.

The work feels automatic, but the air is anything but. Every movement I make feels amplified, brushing up against something unspoken that hovers on the edges of the space between us—and every time I look up, I swear I catch his eyes before they can drift away.

"Your cottage is walking distance, right?"

The question drops casually into the space. But its effect is anything but casual. I falter for just a moment, the rag pausing midair as his words land sharper than they should. "How do you know I have a cottage?"

"Ruth mentioned it." He leans back, his sweater shifting against his broad shoulders. "Something about a colorful door you painted yourself."

"Of course she did." I force my hands to move again, dragging the cloth in slow circles over the table to center myself. "It's just a few blocks. Small. Sufficient." My tone is flat, clipped, but my mind races with the possibilities behind his question.

"Better than The Aspen Cabin," he says, his casual tone wrapping around something unspoken. "Great view, but a longer walk."

He rises as he speaks, slowly stretching his arms over his head. My heart trips over the sight of his sweater lifting, exposing a strip of skin, sharp hip bones carved against the waistband of his jeans. Heat flushes under my skin before I can stop it.

"The property manager keeps pushing guest mixers," he continues, letting his arms drop as he adjusts the weight of his bag on his shoulder. "Apparently, I'm antisocial."

I snort weakly, still stuck in the vision of him. "Imagine that."

He chuckles low, the sound rippling under my ribs, deeper inside me. I force myself to turn, to refill a carafe, break the magnetism still simmering between us. It's ridiculous. I've spent hours with him this week, but for some reason, tonight feels different.

I turn to the bar and start a fresh pot—piloncillo crumbling in my palm, cinnamon stick cracking, orange peel expressing a bright ribbon over the steam.

I cross to his table with a small clay mug. "Café de olla. Spiced. Comfort in a cup." I set it down; his fingers wrap the heat, our hands a breath apart.

He inhales. The guarded line at the corner of his eyes eases. One sip, then another—longer—the kind of appreciation that feels like a thank-you without words, but that's not Max's style. "Thank you," he adds, fingers tightening around the mug. "For this."

"It's what I do." The cloth finds one last circle on the nearest table.

He rises, slings the bag over a shoulder. "And you do it extraordinarily well." Closer now by the door, the small space pulling heat between us. "Goodnight, Lily."

The way he says my name skims along skin. I hold his gaze a beat too long and pretend it's the deadbolt I'm reaching for and not air.

He doesn't offer to walk me home.

By the time the lock clicks shut behind him, I'm left in the heavy quiet of my empty shop, wiping the same counter space clean while my mind spins with the questions he never asked.

Because if he'd offered—if he'd said, *Let me walk you home, Lily,* in that deliberately low voice of his—I might've said yes. Hell, no—I'd have probably asked him inside. Just to see what he'd do.

And what I might let him do to me.

I'm almost done with closing when Darlene knocks at the

back, rings of keys chiming against the glass. I let her in, one brow up.

"You're missing the party," she announces, removing her coat. "The PickAxe is packed for Doc Blake's band, and I thought you might reconsider."

"I've got inventory to finish."

"Inventory can wait. Life can't." She studies me for a moment. "Your tech boy hasn't shown up either."

I busy myself counting coffee bags. "Not surprised. He just left the shop."

"Oh, honey." Darlene's laugh is soft. "You should've asked him to join you at the PickAce."

"Why would I do that?"

"You're not fooling anyone but yourself."

"Is there a point to this visit, or are you just here to offer unwanted observations about my personal life?"

"Both." She hops onto the counter, swinging her legs. "Ruth sent me to tell you that your boy genius asked some very specific questions about you the other night."

"Me?" My hands still. "What kind of questions?"

"How long you've been in Angel's Peak. Where you came from before. If you've always been in the coffee business." Darlene watches my reaction carefully. "Ruth didn't tell him anything specific, just that you showed up two years ago and opened the best damn coffee shop Angel's Peak has ever seen."

Relief and anxiety war in my chest. "Good."

"He seemed pretty interested for 'just a customer,'" Darlene adds, air quotes punctuating her words.

"Drop it, Darlene."

"Fine, fine." She slides off the counter. "But for what it's worth, Ruth thinks he seemed genuinely interested, not creepy-stalker interested. And Ruth's creep radar is never wrong."

After she leaves, I finish closing, my mind churning. Max

asking questions about me isn't necessarily sinister, but it awakens the caution I've lived with for two years. Getting too close, letting anyone dig too deep, could unravel everything I've built here.

Yet as I walk home in the cool mountain evening, the shop safely locked behind me, I can't help replaying our interactions —the careful way he studies me when he thinks I'm not looking, the moments of genuine connection breaking through our respective guards.

I tell myself it's nothing. A temporary diversion in the quiet routine of my life. In three weeks, Max Lawson will return to his world of tech innovations and corporate success, and I'll continue in mine, one of coffee and careful anonymity.

But as I unlock the door to my cottage, the emptiness inside feels more pronounced than usual, as if the space itself recognizes what I refuse to admit—that for the first time in two years, I've met someone who makes me question whether hiding is really living.

Angel's Peak

Chapter 9

THE AIR INSIDE MOUNTAIN BREW HAS SHIFTED. IT'S not the temperature or the cinnamon-rich scent wafting from the pastry case—it's him.

Max Lawson.

Always there, always watching, always absorbing. He claims my booth with quiet arrogance, and integrates himself into my routine as though he's stitched into the fabric of Mountain Brew.

And yet, his presence still manages to unsettle me in ways I don't fully understand—unraveling threads I plucked from the canvas the day I chose this life.

It's impossible to ignore how different Mountain Brew feels since Max Lawson started showing up every day.

Not that he does anything obvious. He never raises his voice, demands attention, or acts entitled to the space he's quietly claimed. No, Max's presence wraps itself into the shop's routine like it belongs there, like *he* belongs.

Except it doesn't feel natural.

Not really.

His presence hums under the surface, a steady, low current

that makes ordinary moments—like twisting the steam wand or wiping down the counter—feel off balance.

Uneven.

Today, like every day this past week, he works in silence, his laptop casting a faint glow over his sharp features. The copper light fixtures above catch on the strong angles of his face, softening him just enough to make him seem like he belongs in the quiet chaos of my café.

He doesn't demand attention, and yet, people still notice him. The moment someone walks through the door, their gaze flickers just slightly toward him, aware of the quiet presence in the corner booth that carries more gravity than it should.

Max Lawson radiates something I'll never understand.

Confidence. Command. Control.

The kind of energy has always felt like *too much to me*, like too bright a light aimed directly at me that I need to shy away from. But with Max, it isn't too much. It's steady. Silent. And worst of all, it doesn't repel me.

It draws me in.

That pull makes everything feel unsteady.

It's not just the way his gaze lands on me when he thinks I won't notice—sharply focused, like he's studying my movements, calculating some answer I can't see. It's not even the deliberate way his attention shifts back to me every time I flit between the counter, the pour station, or the register.

It's the way he's chipped steadily at the veil I've worked so hard to keep between myself and the world.

Now the edges of it feel thin. Worn. And I can't tell if I want to pull it tighter or just let it fall.

During a lull in customers, he breaks the soft rhythm of the café, his voice cutting through the muted hum of conversations and the hiss of steamed milk.

"Those patterns are impressive."

I glance up to find him at the counter, leaning forward, his body relaxed but his attention sharp and singular. His arms are crossed over the breadth of his chest as those infuriating eyes settle on me.

I follow the direction of his nod to the latte art blooming beneath my steady hand. A smooth rosetta curls along the top of the foam, a quiet triumph I've done a thousand times before. But the way he's looking at it—looking at *me*—makes it feel suddenly noticeable.

Important.

"There's a trick to it, isn't there?" Max keeps his voice low and steady.

For a minute, I assume he's talking to someone else. My eyes flick to the room behind me, then back to him, and there's a faint tilt to his mouth that tells me he knows exactly where my head is. The subtle lift of his brow feels like a private joke at my expense.

"There's no trick." I slide the finished latte across the counter to him. My voice is light, almost dismissive, but there's no escaping the way Max's focus stays locked on me, unwavering. "Latte art isn't magic. It's just physics and a steady hand."

"You downplay it." The faint curve of his lips deepens into something that feels just shy of a smirk. "But it's not just skill, is it? It's craft."

I pause, wiping down the counter slowly, his words sitting between us longer than they should. He doesn't look away, doesn't fidget, doesn't fill the silence with anything unnecessary. He just lets me feel the weight of him.

And damn it, it works.

"There's nothing you couldn't learn with practice," I say quickly, with what I hope is a nonchalant shrug. My eyes drop to the cloth in my hand, anything to get away from the way he's looking at me. "I could show you."

The words are out before I have time to snatch them back. Why did I say that?

He leans back, one arm sliding easily along the counter as his fingers drum lightly at the edge. Everything about the way he moves feels deliberate, like he's calculating how far to push.

"Call me intrigued." His voice threads with quiet amusement. "Show me."

Before I know it, we're shoulder to shoulder at the latte station, the tiny workspace only intensifying the quiet current humming between us.

"We'll start you slow," I say, pressing a milk pitcher into his hand. My fingers brush his in the transfer, the warmth of his skin sharp enough to snag my attention and throw me off stride for half a second. I pull back just slightly and pretend I don't notice. "No hearts or tulips. Just a rosetta."

His fingers curl around the metal handle. Up close, his hands seem too large to manage the delicate precision required for latte art. Yet there's a steadiness there I shouldn't find as distracting as I do.

"Hold it lightly," I say, my voice softening as I reach up to adjust his grip. My hand covers his instinctively, guiding the motion. The moment I touch him, my heart skips—not like a *little* flutter, but a full-on stumble, like it's forgotten how to pump altogether.

His hand is strong beneath mine, warm, impossibly steady. He doesn't move. Doesn't flinch. He just waits, watching me with a focus I can feel in my jaw, my ribs, *lower*.

"You've done this before?" I ask to fill the silence, my tone lighter than I feel.

"Never," he admits, tilting his head slightly—but not his hand. He doesn't need to look at me to make me feel like I'm under scrutiny, like he's cataloging every move, every breath I take.

"Okay. Well..." I clear my throat. Focus. His proximity

hammers at the edges of my concentration. "Tilt the cup slightly. It gives the milk somewhere to roll into."

His hand mirrors mine, our knuckles brushing again, barely, but enough that heat gathers low in my stomach. I press forward, trying to force the moment into something mechanical, something professional. "Don't rush. Just a small stream, slow and steady."

The milk glides along the surface of the espresso, tentative but smooth, spiraling out as the soft white contrasts against the dark, glossy base.

"That's it," I murmur, guiding his wrist just slightly. Our shoulders are almost touching now, the space between us closing even though neither of us acknowledges it. The ribbon of milk begins to settle, curling into faint petals.

"You make it look easy," he says, his tone low, closer than I'm ready for.

I glance up instinctively, expecting to find him watching the milk. Instead, his eyes are locked on me.

The rest of the room goes quiet, fading into the background. My heart pounds against the base of my throat, fierce and raw. The air between us seems thinner now, heavier in my lungs. His gaze doesn't waver, and my breath hitches as I try to hold steady—but there's no moving, no looking away.

And somehow, I don't want to.

Max Lawson has stared at me a hundred times this week— enough that I've stopped wondering why and started counting the way it makes me feel. Uneasy. Warm. Alive. Like every time he looks, he scrapes away some layer I didn't know was there. Sometimes I want to yell at him to stop.

Sometimes I want him to look harder.

"What makes the pattern happen?" His question catches me off guard.

"Gravity," I say.

"That's a weak answer," Max counters, his voice still calm

but tinged with amusement. The faintest trace of a smirk curves his mouth. "It's not just gravity. There's precision. Intention."

"It's really just physics," I deflect, repressing the urge to let his focus disarm me. "You watch the flow, decide where to drag it. It's not complicated."

He tilts his head, unconvinced. "If it's not complicated, how come nine out of ten cafés screw it up? Seems like art to me."

"It's about understanding the elements: how the milk folds into the espresso, how steady your hand is." I shrug, wanting to brush it off, even though his focus sets something low in my stomach stirring. "It's not magic."

He exhales, low and controlled, and I swear I catch the faintest quirk of satisfaction in his expression. "You make it look easier than it is."

"It's just—" I turn to answer automatically, and find myself closer to him than I realized. His gaze lowers to meet mine at the same time, clear and intense and searing, pinning me there.

I forget what I'm going to say. The words evaporate completely. Heat prickles along my spine, down my arms. It's not the kind of heat that comes with embarrassment or awkward proximity—it's sharper than that.

Hungrier.

It's awareness.

It's desire.

The liquid in the cup trembles slightly, a ripple breaking across the surface, but neither of us notices. Neither of us looks. My focus is caught somewhere else, somewhere closer. His hand is still beneath mine, steady on the handle of the milk pitcher, but it's not the silk of the foam or the swirl of white against brown that holds us like this.

The room narrows to the infinitesimal space between us as his body leans closer, heat radiating from his skin in invisible waves. The air seems to tilt, gravity shifting when his shoulder brushes mine—the lightest touch unraveling something tight within.

My gaze lifts, drawn to his profile like a compass finding north. He's already watching, eyes sharp and shadowed beneath dark lashes, their weight pulling me under like an undertow. There's a faint catch in my breathing as his attention drops to my lips. The shift whispers through the air between us, subtle yet unmistakable.

It would be so easy.

One tilt of my chin.

One lean forward.

One inch separates the charged air between us from something more.

His lips part just slightly, like maybe he's thinking the same thing, like perhaps he's about to say something, or maybe not say anything at all.

My pulse pounds, wild and erratic. Every part of me leans toward him, toward whatever this is. Toward something I shouldn't want but suddenly, desperately *need*.

But before I can decide—before either of us does anything, the front door flies open with a bright, cheerful *ding*!

The sound shatters the moment, loud and grating in the silence we've wrapped ourselves in. The chilly mountain air spills into the café, dousing the heat between us, followed by the noise of chatter and excited voices. A group of tourists pours inside, four or five of them, their sun-flushed faces scanning the café as they clamor loudly about pastries.

Max straightens, the glint of something unreadable slipping back behind the guarded mask of calm he always wears. A beat passes, his eyes catching mine for one last fleeting second, and my knees almost buckle under the weight of whatever that was.

And then, like it never happened, he steps back. Just one step, but it's enough to unspool the pull dragging me closer to him.

The tourists keep talking, oblivious to what they've interrupted, and I fling myself into action before I can think too much about what I was about to do. "Customer Service Lily" reactivates like a reflex—steps practiced and precise as I duck out from behind the latte station, moving toward the counter like nothing has changed.

My shoulders are stiff, my skin thrumming with heat that refuses to cool, but I keep moving. Keep busy.

To his credit, Max doesn't press. He doesn't call attention to my awkward, flustered retreat or the crimson I'm sure is painting my neck. He doesn't try to pull me back into that magnetic tension that left my mind empty and my body leaning into instincts I'm not ready for.

Instead, he drifts back to his booth like we didn't just stand at the edge of something vast and unspoken.

As for me, I'm not calm, cool, and collected like him. I'm not fine *at all*. Not really. My heart refuses to settle—the erratic rhythm battering against every wall I've built since moving here.

And just like that, another day passes.

Angel's Peak

CHAPTER 10

THE NEXT MORNING, THE BELL ABOVE THE DOOR chimes at exactly 7:02.

Max's arrival slices into the quiet hum of the shop. Outside, the pale morning light has begun to stretch itself across the street, but inside, the air shifts the moment he steps through the door.

There's a brief gust of mountain chill that follows him in, clinging to his cashmere sweater—dark slate today, like the morning sky threatening rain. He pauses near the door, a single nod for me across the room, his mouth curving—barely —at the edges when his gaze flicks to the corner booth.

It's already waiting for him.

The glass water bottle sweats with condensation beside a slim thrift-store vase holding two sprigs of purple lupine and a daisy, fresh from the side garden. In front of the vase, propped against the salt cellar, sits a small hand-lettered card:

Today: Single-origin Yirgacheffe — pour-over.
Flavors: Blueberry, cocoa, and jasmine as it cools.

Max studies the card for a moment, the smallest crease forming between his brows before his hand drops to brush the corner of it with one finger—gentle, deliberate. His laptop and notebook fall into their usual lineup on the table, his pen sliding parallel to the edge. His phone is face down near the water, as always.

When he settles into the booth, his shoulders lose the tension he carries through the door, like he's shrugging off weight that doesn't belong in here. The quiet of the shop seems to wrap around him the way it does me before opening hours.

His finger trails across the edge of the card again, his touch reverent. He doesn't pick it up, doesn't distract with chatter, nods slightly, the curve of his mouth deepening.

The grinder hums as I measure the beans, the aroma of blueberry and soft cocoa pressing into the warm air. The coffee blooms beneath the first pour, soft spirals of water teasing jasmine into the steam. Each pass of the kettle is steady, deliberate.

My body has memorized this movement. My hands move mechanically, but my focus remains fractured, trailing back to him—to the careful way he cradles his water bottle and scans the rising steam from the coffee, to how this all feels automatic now, like he belongs here as a fixture of the shop.

I walk over his first cup of the day, steam blooming from the rich roast.

"Pour-over to start," I murmur, stopping beside the table. "You'll get the blueberry if you let it sit."

"Thank you."

When I set the ceramic mug beside him, he doesn't reach for it right away. His hands settle around the cup like he's absorbing its warmth through his skin, holding onto the moment before the sip.

His lashes brush once against his cheek as his eyes shut for a heartbeat, and when he raises the cup to his lips, his shoulders drop another fraction. The simple act of drinking coffee looks like something sacred when he does it.

It's unnerving. And captivating.

The bell jingles again, pulling my gaze from him. Eleanor shuffles inside, her thick scarf tucked into her coat, fingers tight around her coin purse. Her movements are slower than usual, and her left knee appears to be stiff.

"Morning, Eleanor." I offer her a warm smile. "Doing okay?"

"Ah, yes. It's just the weather. A storm's blowing in. At least, that's what my knee's telling me. It's more reliable than the weatherman, you know."

"I know." I laugh at her weather knee, and she's not wrong. It's more reliable than the weatherman. "Dark roast today?"

"Yes, please. You know what I like."

Max looks up from his table. His mouth curves into that faint smile of his, the one I'm starting to see as a replacement for words he'd rather not say. The tension that always lingers in his frame has slipped away entirely, and he stands, his hands loose at his sides, easy as ever.

"Have a seat," he says, his voice mellow, his movements fluid. "I'll run it over."

"Oh," Eleanor says, startled but smiling all the same. She waves one hand dismissively, but it does nothing to stop him as he steps closer to the counter. "You don't have to, but that's so sweet of you." She tucks herself into her favorite corner table near the window, wincing only slightly as she eases into the chair across from Max.

Her gaze shifts to me, glinting in the morning light, to where I stand behind the counter, watching, assessing, calculating.

Meddling.

Max holds my gaze briefly as I prepare Eleanor's dark roast

behind the bar. The mug fills, steam rising in soft ribbons through the air.

When I slide it to the end of the counter, he's already there waiting, his hands braced lightly on the edge. His fingers curl around the mug—careful, delicate—as though he's holding something breakable. There's a casual sort of ease about him now, but there's also something intentional in the way he moves, like he enjoys anticipating the steps before they need to happen.

As he walks the mug to Eleanor's table, he dodges a group of high schoolers who rush in and salivate over the pastry case.

"You'll spoil me," Eleanor says as the dark roast touches the table in front of her.

"Working on it," Max replies, the line almost cocky but landing softly instead, some subtle warmth threaded through his words.

She clasps her hands, blowing lightly on the surface of the coffee. "Lily never spoils me like this."

The interaction is short and simple. He doesn't look at me when he slides past the counter again, but my body betrays me regardless—my chest tightening, stomach flipping against my will.

Eleanor's eyes twinkle with mischief as she turns her attention to me. "You should know that Ruth Fletcher is planning to corner you about the Rocky Mountain Coffee Championship."

My hands still on the coffee carafe. "What about it?"

"It's being held in Riverdale next month. First time it's been this close to Angel's Peak." She watches my reaction closely. "Ruth thinks your specialty lattes should be entered. Said your cinnamon latte is 'competition-worthy.'"

"I happen to agree." Max turns to me. "Your blends are special, Lily. The kind that deserve recognition beyond this town."

I busy myself wiping down the already spotless counter, mind racing. The Rocky Mountain Coffee Championship is a prestigious event in the specialty coffee world. Winners often receive national attention, distribution deals, opportunities to expand. The kind of exposure I've deliberately avoided since leaving BrewTech.

"I don't do competitions," I say finally.

"Maybe you should." Eleanor sips her coffee, studying me over the rim. "Hiding your light under a bushel serves no one, least of all yourself."

Before I can respond, a group of hikers enters, saving me from further discussion. The morning continues in a flurry of activity—the pre-storm rush as locals stock up on caffeine before hunkering down at home.

The last hiker shuffles away, backpack jingling. Max's empty cup slides across the bartop. He taps twice on its rim—our signal that has evolved without ever being discussed. When I approach, his eyes lift from the glass, meeting mine with that careful neutrality he's perfected.

"Surprise me," he says, voice pitched low enough that only I can hear. "Something you'd drink." The request hangs between us, more intimate than it should be—as if he's asking to taste something of me, not just liquor. His mouth twitches —just barely—the edge of his jaw tightening over some thought I want to reach out and pluck from his head.

Ice clinks. Tonic fizzes clear. I pull a tight double—crema banded gold—then float it over the bubbles. Orange oils spray under my thumb, perfuming the glass.

Max doesn't rush the drink, letting the orange and coffee mingle across his tongue like it's worth savoring. His fingers rest lightly on the side of the glass, tracing lazy circles over the condensation. He glances up then, catching my eye as I pass near his table.

"Damn," he says, voice low but cutting through the soft

hum of the café. His lids lower like he's enjoying some private relief. "That's good." One corner of his mouth tugs up, the smallest smile curling there. "I'd say you're spoiling me, but I don't want it to stop."

He says it like it's a joke, but something flickers in his tone, quiet, almost unguarded. The words land square in my chest, making me grip the edge of my towel tighter than necessary.

I tilt my head at him instead, unfazed. "Careful, Lawson," I say, sliding a small dish of candied orange peel toward the corner of his table. Its sticky sweetness glistens faintly in the muted sunlight. "You'll start to expect special treatment."

His fingers reach for the dish. He plucks a thin strip of orange, holding it between his thumb and forefinger like it's evidence of some larger truth. "Expect?" His brow arches. "I'm already ruined by it." He gestures with the glass in a small tilt toward me. "By you." His voice loses its mock gravity, dropping quieter. "I mean, let's be honest—how am I supposed to drink coffee anywhere else now?"

I laugh under my breath, ignoring the heat crawling up my neck. "Pretty sure Starbucks'll survive if I stop ruining you."

If there's a compliment lingering underneath, I don't acknowledge it. I don't trust myself to. Instead, I return behind the bar as the door jingles and two contractors step inside, sawdust and cold clinging to their heavy boots.

Their boisterous energy breaks the thread of wherever our conversation was going, and I busy myself by pulling a double shot for their macchiato order.

A few minutes later, while the contractors dig into their coffees and warm blueberry scones, I clear a stray cup from a nearby table to give myself an excuse to glance toward Max again.

The scene hasn't changed much. His laptop glows faintly, a notepad sits slightly off-center next to it, and his sleek pen now lies down at an angle across the page, as though it had been dropped mid-thought. His left hand hovers over the espresso tonic, circling the glass absently while his mind works in quieter ways than those contractors ever could.

The corner booth matches him, now more his space than mine. The glass water bottle glints in the sunlight streaming through the window, the thrift-shop vase leaning slightly with its lupines and solitary daisy, and my card—our small, running catalog of drinks and recommendations—is propped upright where he leaves it.

He settles seamlessly into the heartbeat of the café, like he's always belonged here, though it feels unnerving for all the ways he hasn't. And yet, it's impossible to untangle his rhythm from mine now—he's a fixture. Expected. Predictable, but quietly disruptive in all the ways that matter.

I return to the machine, falling into my own rhythm, weaving between incoming orders and stolen glances toward his booth. Another hour ticks by, and even in the midst of the small mid-morning crowd, the soft taps of his keyboard somehow thread through the space, syncing with the scrape of mugs, the occasional burst of laughter, the low hum of conversations.

A quiet exchange we've never discussed but have come to understand the rules of—he doesn't look at me when he places the empty glass at the edge of his table, leaving just enough room for something new.

I step toward the back bar where I've already set the ingredients for the next drink.

Am I spoiling him?

Possibly.

But spoiling him offers a strange kind of satisfaction I haven't felt in years, and somehow I don't want to stop.

By eleven, I switch the card at his table again.

Next: Maple-cinnamon cortado. Short. Intense.

I tamp a tight basket, watch the first amber strands strip

into tiger-tailed crema. Milk, not quite as hot; cinnamon dusted fine, maple folded through the foam. I set the glass down and wait. He lifts it, inhales like he's memorizing the scent. The sip is small, deliberate. Tongue pressing to his palate to catch the spice.

"Dangerous," he murmurs, and the word skates under my skin.

The lunch lull settles. The afternoon passes, and I set the next card down at his table when he steps away to take a call. When he returns to the booth, he lifts my card.

If you make it to four p.m.: Dark-chocolate chili mocha. Heat under sweet.

He taps the edge with his pen, eyes lifting to meet mine across the room. No smile. Just recognition. A promise that he'll be here at four.

I turn to the grinder, cinnamon and cocoa already waiting, and tell myself this is good business. The steam rising from the pitcher argues otherwise.

Angel's Peak

A STORM ALERT CUTS THROUGH THE LINGERING rhythm of the café's afternoon lull, sharp and undeniable.

"Angel's Peak and surrounding communities should prepare for severe winter conditions," the weather announcer's voice crackles through my phone speaker. *"The National Weather Service has issued a winter storm warning beginning this afternoon through tomorrow morning. Accumulations of two to three feet are expected at higher elevations, with wind gusts up to forty miles per hour creating white-out blizzard conditions. Travel will be impossible in many areas. Residents are advised to prepare for power outages and—"*

I silence it with a tap of my thumb, already glancing toward the windows. The glass fogs faintly at the edges, but I can still see the sky outside, dull and heavy with thickening clouds that cling to the peaks and spill downward like smoke.

Snow hasn't started falling heavily yet, just the occasional flurry dusting the street like sugar, but the familiar pressure sits low in the air, warning me it won't hold for long. Storms in Angel's Peak might start slow, but when they arrive, they have teeth—sharp, dangerous, and unpredictable, catching even locals off guard.

The bell jingles, and I blow out a breath, glancing reflexively toward the door.

"Afternoon, Lily."

Not Max.

Mayor Reynolds enters, stamping the dusting of snow from his boots onto the mat by the door. His coat is unzipped —an optimistic sign that won't last long—and he rubs his hands together briskly as he makes his way to the counter.

"Afternoon, Mayor."

"Quite the system moving in." He jerks his chin toward the windows as I move to pour his usual Americano.

"I just heard the alert," I reply, sliding the warm cup across the counter.

He wraps his chilled hands around it, cradling it with visible relief as though the ceramic itself could will the storm away.

"Bad enough to shut the town down?" I ask.

"Highway patrol's already getting ready to close Route 14. Donovan's got his deputies out, keeping an eye on key points. It's going to hit fast and nasty—like a mule kick to the gut. I'd suggest closing up early and getting home while you can. This one's going to be a doozy."

I tilt my head to the windows again, watching as the clouds pull closer like curtains dropping over the peaks. "I appreciate the warning."

He nods and drops an extra dollar in the tip jar before pausing. His smirk, small but deliberate, creeps onto his face. "Where's your shadow today?"

There's no need to ask who he means, and I pretend the light flush creeping into my cheeks doesn't exist. "Outside, on a call."

I think.

His gaze lingers a second longer than it should, teasing without words. "Well...when he gets back, tell him he ought to head back to The Haven sooner rather than later. Once those mountain roads ice over, even four-wheel drive will be no good, and with white-out conditions expected, traveling on foot won't just be inconvenient. It'll be deadly."

The bell over the door jingles, and I freeze. A gust of cold bites at my ankles as the door opens wide. I spin toward the entrance, already expecting to see him standing there.

But it's not Max.

A middle-aged couple stumbles into the shop instead. Their outdoor gear is pristine—bright orange and black jackets layered over tech-savvy thermal pants, their boots barely scuffed from wear. They shed snowflakes in a hurry, their expressions harried as they approach me.

"I'm so sorry," the woman says first, her gloved hands fumbling with the zipper of her jacket. "Do you have some-where...somewhere we could wait out the storm? We didn't realize it was supposed to get this bad."

Her partner follows closely, shaking snow from his hair. "We were hiking down from Sunrise Ridge Trail when it started picking up. By the time we got to the car, the roads were already impossible to navigate."

"Storm's catching everyone off guard." I gesture toward the nearest table. "You can sit as long as you need, but you may want to get back to your lodging sooner rather than later. Let me get you something warm."

The woman wastes no time, collapsing into a chair with a visible shiver while the man lingers at her side, scanning the café as though trying to orient himself. His eyes linger at the corner booth, Max's usual spot—in its predictable order: vase, card, everything waiting exactly as it was.

"Where are you staying?" Mayor Reynolds asks.

"Up at the lodge," the man says.

"You're in luck, I can give you a ride, but Lily's got a point. We need to leave now. The roads won't be passable for much longer."

"Thanks," the woman mumbles. "We really didn't think—"

"You're fine," Reynolds assures them. "I'm headed up there as it is. More than happy to give you a lift." He turns to me. "Lily, make sure you close up and head home before it gets much worse."

"I'm on it."

After the mayor leaves with the couple, I prep for an early closure. My steps are quick, my movements more deliberate than usual as I count the till, stack pastry boxes, and double-check the windows against the wind that howls harder with every passing minute.

The storm outside is relentless—snow swirling in thick, chaotic gusts past the streetlights, clawing at the glass. It's only mid-afternoon, but the heavy, low-hanging clouds make it feel like dusk.

I'm just finishing a final wipe of the counter when the bell chimes. My heart jumps—half from relief, half from the nervous energy that's been building between glimpses at the clock.

Max steps inside, a cold-stung blur of gray wool and damp edges. His coat and boots are coated in thick layers of fresh snow, flakes clinging stubbornly to his sleeves and collar, while stray droplets melt and streak down his cashmere scarf. His dark hair is damp too, dripping slightly at the ends, a few beads of water slipping down the curve of his cheekbone and jaw.

He stops just inside the door, planting both feet firmly on the mat, and stomps hard to shake off the snow. One gloved hand drags across his jaw, swiping away some of the damp before he glances toward me, his chest rising with a sharp breath like he's just walked straight through a blizzard.

"Have you seen what's happening out there?" he asks, voice clipped but tinged with something lighter, something that sounds closer to relief than frustration. He unwinds his scarf, tugging it loose and tossing it into his palm. "The road to The Haven is already nearly impassable."

"You're frozen." I can't stop staring at him for a moment, taking in the mess of snow and cold against his otherwise sleek, comfortable exterior. "Did you drive down in this?"

"No."

"Then how did you—"

"Walked. Thought I'd enjoy the snowfall." He exhales sharply. "Did not expect how fast the storm would get."

"Walked? You shouldn't even be outside."

"I know. But I wanted to see if you needed any help." He shrugs, a faint curve at the edge of his mouth, though his movements are stiff with cold. Snowflakes scatter from his sleeves as he tugs at the zipper of his coat.

"Help?" I tilt my head toward the gray-white chaos outside.

"Yeah." He exhales, short and sharp as he pulls free of his coat, draping it over his arm. Despite the cold clinging to his skin, he looks warm in that steady, self-possessed way I've learned is just him.

His hand runs through his damp hair where the snow's melted, a casual kind of gesture that seems more like instinct than thought.

My eyes flick toward his booth, unchanged since this morning. The card propped by the vase. I'd almost forgotten it was still there, like a quiet placeholder for every moment I spent glancing toward the door, waiting for him to walk in.

I fold the towel and lean back against the counter. "You shouldn't have risked it."

"And miss the chance to play hero? Never." His lips twitch, that faint smile appearing again as he steps deeper into the warmth of the café, snow trailing in damp patches across the hardwood.

There's enough lightness in the words to make me roll my eyes. But the way his smile lingers—gentle at the edges, something a little too close to sincerity glinting just behind it—keeps my response lodged in my throat.

Instead, I nod toward the corner booth. "Well, your booth is still waiting. Untouched."

"Good," he says, stepping away with a new ease, peeling off a glove and dropping it into his coat pocket. "Didn't want to risk losing my card collection. Wouldn't know what to drink without you."

Heat blooms across my cheeks, but I shake my head, letting out a soft laugh I hope will deflect the strange little ache threading through his words.

"We've got work to do if we're getting out of here before the roads disappear. The storm's accelerating, and everyone is hunkering down." I study his appearance more carefully, noticing the shadows under his eyes and tension in his jaw. "You really should head back if you want any chance of making it."

His brows furrow.

"Everything okay?" I ask, surprising myself with the concern in my voice.

"Just..." He runs a hand through his snow-damp hair. "Technical difficulties. Been working since four this morning trying to solve an encryption issue."

"Wait here." I study him for a moment, then make a decision.

In the back room, I pull out ingredients I've been saving for a special recipe—cardamom, cinnamon, a touch of saffron, and my secret weapon, a dark chocolate infused with chili.

The preparation takes precision and patience, the aroma rich and complex as it comes together.

When I return, Max stares out the window at the intensifying storm, shoulders tight with whatever weight he's carrying.

"Try this." I place a tall glass mug before him, filled with a creation that looks nothing like his usual order.

"What is it?" He turns, eyebrow raised.

"Off-menu special. The Cognitive Reboot."

Skepticism crosses his features, but he takes the mug, inhaling the aroma first—a habit I've noticed and appreciated. His first sip is tentative, followed immediately by a second, longer one. His eyes widen slightly.

"This is..." He takes another sip, closing his eyes briefly. "What's in it?"

"Trade secret." I lean against the counter. "How's the encryption problem?"

"How did you know it was encryption?"

I pause and cock my head. "You literally just said you were trying to solve an encryption issue."

"Did I?"

"Yes." I don't mention that I understand exactly what he's working on from the snippets of calls I've overheard.

His eyes narrow slightly, studying me with renewed interest. "You know, for someone who runs a small-town coffee shop, you have a surprisingly technical vocabulary. Yesterday, you referenced API integration when talking about online ordering systems."

"I read a lot." Heat crawls up my neck.

"Mmm." He doesn't look convinced. "And last week, when my laptop was glitching, you suggested it might be a memory allocation issue rather than a software conflict. Most people wouldn't make that distinction."

I busy myself wiping down the counter, avoiding his gaze.

"I picked up some tech knowledge over the years. Hazard of living in the digital age."

"Some knowledge." The skepticism in his voice is clear. "You diagnosed a recursive function error by glancing at my screen. That's not casual tech knowledge. That's computer science expertise."

My chest tightens with familiar anxiety. This is exactly what I've been afraid of—someone connecting the dots between who I am now and who I was before.

"I took some courses in college," I say, finally, the partial truth easier than outright lies. "Before I realized coffee was my true calling."

"Must have been quite the program." He doesn't press further, but his expression tells me he's filed this information away for future reference. "This drink really is remarkable. The cardamom's a brilliant touch."

"I designed it for focus and mental clarity." I allow the subject change, relieved. "The combination of compounds in the spices and chocolate triggers specific cognitive responses."

"You approach flavor like a scientist." His observation hits uncomfortably close to home. "Systematic, precise, with clear intended outcomes." He studies me over the rim of the mug, eyes narrowing slightly. "There's something about you, Lily Brock."

"I get that a lot. Usually followed by requests for free coffee."

His laughter is unexpected, warming the space between us more effectively than any heater. "The way you approach flavor reminds me of coding. Precision, balance, unexpected combinations that somehow work perfectly together."

If he only knew, but if he did, he'd run away from me as fast as he could. My reputation within the tech world is a shambles. The comparison surprises me, along with the fact that it doesn't immediately put me on the defensive.

"I never thought about it that way."

"It's all science in the end." He takes another sip, expression thoughtful. "Whether it's coffee or code. Finding the perfect balance of elements to create something greater than the sum of its parts."

"Spoken like a true tech philosopher."

"Spoken like someone who recognizes craft when he sees it." His gaze holds mine, unexpectedly sincere. "What you do here—it's art. Don't let anyone convince you it's just coffee."

The compliment catches me off guard, settling warm in my chest. Before I can respond, a violent gust of wind rattles the windows, drawing our attention to the worsening storm.

The bell chimes, snow gusting in with a blast of frigid air. Hannah Lewis enters, her auburn hair tucked beneath a knitted cap, arms laden with books.

"Lily! Thank goodness you're still open." She hurries to the counter, depositing her library books with a thud. "I'm making emergency deliveries to the elderly residents before the roads close. Could I get four chai lattes to go? Mrs. Peterson and her bridge club refused to cancel their weekly game despite the weather."

"Coming right up." I move to prepare the drinks, noting how Max automatically shifts to make room for Hannah at the counter.

"You must be the tech wizard everyone's talking about," Hannah says, extending a hand to Max. "Hannah Lewis, town librarian and unofficial gossip clearinghouse. Well, almost. I think Eleanor or Ruth might have me outmatched, but can't blame a girl for trying."

"Max Lawson." He shakes her hand, a hint of amusement in his eyes. "And what's the gossip saying?"

"Oh, the usual small-town speculation." Hannah waves dismissively. "Secret billionaire? Corporate spy? Heartbroken recluse seeking mountain solitude to heal? The theories get wilder by the day."

I nearly drop a chai tea bag at the "corporate spy" mention, but Hannah continues, oblivious to my reaction.

"Personally, I'm betting on the 'burnt-out genius seeking inspiration' theory. We get at least one of those each year, though usually they're novelists, not tech moguls."

"And what makes you think I'm burnt out?" Max asks, seeming genuinely curious.

"The way you stare at the mountains when you think no one's looking." Hannah's assessment is surprisingly insightful. "Like you're trying to absorb some essential truth from them. Classic sign of someone who's lost their north star."

An uncomfortable silence follows her observation. I busy myself with the chai lattes, giving Max space to respond or deflect as he chooses.

"Perhaps you're in the wrong profession, Ms. Lewis," he says finally. "With that kind of perception, you'd make an excellent psychologist."

"Oh, I considered it. But books are far less complicated than people." She accepts the carrier of chai lattes I hand her. "Though sometimes just as revealing." She gives Max a significant look. "Your choice of reading material says a lot about you."

"Does it?" His tone is carefully neutral.

"Mmm. 'The Ethics of Privacy in the Digital Age' isn't casual beach reading." She smiles at his surprised expression. "I'm a librarian. I notice what people read. You've been using our research terminal during our extended hours."

I hadn't known Max was visiting the library. The revelation that he's been integrating himself into Angel's Peak beyond just Mountain Brew creates a strange feeling in my chest—not quite jealousy, but something adjacent. A sense that he's building connections in my town, my sanctuary, that exist independent of me.

"Anyway, I should get these delivered before they cool." Hannah nods toward the window, where the snow falls more heavily now. "Lily, don't stay open too late. This storm is moving faster than predicted."

After she leaves, Max returns to his mug, a thoughtful expression on his face. "Interesting woman."

"Hannah sees everything." I begin preparing for closing, aware of how quickly the weather is deteriorating. "And remembers everything. She's been cataloguing Angel's Peak's secrets since she was old enough to read."

"Including yours?" His question is casual, but his eyes are intent.

"I don't have secrets. I make coffee, and you should probably go." The words feel strange in my mouth, reluctant. "It's getting worse by the minute."

Max glances at his watch, then back at the storm. "What about you? When will you head home?"

"After I close up. My cottage is only a few blocks away."

He stares into his coffee for a moment, seemingly debating something. "Mind if I stay a bit longer? That drink is doing something to my brain chemistry, and I think I just figured out the encryption solution." He pulls his laptop from his bag, clutching it against his chest.

"Told you. Cognitive Reboot." I gesture to his usual booth. "Stay as long as you need. I'm officially closed anyway."

While Max works, I complete my closing routine, occasionally stealing glances at him. The tension has eased from his shoulders, replaced by focused intensity as his fingers fly across the keyboard. His presence should feel intrusive in the empty shop, but somehow it doesn't.

Angel's Peak

Chapter 12

"You know, most people go to the mountains to escape work, not bring more of it." I slide a fresh mug beside Max's laptop.

An hour has passed since I officially closed, yet here we are —him typing with monastic focus, me pretending there's still cleaning to do. The shop's silence is punctuated only by his keystrokes and the occasional muttered curse when something doesn't compile.

He doesn't look up, just reaches blindly for the mug. "Most people don't have investors breathing down their necks." His fingers find the handle, and he takes a sip without breaking eye contact with his screen. Then freezes. Blinks. Finally looks at me.

"This isn't coffee."

"Congratulations on your functioning taste buds." I lean against the counter, arms crossed. "It's hot chocolate with a splash of bourbon. Even code-breaking geniuses need sugar sometimes."

He takes another sip, slower this time. The corner of his

mouth lifts—not quite a smile, but close enough to count as a victory. "Not bad. Though I'm not sure mixing alcohol with cryptography is wise."

The corner of my mouth twitches like I'm about to say something smart, but the wind howls against the window hard enough to steal my attention.

Outside, Angel's Peak has vanished entirely, swallowed by thick, blinding sheets of white. From here, you wouldn't even know there were mountains behind the storm. Snow slams against the door in gusting waves, the drifts piling quickly against the front walkway.

Max follows my gaze to the snow-covered glass, his shoulders tightening at the sound of the wind scraping against the corners of the building. My phone buzzes on the counter, cutting through the silence and the weather outside.

We both glance down as the town's emergency alert system flashes across my screen:

ALL ROADS CLOSED. SHELTER IN PLACE UNTIL FURTHER NOTICE.

I glance at him from the corner of my eye, my pulse suddenly louder than the storm outside.

"Well," I say, slipping the phone back onto the counter, trying to sound steadier than I feel. "Looks like you're stuck here."

Max leans back slightly, the faintest ghost of a smile returning to his face. "At least I know the coffee's good."

Perfect.

He glances toward the windows, seeming to register the storm's intensity for the first time.

I turn toward the windows as another violent gust shakes the glass.

"These old windows weren't made for storms like this. I need to secure the shutters."

"Let me help." Max closes his laptop and rises to follow me.

The wooden shutters are original to the building—charming, yes, but nothing about them is designed for convenience. Each has to be manually closed from the outside, then secured from the inside with iron hooks. During a blizzard, even twenty minutes of work stretches into an endless, exhausting battle against the wind.

Max works beside me, matching my motions as if he's been doing this for years. The quiet between us feels companionable, but there's an edge to it, a tension unfurling in the spaces between glances, touches, and breaths. Every gust of wind that rattles the windows feels like it tightens something invisible between us.

"Last one," I murmur, stepping toward the final window. The iron hook dangles loose against the frame, swinging gently as I reach for it.

Max moves at the same time. His hand collides with mine, warm despite the cold radiating through the glass.

The light contact sends a thin, shimmering current straight through me. His fingers brush over the back of my hand, firm and sure, before resting there, as though if he let go, the hook might disappear entirely.

I should pull away. But I don't.

And then neither does he.

For a moment, the sounds of the storm fade, the wind's relentless howl disappearing under the steady pulse of my heartbeat hammering in my ears. I turn my head, and his face is closer than I expect—too close, far too close.

Every detail assaults me at once: the faint droplets of water still clinging to his dark lashes, the shadows cast by his sharp jawline, the slightly parted curve of his lips.

His eyes lock onto mine, the blue of them darker now, storm-shadowed and intent. I forget how to breathe as he studies me, his gaze tracing a path over my face, heavy and heated, impossible to turn away from.

"Careful, Lily..." The words come low and rough, barely audible over the storm, but somehow they sink into me like a physical touch.

My name on his lips should be innocuous, even casual, but this time it's something else entirely—a weighted warning, a restrained hunger that tightens around me like a net.

"What?"

His next words are softer, deliberate, but molten with promise. "If you keep looking at me like that, I'm going to have to kiss you."

My throat goes dry. Every nerve in my body tightens in anticipation. I don't remember deciding to look at him like anything. But now, I know exactly what he means.

Logic screams at me to step back, to break this before it breaks me. But somehow, I can't. I couldn't stop the way my body leans in, even if I wanted to—and I don't want to, not even for a second.

Max moves first, unhurried and deliberate, like he's testing that fragile line between hesitation and inevitability. His free hand lifts, warm fingers brushing along my jaw until they find my chin. His touch is gentle but firm, tipping my face until there's no space left for pretense.

His thumb grazes the faint curve of my jaw as he tilts my head, a steadying motion that sends sparks scattering through my skin. The contact burns, but it's the look in his eyes that leaves me molten—molten and rooted, unable to move or think or breathe.

The storm rages outside, snow slamming against the glass, the shutters vibrating faintly with every gust of wind. But I barely hear it. All I can hear is the rasp of his breath, low and warm, mingling with mine. All I can feel is the tension crackling between us, a current building so intensely it's unbearable.

And then, finally, he lowers his head, his lips brushing mine softly at first—a tentative exploration, as if giving me one last chance to pull away.

I don't.

My response is immediate and uncontrollable. I press closer, my hand lifting on instinct to press flat against his chest. His heartbeat beats against my palm, hard and fast, matching my own—or maybe it's the other way around.

Max deepens the kiss, his mouth moving over mine with an intensity that steals whatever breath I have left. Heat floods through me, gathering low and urgent, as my fingers curl into the soft wool of his sweater for balance.

His hand slips from my chin, thumb lingering momentarily at the corner of my mouth. His fingertips drift downward, mapping the curve where my jaw meets my neck, hovering over my pulse—a ghost of contact that somehow burns hotter than a direct touch. His palm follows, skimming the column of my throat where each swallow becomes embarrassingly visible to him.

His touch skates across my collarbone, tracing its ridge like a cartographer memorizing coastlines. His fingers fan out, spreading across the slope of my shoulder, then reunite to trail down the length of my arm—one continuous, unbroken line that leaves goosebumps rising in its wake. His hand circles my elbow, thumb stroking the sensitive inside bend before continuing its journey.

When his fingers reach my wrist, they pause to count my heartbeats, then slip to my side, palm flattening against my ribs where each breath pushes me further into his touch. His hand slides around to the small of my back, fingers splaying wide, claiming territory as they settle at my waist—low and possessive. He pulls me flush against him, and I go willingly, my body arching to meet him as though it's impossible to avoid.

It isn't enough.

The cold of the window against my back shocks me slightly when he presses me against it, but it only seems to fan the fire growing between us. Max braces one hand beside my head, his other tangling into my hair, his grip firm yet achingly gentle. The sensation sends a shudder down my spine, and I press up into him, craving his warmth, his weight, his presence.

The kiss demands more from me than I know how to give —but I give it anyway, my lips moving eagerly against his, answering the wordless hunger in every movement. His scent surrounds me, a mix of coffee, woodsmoke, and cold air, making me dizzy.

Max groans low in his throat, the sound vibrating through both of us as his lips part mine deeper, coaxing, commanding, but with a tenderness that steals the ground out from under me.

My fingers find his neck, brushing the soft, damp hair there before tracing down the hard line of his collar. The smooth fabric of his shirt beneath my fingertips almost feels too delicate for the strength thrumming through him.

The lights flicker violently above us, plunging the shop into a brief, heavy darkness. The backup generator kicks in almost immediately, sending a dim glow over the space, but the momentary shock doesn't pull us apart.

We break the kiss only when the need for air overrides everything else, our breath mingling as he rests his forehead against mine. His grip on my waist remains firm, his thumb stroking my hip in slow, grounding circles even as his breaths come sharp and uneven.

"I'm sorry. I shouldn't have done that," he murmurs, voice

rough and low, his words betraying the unsteadiness sharp in his chest.

"No," I reply, my hands still clutching him tightly, my fingers curling possessively under the collar of his shirt. The heat of his skin burns against my fingertips, and I can't bring myself to let go. "You shouldn't have."

The hint of a smirk flickers on his lips, dangerous and knowing. His pupils dilate as his gaze drops to my mouth again, darkening his eyes to midnight.

"But I did." His thumb strokes my cheek again, softer now but just as possessive. The callus on his thumb catches slightly on my skin, sending shivers down my spine.

"You did." My voice emerges as barely more than a whisper, the two simple words carrying the weight of surrender.

"I don't regret it, but you need to be careful." His jaw tightens, a muscle there jumping beneath his skin as he fights some internal battle.

"Of what?" I lean back just enough to search his face, my fingers unconsciously tightening on his shirt, pulling him closer even as I create space between us.

He dips his head, lips brushing the shell of my ear as his voice drops to a rough whisper. "Because what I want is to back you against that counter, lift you onto it, and ravage you the way I have every night in my dreams."

His breath catches, warm against my skin. "I want to worship every inch of you until you're singing my name like a prayer." His fingers tighten fractionally at my waist, the tremble in them betraying how tightly he's holding onto his control. "But I should warn you—I'm not good at denying myself what I want. If you say yes..." His voice roughens, breaking slightly on the next words. "I'll take everything you're willing to give. And I've imagined so much."

I feel his words everywhere—heavy, electric, promising things that make my pulse stutter. For a heartbeat, all I can do is stare up at him, breathless, savoring the sharp, wild ache he's kindled inside me. I press my hips a little closer, making sure he feels my answer in the flush of my body against his.

"Yes." The word escapes before I can think better of it, and my voice is unsteady, wrecked with wanting. I swallow hard, then meet his gaze directly. "What exactly have you fantasized about?" My question carries surrender in its edges, an offering.

"Your back against this wall." His eyes darken impossibly further, and his voice roughens. "My hands exploring every inch of you, taking you right here where anyone could walk in." He studies my reaction carefully. "I've imagined you sprawled across this counter, on the desk in your back office, in my shower with steam rising around us." He pauses, gauging me. "And yes, on your knees, looking up at me." His thumb traces my lower lip. "Too much? Or not enough?"

A shiver runs through me, not from fear but anticipation. My breath comes faster, my skin flushing hot beneath his gaze.

"Not enough," I whisper, surprising myself with my boldness.

His grin turns wicked, his hand flexing on my waist. The promise between us, old as the storm outside, is no longer just a maybe. His eyes darken to obsidian as they lock with mine, raw hunger barely contained beneath his careful control. The tension in his shoulders shifts from restraint to purpose, his body coiling like a predator finally given permission to hunt.

When his thumb traces the curve of my lower lip, the callused pad catches slightly, sending lightning down my spine that pools molten in my core.

"Good," he breathes, the single word carrying the weight of every night he's spent wanting this—wanting me. "That was just the prelude." His grip tightens, possessive. "I have desires that would make you blush in places no one can see, appetites that would leave marks on your skin for days." His voice drops to a near-growl. "I want to push you to edges you didn't know existed, then catch you when you fall." His breath caresses my ear. "The question is whether you're brave enough to discover them." His challenge hangs between us, a door opening to something both frightening and irresistible.

His other hand slides to the small of my back, pressing me impossibly closer while his fingers slip beneath the hem of my shirt to find bare skin. He makes a sound—half groan, half sigh—as though touching me has unlocked something primal within him. His palm splays wide, claiming territory as he bends to recapture my mouth.

Outside, winter rages. Inside, with him, I am already burning.

Before I can respond, my phone rings—the emergency tone I've assigned to official calls. The harsh electronic sound slices through the heated air between us. For a moment, we freeze, connected at every point, neither willing to be the first to break away. The phone rings again, insistent.

Reluctantly, I extract myself from Max's embrace, pulse still racing as I answer. His hands linger until the last possible moment, fingertips trailing across my skin like a promise postponed rather than broken.

"Lily, it's Sheriff Donovan." His voice crackles with static. "Just checking you're safe at home."

"I'm still at the shop." I try to steady my breathing, acutely aware of Max watching me, his eyes still dark with unresolved hunger.

"The shop? Dammit, Lily, I thought... I told you to head to your cottage hours ago."

"Sorry, but I got caught up with closing procedures." It's not entirely a lie. My free hand unconsciously touches my lips, still swollen from Max's attention.

"Well, you're staying put now. Roads are completely impassable, and we've got power lines down all over town. Not to mention, it's blizzard conditions out there. Complete whiteout. Whatever you do, please do not leave your shop until this blows over." The sheriff's tone brooks no argument. "The shop's sturdy, and you've got that old generator, right?"

"I do." However, I've failed to do its annual maintenance for two years now. Not that I'll admit that to him.

"You'll be fine there until morning when my crews can clear the main roads."

"I will."

"Anyone else stuck there with you?"

I glance at Max, who has returned to his spot by the counter, leaning against it with deceptive casualness. The intensity in his gaze belies his relaxed posture. "Max Lawson. He came in before the worst hit."

"Well, that's lucky, at least. Two is better than one in these situations. You've got food, water?"

"Enough cookies, biscuits, and coffee to manage." My voice sounds strained even to my own ears.

"Good. Check-in if anything changes; otherwise, sit tight. This system should blow through by morning."

After hanging up, I stand frozen in the middle of the shop, reality crashing down.

Trapped overnight.

With Max.

After that kiss.

"I take it we're stuck here?" Max asks, expression unreadable, though his eyes still smolder like banked coals.

"Until morning at least." I run a hand through my hair, trying to regain composure.

The space between us feels electrified, charged with potential energy. Every movement seems magnified—the rise and fall of his chest, the way his fingers tap against the counter edge, the slight shift of his weight. The few feet separating us might as well be a minefield of unspoken promises.

"I should check the generator." I clear my throat, but it does nothing to dispel the thickness in the air.

"What can I do to help?" His voice has a ragged edge that sends a shiver down my spine. When I hesitate, he adds, "Put me to work."

"You could..." My mind scrambles for a task, anything to create distance. "Check the storage room for extra blankets? Second door on the left, past the restrooms."

He nods, pushing away from the counter. As he passes me, our shoulders nearly touch, and I swear I can feel heat radiating from him like a furnace. The ghost of his touch lingers on my skin.

An awkward silence descends, the air still charged with the energy of our interrupted moment. I busy myself checking the generator, assessing supplies, anything to avoid addressing what just happened. But when he returns with an armful of blankets, I can't avoid looking at him—the way his arms flex under the weight, how his eyes never leave mine as he sets them down on a nearby table.

With the Sheriff's words of caution, it's clear this storm has shifted from an inconvenience to a potential danger. I move purposefully through the shop, gathering flashlights and candles from behind the counter. All the while, the heat between us remains palpable, an invisible current that makes the hair on my arms stand on end whenever we pass too close.

His words echo in my mind—desires that would make me blush, appetites that would leave marks—and I fumble a stack of emergency candles, sending them clattering to the floor.

Max is there in an instant, helping me gather them. Our fingers brush, and we both freeze, the contact burning like a brand.

"Sorry," I mutter, though I'm not sure what I'm apologizing for.

His expression softens slightly. "Don't be." The words

carry weight beyond this moment, a reassurance about everything that passed between us.

Max gathers the remaining candles with efficient movements, his hands steady where mine had trembled. He arranges them in a neat row on the counter, then pauses, watching me fumble with the matches.

"Here," he says quietly, taking them from my unsteady fingers. His hands close over mine for just a moment, warm and grounding. "You're shaking."

I pull back, crossing my arms. "Just cold," I lie.

His mouth quirks up at one corner, seeing through me instantly. "Lily." Just my name, but spoken with such certainty that I have to meet his eyes. "Take a breath. Nothing's going to happen tonight that you're not ready for."

The tension in my shoulders eases slightly. "I didn't think—"

"You did." His smile is gentle now, though no less potent. "And I'm not sorry for finally telling you what I want." He strikes a match, lighting the first candle with deliberate focus. "I've waited too long to pretend I don't feel this." The flame illuminates the angles of his face, casting shadows that emphasize the intensity of his gaze. "But I am patient. Very patient, when something matters."

The way he says it—like I'm something precious to be savored rather than rushed—sends a different kind of heat through me, one that warms rather than burns.

"I've found that control is essential," he continues, lighting another candle, his movements precise, measured. "In all things worth having."

The words sink in slowly, then all at once. My breath catches as understanding crystallizes. The dominance in his stance, the careful restraint in his touch, his talk of appetites and desires—they weren't just heated words in the moment.

This is who he is.

What he wants.

What he needs.

Max Lawson—my quiet, brilliant regular with his coffee order I could recite in my sleep—is telling me exactly who he is beneath that composed exterior.

My cheeks flush hot, but not from embarrassment. Something primal stirs in response, a recognition I wasn't prepared to feel. The thought of surrendering control to him sends a liquid warmth through me that has nothing to do with the candles he's lighting. I've never thought about power dynamics beyond the occasional fantasy, but the steady assurance in his hands as they perform this simple task makes me wonder what those same hands could coax from me if I let them.

His eyes flick to mine, catching me watching him. Something knowing passes across his features—he sees my reaction, reads it like it's written in neon across my face.

I turn away abruptly, needing space to process this revelation. "The good news is, we have plenty of food," I announce, my voice slightly higher than normal as I busy myself cataloging the day's unsold pastries and sandwiches. "And obviously, no shortage of coffee."

The mundane words feel ridiculous after what just passed between us, but they give me a lifeline back to normalcy, a moment to catch my breath and consider what I want—and whether what I want terrifies me more than it excites me.

"What about the generator?" Max asks, following me to the utility closet. The way he says it—casual, professional— tells me he's giving me the space I need.

For now.

"Eight hours at full capacity. Longer if we're conservative." I check the fuel gauge, frowning slightly. "Though it hasn't had maintenance in... a while."

"Define 'a while'."

"Two years, give or take."

Max's eyebrows rise. "That's not ideal."

"I've been busy."

"Want me to take a look? I'm decent with engines."

I hesitate, weighing my independence against practicality. "You know how to service a generator?"

"My father was a mechanical engineer before he lost his job." He says this without self-pity, a simple statement of fact. "I grew up rebuilding engines with him. Generators are pretty straightforward by comparison."

I step aside, gesturing toward the machine. "Be my guest."

While Max examines the generator, I continue preparing for a night of sheltering in place. The shop's back office has a comfortable couch where I sometimes nap during busy seasons. With blankets and pillows, it will serve as our sleeping quarters for the night.

The intimacy of these preparations—gathering blankets, creating a makeshift bed we'll have to share—feels weighted with implications I'm not ready to face. The kiss lingers between us, unacknowledged but impossible to forget.

"You need a new air filter," Max calls from the utility closet. "And the oil should be changed. But I can get it running more efficiently with what's here."

"There should be basic maintenance supplies on the shelf above," I call back, arranging candles strategically around the shop.

Working together, we transform Mountain Brew from a coffee shop to a storm shelter. Max tends to the generator while I inventory supplies and secure anything that might be damaged if the temperature drops significantly overnight.

When there's nothing left to prepare, we find ourselves standing in the center of the shop. The kiss, his whispered desires, the way I pressed against him—all of it hangs in the air between us, electric and undeniable.

"Lily." His voice stops me as I wipe down a counter that's already clean. "We should talk about what happened."

I keep my eyes on the rag in my hand, suddenly unable to meet his gaze. "It's been... a long day." My voice emerges softer than intended, betraying my uncertainty.

"Look at me." He doesn't move closer, giving me space I both appreciate and resent. When I finally raise my eyes to his, the intensity I find there steals my breath. "I meant everything I said earlier."

A flush creeps up my neck. "That's... a lot to process."

"I know." His voice gentles. "And I shouldn't have over-whelmed you like that."

"No, it's not that." I struggle to find words for the storm of emotions inside me. "I just didn't expect... any of this. You've been coming here for days, and I never knew..."

"That I wanted you?" His directness makes me shiver. "I've wanted you since the first day when I literally ran into you, but there's a difference between wanting and acting."

"Thanks." I swallow hard. "Ummm....the back office has a decent couch. There are extra blankets and some emergency supplies. We'll manage for one night."

"One couch?" His question carries weight.

"One couch." I meet his gaze briefly before looking away again. "But it's better than the floor."

"I'll take the floor." His tone brooks no argument.

"Don't be ridiculous. The couch is big enough for both of us." Even as I say it, I know it's not true—not with the current running between us.

"No." The word is soft but final. "It's not about space. It's about the fact that if I lie next to you all night, feeling your body heat, smelling your skin..." He inhales sharply. "I'm only human. And after what happened earlier, after telling you exactly what I want to do to you, and seeing how your body responded—" He cuts himself off, jaw tight with restraint.

"The floor is the only place I can guarantee your safety tonight."

My heart stutters at his admission. I want to tell him I don't need guarantees, that maybe I want what he's offering, but the words stick in my throat. Everything is happening too fast, desires I didn't know I had surfacing under his steady gaze.

"I..." I trail off, uncertain what I'm trying to say.

His expression softens with understanding. "You don't have to decide anything tonight." He takes a small step closer, still maintaining distance. "Just know that when I said I'm patient, I meant it."

The sincerity in his voice touches something deep inside me. "I should check the generator again," I whisper, needing space to think clearly. "Make yourself comfortable. There's food in the mini-fridge if you're hungry."

"I'm not hungry for food." His gaze follows me, intense and knowing.

I retreat to the back office, my fingers trembling as I press them against my lips. They still tingle from his kiss, a sensation that lingers like a brand. My body feels foreign to me—hypersensitive, aware of itself in ways I've forgotten or never known.

This attraction is inconvenient at best, dangerous at worst. Max represents everything I fled from—the tech world, powerful men with secrets, complications I can't afford. A man who speaks of control as essential, who admits to darker desires without shame. A man whose mere presence makes me forget every carefully constructed boundary.

Yet, as I listen to him moving around in the front of the shop, I can't deny the pull between us, stronger than professional boundaries or common sense. His words echo in my mind—desires that would make me blush, appetites that would leave marks—and a small, hidden part of me wonders what it would be like to surrender to those desires, to let him take control in the ways he'd hinted at.

One kiss. That's all it was. But something fundamental has shifted between us, something neither the approaching blizzard nor my better judgment can stop.

We're an inevitability.

And now we have an entire night ahead of us, alone in the dark with nothing but a couch, a floor, and the dawning realization that I might want exactly what he's offering—if only I'm brave enough to take it.

Angel's Peak

CHAPTER 13

"You're surprisingly well-prepared for emergencies." Max helps me drape a heavy wool blanket over the worn leather couch, knuckles grazing mine—unintentional, but each contact still sizzles beneath my skin.

"Angel's Peak lesson number one: winter storms don't care about your plans." I retrieve emergency candles from a cabinet and arrange them on the desk. "I've been caught unprepared exactly once. Never again."

"What happened?"

He settles on the edge of the desk, and the soft glow from a candle flickers over the stubble along his jaw, drawing my eyes to his mouth. I force myself to focus on the battered matchbox in my hands.

"Power outage, middle of February, my first winter here. I nearly froze in my cottage before Noah Morgan realized I hadn't checked in and came to my rescue." A small, involuntary shiver runs through me—part memory, part the way Max is watching me, intent and unblinking. "After that, I stocked emergency supplies everywhere—home, car, shop."

"Smart." A rare softness skims across his features—something akin to respect, or maybe acknowledgement. He's close enough that I can still taste the memory of his mouth, and I wonder if my skin looks as flushed as it feels.

I light the last candle. Shadows flicker wildly along the ceiling, amplifying the hush between us. The space smells of melting wax, woodsmoke, and faintly, of him.

The back office is small but functional—just enough space for a desk, a filing cabinet, and the couch that doubles as my nap spot during busy seasons.

"Dinner options are limited." I rummage through the fridge. "Yogurt, cheese, some fruit. There's granola in that cabinet, and I've got emergency protein bars that taste like sweetened cardboard but will keep us alive."

"I've survived on worse during coding marathons." Max smiles, the expression transforming his face, softening the sharp edges of his usual intensity.

He takes a seat at the desk, legs wide, arms folded. He looks completely at home, but nothing about his gaze is casual —every sweep of his eyes makes my stupid heart trip over itself. He tears a protein bar in half, holding out a chunk, his fingers lingering a split second longer than necessary as I take it.

"The glamorous life of a tech CEO."

"Hardly glamorous." He leans against the desk, watching me arrange our makeshift meal. "More like unhealthy obsession masquerading as an impossible work ethic."

"At least you're self-aware."

We settle onto opposite ends of the couch with our improvised dinner spread between us. Outside, the wind howls around the building's corners, and snowflakes are occasionally visible through the tiny window near the ceiling. The candles cast dancing shadows across the walls, creating an intimate atmosphere I'm trying desperately to ignore.

"So," Max begins, selecting a slice of apple, "how does

someone with your coffee expertise end up in Angel's Peak? Not exactly the specialty coffee capital of the world."

The question is casual but perceptive. I consider how much to reveal.

"I needed a fresh start." The truth lurks between the words, shadowed by regrets I'm not sure I want to unearth tonight. I focus on arranging cheese on a cracker while desperately trying to figure out how to redirect this conversation.

He leans in, the edge of his sleeve brushing the side of my leg. "Sounds like a story there."

"Nothing interesting. I'm much more interested in you. What is it you do that sends you to Angels Peak and keeps you coding all day?"

"I started Nexus Systems six years ago. My roommate, two laptops, entirely too much caffeine." He breaks off granola, his thumb skimming along the edge, the casual movement sparking heat low in my belly. "The bigger we got, the messier everything became. Some people hunt for blood when they smell success."

"And competitors." My words are sharper than intended, but Max doesn't flinch—just holds my gaze, eyes shadowed and knowing.

The silence hangs, taut as a drawn string.

He passes a slice of cheese, his fingers brushing mine deliberately.

That touch, more than any words, makes my pulse leap.

"True." His eyes meet mine across the candlelight. "Though often the most dangerous ones are closer to home."

"That may be, but sometimes the innocent are branded as sharks by those with inscrutable morals." We're talking generally, but I can't help but defend myself.

The statement hangs between us, resonating uncomfortably with my experience. He gives me a strange look, and I immediately shift the conversation.

"Why Angel's Peak? Of all places to work on your top-secret project?" I push past the ache in my chest, fixing my gaze on the candle flame.

He takes a sip of water. "Completely random. I needed a place that was isolated, had decent internet, and where no one knew me. Threw a dart at a map of mountain towns within driving distance of Denver, and here we are."

"Destiny by dartboard?"

"Random chance." He smiles again, more relaxed now. "I've got a few more weeks to finish this update before launch. After the security breach last quarter, the board is breathing down my neck. The pressure in San Francisco was... suffocating."

"A few weeks?" The timeframe lands like a stone in my stomach. Against my better judgment, my body sways fractionally toward his. I'm close enough to see where his lips curve around the words.

"That's the deadline. Back to reality after that."

Back to reality. As if this—this town, this shop, this moment—is some fantasy interlude in his real life.

"What's the project?" I ask, redirecting my thoughts.

"An enhanced security protocol for small businesses." His expression animates with genuine passion. "The current system protects data, but the update will create secure pathways between physical point-of-sale systems and cloud storage that even sophisticated hackers can't breach."

Despite my determination to maintain emotional distance from anything tech-related, his enthusiasm is contagious.

"Like for coffee shops?" I find myself asking. "Sounds expensive," I whisper, unable to keep the longing from my tone.

"As I told Hunter Morgan, small businesses are the most vulnerable to data theft because they're the ones who can least afford enterprise-level security." He leans forward, eyes bright.

"Imagine knowing your customers' payment information is as secure as any major corporation's, without needing an IT department or expensive infrastructure."

The air tightens again—now layered with want, yearning, the brushfire spark between us that neither of us quite dares stoke, not yet.

Our knees jostle, legs tangling in the tight shuffle for space. He doesn't pull away, and I don't either. The candle shadows stretch, flicker across his jaw, and his eyes linger on my lips. For one long moment, silence blooms: lush, full of all the things that first kiss woke inside us.

"That's... actually useful."

"Try not to sound so surprised." The corner of his mouth quirks up. "Some of us tech bros occasionally create things that help real people."

I laugh, surprising myself. "Fair point."

Our conversation flows more easily as we finish our makeshift dinner. Max describes his journey from scholarship kid at Stanford to reluctant CEO. I share sanitized stories about my coffee training, my travels to source beans directly from farmers, and my dream of eventually creating my own roasting facility.

Carefully, we navigate around the dangerous edges—his current project's specifics, my reasons for leaving San Francisco. The candlelight creates a bubble where only selected truths are permitted.

"Your turn." He gathers our empty plates in slow, deliberate movements—never breaking eye contact, never breaking that shimmering tension. "How did Lily Brock become a coffee sorceress in a mountain town?"

His question lands as soft as velvet but as charged as lightning, and demands more honesty than I've offered so far. I stare into my water glass, debating, but there's really only one path forward. My heart pounds so loudly I'm certain he must hear it too. I tuck my hair behind my ear, shivering at the memory of why I ran, and what I lost.

Under the blanket, our thighs almost touch. One subtle shift and we'd be tangled, skin to skin, beneath wool and candlelight's half-shadow. It's easier to focus on a safer subject, such as work, coffee, or an old injury—anything but the wicked curiosity whispering through me.

Max stretches his arms along the back of the couch, his shirt riding up just enough to reveal the hard edge of his stomach. The movement is casual, but nothing about it feels innocent—not when I've just learned what lies beneath his composed exterior.

I can't help but trace the exposed strip of skin with my eyes, remembering his whispered promises against my ear. That he wanted to back me against the counter, lift me onto it...

My throat goes dry at the memory of what followed, how he'd wanted to taste every inch of me.

Even in his gentle posture, there's coiled intent, leashed strength. The same control he spoke of earlier—the power he found essential "in all things worth having."

Is that what I am to him? Something worth having? Something worth controlling? The thought sends a contradictory shiver through me—half apprehension, half thrill.

How did I become a coffee sorceress in a mountain town? Good question. Something I'm not going to answer with anything approaching the truth.

"I needed a fresh start. Wanted something real." My voice is steadier than my nerves.

"That's not the whole story." His voice drops—soft, unmistakably commanding. The arm behind my shoulders tightens, corralling me just a little closer. His thigh angles into mine, a subtle but territorial press.

He waits, silence thick and thrumming.

When I don't answer right away, his hand slides behind my neck—not quite touching skin, but hovering just close enough that I feel his warmth ghosting along my hairline.

"Open up, Lily. I want the truth, not the PR version. Tell me what you've told no one else."

His eyes hold mine, steady and unyielding. There's no room for misdirection in the space carved out by that dark, expectant gaze. My breath hitches; the room feels smaller, Max suddenly so close I could taste the command in his words if I dared.

My throat tightens, not in fear, but from the exhilarating pressure of being seen, of being given space to let down my guard. The part of me that craves honesty—the same part that craves surrender—sits up and listens.

"The story I've told no one?"

"Yes." He shifts slightly, his expression softening, though his intensity remains. "True intimacy isn't physical. It's the act of confiding our worst fears, of taking that giant leap and being truly seen." His fingers finally make contact with my skin, a featherlight touch at my nape that sends goosebumps cascading down my arms. "I want the parts of you that you keep hidden. The truths you guard."

I swallow hard, torn between the desire to open up and the certainty that my past will extinguish whatever is kindling between us. A tech executive like him would run at the first mention of corporate espionage. The words "corporate spy" have a way of ending conversations, ending possibilities.

But his eyes stay locked on mine, patient and expectant, and I find myself wanting to trust him with this buried piece of myself. So I do the one thing I decided I'd never do. I give him the truth.

I start, "I worked for a tech company in San Francisco. We were developing analytics software for specialty coffee preparation." The confession feels like venturing onto thin ice, but I keep my eyes forward and the words clipped, as if detachment could protect me.

Max's expression shifts, recognition flickering in his eyes. "BrewTech. They had that scandal a few years back. Something about intellectual property theft."

That was me—or at least the lies spread about me.

"That's the one." My heart rate accelerates. This is the moment when I should tell him everything. Instead, I chicken out and offer the barest outline. "I worked there, and when everything fell apart, I left the tech world behind."

Angel's Peak

Chapter 14

He studies me, head tilted slightly. "There's more to that story."

"There is." I meet his gaze steadily. "But tonight isn't about BrewTech."

His hand finds my wrist, fingers circling it completely, the pressure gentle but unmistakably commanding.

"You're right, Lily. It's not about BrewTech." His voice drops lower, that same tone that had sent shivers through me earlier. "It's about you. And I want to know *your* story."

The way he says my name—like he's tasting it, claiming it—makes resistance feel impossible. His thumb strokes the pulse point at my wrist, a subtle reminder of his earlier words about control.

"Why?" The question escapes before I can stop it.

"Because nothing about you is what I expected." His eyes hold mine, unyielding. "I've watched you for days, learning your rhythms, your expressions. But tonight I'm discovering who you really are, and I want all of it. All of you." He pauses, his grip tightening fractionally. "So tell me."

The authority in his voice wraps around me like a physical

touch, and I find myself responding to it before my mind can catch up.

"I developed the core algorithms that made BrewTech's product revolutionary." The confession spills out, unstoppable now that it's begun. "Eric Denton—he was my boss, and my boyfriend. I'm not proud of that, but I was young and he was..." The word tastes bitter.

"Your boss." Max's lips twist, but he waits for me to continue.

"When the company started getting acquisition offers, he stole my work, erased my contributions from the system, and when I confronted him, he planted evidence suggesting I was trying to sell proprietary code to competitors."

Max's expression remains perfectly controlled, but something flashes in his eyes—sharp, dangerous.

"He was thorough," I continue, unable to stop now. "By the time the investigation concluded, my reputation was destroyed. Labeled a corporate spy, blacklisted from every tech company in the Valley. I was unhireable." My laugh sounds hollow even to my own ears. "So I came here. Where no one would know or care about tech world scandals, and I brew coffee in Angel's Peak, at least until I'm kicked out."

"Kicked out?"

"I'd rather not talk about that, if that's okay."

"Of course." He places a hand on my knee. "I'm interested in you. Very interested, but I'm not interested in pushing past boundaries you're not willing to cross. We'll table that until you're ready."

"Thanks."

His thumb continues its rhythmic stroke against my wrist, the only indication that he's processing what I've told him. For a long moment, he says nothing, and I brace myself for the withdrawal, the coolness that inevitably follows when people learn my story.

"Eric Denton," he finally says, the name precise and clinical on his tongue. "The same Eric Denton who's now CTO at Meridian Tech?"

I nod, surprise flickering through me. "You know him?"

"By reputation. His security protocols are inadequate, and he's reckless." Something shifts in Max's expression, a calculated darkness that sends a different kind of shiver down my spine.

The observation hangs between us, loaded with meaning I can't quite decipher. Then his free hand lifts to my face, fingers tracing my jawline with unexpected tenderness.

"Thank you for sharing." His voice gentles, though that underlying steel remains. "For trusting me with this."

The relief that floods through me is so intense it's almost painful. He believes me. More importantly, he isn't pulling away.

We sit in silence for a moment. His stance shifts, shoulders drawing back slightly, jaw tightening. The tech executive emerges in his posture, replacing the man who just whispered his desires against my skin.

His gaze drops to my lips, lingers there for a heartbeat too long before returning to my eyes. Something measured and cautious replaces the hunger that was there before.

I should have expected this. He represents a world I fled, a culture that values proprietary knowledge above all. Even the hint of scandal would make a man like him wary. The word "BrewTech" alone created this new distance between us.

My breath catches as I remember how he looked at me earlier, how he whispered those promises.

Heat flares under my cheeks. My ex had been... serviceable, focused on his own pleasure, over before I'd even begun to float. Faux-chivalry but nothing tender, certainly nothing wild.

I sneak a glance at Max's hands—broad, capable. I picture

them splayed against my bare skin, pinning me down, stroking me open. Something deep in my chest flutters, a sharp, secret throb. He held my chin earlier—strong, unyielding. The memory of his control, of that brief moment when he claimed me with nothing more than a touch, sends heat pooling low in my abdomen.

But that was before the word "BrewTech" poisoned the air between us.

"What are you thinking right now?" His voice cuts through my thoughts, low and knowing.

I can't tell him the truth—that I'm shocked by his acceptance, overwhelmed by his continued closeness. Wary by his withdrawal. So I remain silent, vulnerable in my gratitude, unable to find words to express my fears.

His eyes darken as he moves closer, the space between us narrowing to almost nothing. "Your pulse is racing," he observes, his gaze dropping to the hollow of my throat where my heartbeat betrays me. "Tell me why."

I sway slightly toward him, drawn by the gravity between us.

"I thought..." My voice catches. "I thought once you knew who I was—what people say about me—your interest would cool." I force myself to meet his gaze. "A tech mogul like yourself shouldn't be seen with a woman blacklisted for corporate espionage. There's no future in it."

His expression softens. "Is that what you're worried about? My reputation?"

"Partly." I swallow hard. "And partly that the things I've imagined between us aren't real."

"Tell me what you've imagined." The command is gentle but unmistakable.

Heat floods my cheeks. "My ex, he was..." The confession feels dangerous, exposing. "Serviceable. Focused on himself. Always over before I'd even begun to..." I can't finish the sentence, but his darkening eyes tell me he understands.

"And with me?" His voice drops lower. "What do you imagine with me?"

"That it might be different." The words come out in a rush. "The way you look at me, the things you said earlier—I thought you might be the kind of man who..." I trail off, unable to articulate the longing, the curiosity.

"Who doesn't leave you hanging?" A hint of amusement flickers in his eyes, but the hunger beneath it is unmistakable. "Who makes sure you get what you need?"

I nod, relief washing through me at his understanding, but still that self-doubt lingers. "But I understand, now that you know who I am, that..." The words simply won't come.

He exhales slowly, running a hand through his hair.

"Jesus, Lily. I don't care about BrewTech, except that what that asshole did to you is a crime." The rawness in his voice sends a shiver down my spine. "After what I told you earlier— the things I want to do to you—and you're still standing here?" His eyes search mine, something vulnerable beneath the desire. "You have no idea what that does to me."

"You're still..." I lean back and take a breath. "You still want to..."

"God yes." His voice drops to a rough whisper as he leans in, the space between us charged with electricity. "I've wanted you from the moment I saw you. Nothing's changed that." His fingers graze my cheek, his touch almost reverent despite the heat in his eyes. "If anything, knowing what you've been through just makes me want to show you how much I..." He swallows hard, struggling to contain something powerful. "How much I want this. Want you."

"I'm—" I struggle to find the right words. "I'm interested. But it's also scary. Exciting, but terrifying." My voice drops to barely a whisper. "I've never been with someone who wants...

what you described. And I worry about being just a fling, disposable once you've had your fill. I'm not sure I'm wired that way."

"First, let me be clear about something." His expression hardens with sudden intensity. "What your ex did—stealing your work, destroying your career—men like that are weak, pathetic." Something dangerous flashes in his eyes. "I'll do everything in my power to clear your name. That's not negotiable."

"You don't have to—"

"As I said, not negotiable." He cuts me off with a finality that leaves no room for argument. His jaw clenches, a muscle working beneath the skin. "I have connections. People who owe me favors. Forensic experts..." His eyes never leave mine, unwavering. "What he did was theft, plain and simple. And I protect what's mine."

The possessiveness in his voice sends a rush of heat through me. He hasn't even touched me, but the intensity of his gaze makes me feel claimed.

"As for the rest..." His voice softens, though the undercurrent of desire remains. "I don't do disposable." His fingers trace a path from my cheek to my collarbone, leaving goosebumps in their wake. "What I want is to take my time. Days, weeks... however long it takes to discover exactly what makes you come apart in my hands."

He leans in, his lips brushing my ear as he whispers, "And trust me, what I described earlier? That's just the beginning of what I want to do with you."

The fierce protectiveness in his voice catches me off guard. We've known each other for mere days, yet he speaks as if my vindication is already his personal mission.

"Second, as for us," he continues, his voice softening though the intensity remains, "we have two options. Tonight, we can discover if what's between us is worth exploring further, but if you need time, we'll take a step back and breathe." His thumb traces my lower lip, a touch so light it's almost reverent.

"You're okay if I need time?" The question feels important, a test of his earlier claims.

"Yes." His certainty is unwavering. "I meant what I said earlier—I'm a patient man, especially when it comes to something I want." The look he gives me is possessive, claiming. "And I want you. Not just for tonight. If that means we wait, then that's what we'll do."

"Just like that?" The question comes out smaller than I intended, contradicting my supposed need for time.

"Just like that." His lips curve into that dangerous half-smile. "If that's what you need, that's what we'll do. But let me be very clear—when you finally say yes to me, I'll make damn sure you'll be seeing stars."

The promise in his words sends liquid heat pooling between my thighs. This is madness—opening myself to a man who represents everything I fled, who admits to desires darker than I've known, who speaks of patience yet radiates barely controlled hunger.

"And if I say yes tonight?" I sway slightly toward him.

He shifts closer to adjust the blanket over my knees, knuckles grazing the bare skin above my sock. Goosebumps race up my leg. His eyes flick down, linger a moment longer than they should, then travel back up to meet mine.

The spark in his gaze—undeniable, almost predatory—makes my breath hitch. He doesn't hide how he's looking at me, how he might devour me if I'd only let him.

He settles in beside me, his thigh pressed flush with mine at last. The thin barrier of denim and wool can't hide how hot his skin feels against me, how easily I could move into his lap, let him take whatever he wants.

My mind whirls, racing ahead—if I ask, will he show me how dark he can go, how far he'll let me fall? Do I dare?

A part of me says that if this is a fantasy, a storm-trapped dream, I want to taste every inch of it while it lasts. And if Max wants to take control, to show me things about myself I've only ever imagined in secret, maybe—just maybe—I'll finally let myself say yes.

His hand slides up my arm, leaving a trail of fire in its wake. When it reaches my neck, his thumb traces my jawline with deliberate pressure.

"Lily." My name on his lips sounds like a claim, a promise. "Tell me what you want."

The command in his voice makes my pulse jump. His eyes track the movement in my throat, a predator noting weakness.

"I want..." The words stick. How do I tell him I want everything he described earlier—his mouth, his hands, his control—without sounding desperate?

He leans closer, his breath warm against my ear. "Say it."

"You." The confession breaks free. "I want you."

Angel's Peak

Chapter 15

Max's sharp inhale is my only warning before his mouth claims mine. This isn't the hesitant, testing kiss from earlier—this is possession, pure and demanding. His hand fists in my hair, angling my head exactly how he wants it, while his other arm bands around my waist, pulling me flush against him.

I gasp into his mouth, the sound swallowed by his groan. His tongue traces the seam of my lips before delving deeper, tasting, exploring. The controlled strength in his movements—holding me exactly where he wants me, taking what he desires while somehow giving more than I knew to ask for—makes me melt against him.

His teeth graze my bottom lip, a gentle bite that sends sparks racing down my spine. When he pulls back, just enough for me to catch my breath, his eyes are dark with promise.

"More?"

"Yes, please," I whisper, already leaning toward him again.

This time, he slows, his mouth moving with deliberate purpose. His tongue strokes against mine, teaching me his rhythm. One hand slides beneath my sweater to span my lower back, his fingers splaying wide against bare skin. The heat of his palm brands me, anchoring me to this moment, to him.

The generator sputters and dies with a groan that echoes through the cabin. One moment we're bathed in the warm glow of the table lamp, the next—darkness swallows everything except the faint blue-white light reflecting off the snow outside.

Max's muscles go rigid against me. The sudden darkness is disorienting; the intimate cocoon we created shatters as reality intrudes—the howling wind rattles the windows, and the temperature immediately seems to drop.

"Shit," he mutters, his breath warm against my cheek.

I pull back on the couch, the leather creaking beneath me. The loss of his warmth is immediate, my skin prickling with goosebumps. My senses, heightened by desire just moments ago, now register the danger of our situation.

"I need to check the generator," I say, already pushing myself up from the couch. The coffee shop—my livelihood— can't afford equipment damage in this storm, let alone my nonexistent cash reserves.

Max rises beside me. "Let me," he says, his hand finding mine in the darkness. "We go together," he says, his silhouette barely visible against the window's glow as he reaches for his coat.

"Max, this is..." I trail off, suddenly aware of how quickly things had escalated between us.

"Bad timing?" he suggests, his voice tight with frustration.

"Temporary." The word comes out sharper than I intended, my fear making me blunt. "You're leaving in a few weeks." I take a step away, the floorboards cold beneath my feet.

He pauses midway through shrugging on his coat. "A few weeks is better than nothing."

"Is it?" My arms cross over my chest. "In my experience, temporary connections leave permanent damage."

His coat rustles as he moves closer. "I would never intentionally hurt you."

"Intentions don't matter in the end."

Silence stretches between us, broken only by the howling wind outside, sounding closer now without the generator's steady hum. His fingers find my wrist in the dark, his thumb tracing circles on my skin.

Finally, he exhales. "You're right." His voice carries resignation and frustration in equal measure. "Mixing business and pleasure is *grounds* for disaster."

The unexpected wordplay catches me off guard. "Did you just make a coffee pun?"

His teeth flash white in the darkness. "Seemed appropriate for the *espresso* situation."

"That was awful." I laugh despite myself. "Please tell me you don't have a whole *brew* of these."

"I've barely scratched the surface," he says, his hand still loosely holding mine. "Look, Lily—" His voice softens. "There's no rush here. We should fix the generator, and you should take as much time as you need. I want you to be certain. About me. About us. Whatever this is or could be." His thumb continues its gentle path across my skin. "I'll still be here tomorrow. And the day after. We have time to figure it out. As for my puns..."I've *bean* saving them up." His eyes twinkle with mischief. "But I won't force you to *filter* through them all at once."

"Stop!" I groan, shoving his shoulder playfully. "Your puns are *grounds* for termination."

"Ah, but you're smiling, so my *grounds* for continuing are strong. I'm just trying to *perk* you up. Felt you needed space." He gestures between us. "This needs time to *breathe*. Like your incomparable brews. There's no reason to rush this."

The tension between us transforms into something lighter, though the underlying attraction remains, steady, persistent, impossible to truly ignore.

We reset the generator and settle into preparing for the night. While the couch is comfortable for sitting, it clearly presents challenges for two adults to sleep on.

"I'll take the floor." Max gestures to the narrow space beside the couch.

"Don't be ridiculous. It's freezing down there."

"I run hot."

"Even your CEO superpowers won't prevent a stiff neck from sleeping on the hardwood." I arrange the blanket on the couch. "The couch is big enough if we're... economical with space."

His eyebrow raises. "Economical."

"You know what I mean." Heat creeps up my neck. "Just sleeping."

"Just sleeping," he agrees, voice neutral but eyes betraying something deeper.

The logistics prove awkward—removing shoes and outerwear while avoiding eye contact. Max sits on the edge of the couch, unlacing his boots while I busy myself with the blankets, smoothing them unnecessarily.

"Should I—" He gestures vaguely at his jeans.

"Whatever's comfortable," I say too quickly, then add, "Within reason."

A smile tugs at his lips. "Within reason," he echoes, unbuckling his belt and slipping it through the loops with a soft hiss of leather. He leaves his jeans on.

Max lies down first, pressing his back against the cushions and stretching his long frame along the couch. He lifts the blanket, creating a space in front of him.

"Come here," he says softly, patting the narrow strip of couch before him.

I hesitate, suddenly shy despite everything we've already shared. With a deep breath, I extinguish all but one candle, casting the room in flickering amber light, and ease myself onto the couch. Max's arm wraps around my waist, drawing me back against his chest, his body curving perfectly around mine.

"Comfortable?" he asks, his breath warm against my ear.

"No." Every nerve ending in my body is hyperaware of his proximity, his solid chest against my back, his thighs cradling mine.

"Neither am I." He laughs, but there's a strain in it. His body is rigid behind me, the hard outline of his arousal unmistakable against my lower back. "Truth is, I'm aching."

"I'm sorry," I whisper, guilt mingling with my own frustrated desire.

"Don't be." His voice is gentle but firm. "I meant what I said earlier. I want you to be certain. I can wait." His fingers find mine, intertwining over my stomach. "Just let me hold you tonight. That's enough."

The tension in his body eases gradually as his breathing slows. Mine follows suit, syncing with the steady rise and fall of his chest against my back.

"Goodnight, Lily," he murmurs into my hair.

"Goodnight, Max."

Sleep is impossible with him so close, his body heat radiating across the small gap between us. I listen to his breathing, expecting it to deepen with sleep, but it remains as irregular as my own. Neither of us is unaffected by this forced proximity.

"Max?" My voice sounds loud in the quiet room.

"Hmm?"

"Why did you kiss me?"

A long pause follows. For a moment, I think he might pretend to be asleep.

"Because I haven't been able to think about anything else

since I met you." His voice is low, honest in the darkness. "You're the most fascinating contradiction I've ever encountered."

"Contradiction?"

"Sophisticated coffee expertise with small-town simplicity. Technical knowledge hidden behind artisanal craftsmanship. Warmth and welcome for everyone except me, at least initially." I feel him shift slightly. "You're a puzzle I can't solve, and I find that... irresistible."

His admission settles in the space between us, too honest for comfort, too compelling to dismiss.

"Well, you did run into me and spill my latte art all over the floor," I say softly, grateful he can't see my face flush in the darkness. "But I'm slowly warming up to you now."

His arm tightens around me, just enough to notice. "Good," he murmurs, his voice dropping to a register that sends heat spiraling through me. The single word carries weight, promise, and just enough suggestion to make my pulse quicken.

His lips brush against my ear, his breath warm and controlled. "Now go to sleep, Lily," he commands, the authority in his voice unmistakable. "Before I forget I'm trying to be a gentleman."

My heart hammers against my ribs, the cadence of his words igniting something primal within me. It's not just the command itself, but the restraint behind it—the promise of what waits beyond his control. I remember his earlier words, the dark, delicious things he whispered he wanted to do to me. Not gentle, vanilla intimacy, but something else entirely— something that makes my skin flush and my breath catch.

I close my eyes, but sleep seems impossible now. My mind races with images of his hands pinning mine, his voice telling me exactly what he wants, what he expects. The promise of surrender, of being completely at his mercy while knowing I'm utterly safe.

His steady breathing eventually slows behind me, but my dreams, when they finally come, are anything but restful—filled with shadows and whispers and the exquisite tension of anticipation.

With the protective curl of his body around mine, listening to the storm rage outside, I'm left wondering how something so new could already feel like coming home.

Angel's Peak

Chapter 16

Morning arrives with blinding brightness, sunlight reflecting off fresh snow through the small window. I wake slowly, comfortably warm despite the shop's chill.

Too comfortable.

Awareness dawns as I register the weight of an arm draped across my waist, solid warmth pressed against my back. Somehow during the night, our careful arrangement dissolved, and we've ended up fitted together like nested spoons, Max's body curled protectively around mine.

His breathing remains deep and even against my neck, still asleep. I should move, establish proper distance, but my body betrays me, melting into the comfort of his embrace.

This is dangerous—far more dangerous than a heated kiss. This quiet intimacy, this sense of security in his arms, threatens the walls I've carefully constructed.

As if sensing my thoughts, Max stirs, his arm tightening briefly around me before awareness hits him too. His body tenses slightly.

"Sorry," he murmurs, voice rough with sleep. "I apparently migrate in my sleep."

"It's fine." I carefully extricate myself, sitting up and running a hand through my tangled hair. "At least we didn't freeze."

He laughs softly, stretching as he sits. Morning light catches in his hair, turning the dark strands nearly blue-black. He should look rumpled and ordinary after sleeping in his clothes, but somehow he manages to look unfairly attractive, with stubble shadowing his jaw and sleep-softened eyes.

"How bad is it out there?" He nods toward the window.

I stand on tiptoe to peer outside. "Clear skies. Lots of snow, but the plows are already working on Main Street."

"Back to reality, then."

"Apparently so." The awkwardness between us feels both teenage and profound.

My phone buzzes—a text from Sheriff Donovan confirming the roads to The Haven are now passable. I relay this to Max, relief and disappointment warring within me.

We moved through the morning routine, restoring the office to its original state and checking the shop for any storm damage. The generator performed perfectly, and Mountain Brew weathered the blizzard unscathed.

"I should get back." Max lingers by the front door. "Change clothes, check in with the office."

"Of course."

"Thank you for the hospitality." His tone is too formal, creating artificial distance from the intimacy we shared.

"Anytime. Well, not anytime. Preferably not during another blizzard."

His smile returns, genuine and warm. "I'll see you later?"

The question carries more weight than its simple words suggest.

"The shop's closed today for storm recovery. But tomorrow... your booth will be waiting."

Something shifts in his expression—pleasure mixed with an emotion I can't quite identify. "Tomorrow, then."

After he leaves, I lock the door behind him and lean against it, exhaling slowly. The shop feels emptier than usual, or perhaps I'm simply more aware of his absence after hours of his company.

I gather my belongings, eager for the comfort of my cottage, a hot shower, and clean clothes. The walk home takes twice as long as usual, navigating through snow piled shoulder-high along the plowed walkways.

My cottage welcomes me with familiar simplicity—colorful pillows on the secondhand sofa, mismatched coffee mugs hanging from hooks in the tiny kitchen, and the patchwork quilt Eleanor made me draped across my bed.

It should feel like a sanctuary.

Instead, it feels strangely hollow, as if something is missing that wasn't missing before.

In the shower, hot water beats against tense muscles, but does nothing to wash away the memory of Max's arms around me. The phantom warmth of his body lingers like a ghost against my skin.

Three weeks. That's all he has in Angel's Peak. I can handle three weeks of attraction without losing my heart—can't I?

The phantom warmth of his body still pressed against mine, however, suggests otherwise.

I spend the remainder of the day in a haze, going through the motions of normalcy. Laundry. A half-hearted attempt at reading. Preparing recipes for tomorrow's pastry case. But underneath it all runs a current of anticipation, a countdown to seeing him again.

Morning comes both too quickly and not soon enough. I arrive before dawn, the familiar ritual of opening—grinding beans, wiping counters, warming ovens—a comforting anchor in my sea of uncertainty. By the time the first customers arrive, the café smells of cinnamon and coffee, and I've almost convinced myself I can face Max with professional detachment.

Outside, the world is transformed—tree branches heavy with snow, the street a pristine white canvas broken only by a few early footprints.

"You're brewing the dark roast too hot again." Mabel's voice breaks through my distracted haze as she slides onto her usual stool at the counter. "Two degrees cooler would bring out the caramel notes."

"Good morning, Mabel." I adjust the temperature setting on the machine, knowing she's right. At seventy-eight, she doesn't miss a thing, especially when it comes to coffee. Her guesthouse has hosted visitors to Angel's Peak for nearly forty years, and her palate remains unmatched.

"Your mind's elsewhere this morning." Mabel's shrewd eyes narrow as I prepare her usual medium roast, a splash of cream, served in the yellow mug with painted daisies. "Heard you had company during the storm."

News travels at supersonic speed in Angel's Peak. "Max Lawson was here when the roads closed. We had to make do."

"Make do." Mabel's silvery eyebrows rise with enough skepticism to fill the Grand Canyon. "That's what the kids call it these days?"

Heat rises to my cheeks. "Nothing happened."

"Your face says otherwise."

I busy myself with wiping down the already-clean counter. "We talked. Slept on opposite ends of the couch. That's it." It's the tiniest of tiny white lies, but I don't need all of Angel's Peak knowing every detail.

"Mmhmm." Mabel sips her coffee, watching me over the rim. "And now?"

"And now nothing. He's a customer."

"A customer who looks at you like you're the secret ingredient in his favorite dish." Mabel sets her mug down with a decisive click. "I've seen that boy every morning at The Haven's breakfast, checking his watch every thirty seconds until it's time to come here."

My traitor heart stutters. "He's just eager to work. The coffee shop is quieter than the resort."

"Lily Brock, you can lie to yourself all you want, but don't waste your breath trying to fool me." Mabel's voice softens. "Just be careful, sweet pea. Tourist romances burn hot and fast. Unfortunately, they often leave nothing but ashes when they end."

"It's not a romance."

"If you say so." Mabel pats my hand, her palm warm and paper-dry against mine. "Just remember—three types come to Angel's Peak: those passing through, those hiding out, and those who've found home. Make sure you know which one he is before you give away pieces of yourself that you can't get back."

Her words stay with me long after she leaves, echoing as I move through the morning routine. Max hasn't arrived yet, his corner booth conspicuously empty. The absence shouldn't matter—shouldn't create this hollow feeling in my chest—yet I find myself glancing at the door each time the bell chimes.

By eleven, I've convinced myself he's not coming. Perhaps the night in the coffee shop clarified things for him—showed him the attraction was merely proximity and circumstance, nothing worth pursuing. Or worse, maybe our conversation about BrewTech gave him second thoughts.

Corporate spy.

The label might have finally registered, overriding whatever chemistry flared between us.

I wipe down the already spotless counter, reorganize the pastry case that doesn't need reorganizing, and check my phone three times to confirm it's working. The memory of his hands on my skin, his mouth against mine, refuses to fade. I can still feel the gentle scrape of his stubble against my neck, still hear the low rumble of his laughter at his own terrible puns.

Pathetic. One kiss—well, several kisses—and I'm acting like a lovesick teenager.

Mabel catches me staring at the door for the fifth time in as many minutes. "Waiting for someone?" Her knowing smile makes me flush.

"Just watching the snow." The lie falls flat even to my own ears.

"Mmhmm." She turns back to her drink, but not before I catch her smirk. "The snow that's been falling continuously for three days. Must be fascinating."

I ignore her, focusing instead on the intricate latte art I'm creating—anything to keep my hands busy and my mind off Max. The foam swirls into delicate patterns beneath my practiced touch, a temporary masterpiece soon to be consumed and forgotten. Like whatever this thing with Max might become.

Would it be so bad?

I wish I had an answer for that.

Mabel's warning plays on repeat: *Tourist romances burn hot and fast. Unfortunately, they often leave nothing but ashes when they end.*

The bell chimes, and there he stands, windblown and winter-bright. My heart performs an embarrassing acrobatic routine. Snowflakes cling to his dark hair and the shoulders of his charcoal peacoat, melting rapidly in the shop's warmth. His cheeks are flushed from the cold; his eyes are bright and seek mine immediately. The intensity in his gaze knocks the air from my lungs.

"Sorry, I'm late." He approaches the counter with purpose,

no sign of awkwardness after our night together. "Had a video conference that wouldn't end."

"Your usual?" I reach for a mug, hoping my hands appear steadier than they feel.

"Actually..." He hesitates, then places his tablet on the counter. "I need your help with something."

"My help?" Suspicion flickers. "With what?"

"Part of our update includes a visual recognition component for small food businesses." He activates the tablet, revealing what appears to be a prototype app. "It helps catalog inventory, suggest pairings, and creates customized recommendations based on customer preferences."

I stiffen, memories of BrewTech surging unwelcome. "What does that have to do with me?"

"I need to test it with actual products. Coffee seems ideal—complex flavor profiles, visual distinctions, quality variations." His eyes meet mine, unexpectedly earnest. "Would you let me photograph and catalog some of your offerings? The data stays local, completely secure."

The irony doesn't escape me—asked to test technology for the very industry that burned me. Yet Max's expression holds none of Eric's calculated charm, only genuine excitement about his creation.

"Why me?" The question comes out softer than intended.

"Because you understand both the technical and artistic aspects of coffee craft. You'll see flaws and possibilities I might miss." He leans slightly closer. "And because I trust your judgment."

Those simple words—"I trust your judgment"—strike a chord Eric never touched. My expertise had always been a tool for him, never something valued for its own sake.

"What would it involve exactly?"

Max's smile warms his entire face. "Basically, an afternoon playing with coffee and technology. Taking photos of different preparations, logging tasting notes, testing how the app catalogs and connects flavor profiles."

"Like a digital sommelier for coffee?"

"Exactly. Only with higher security protocols than the Pentagon."

The tech side of me—the part I've kept buried since Brew-Tech—stirs with interest. "I suppose I could spare a few hours. For research purposes."

"Of course. Strictly professional." The twinkle in his eyes suggests otherwise.

We spend the afternoon in a rhythm that feels surprisingly natural. Max photographs each coffee preparation from multiple angles while I describe the origins of the beans, the roasting process, and the optimal brewing methods. His app catalogues everything, creating interconnected webs of flavor profiles and preparation techniques.

Between regular customers, we huddle over the tablet, Max's shoulder warm against mine as we analyze the results. His enthusiasm is contagious, his expertise impressive. He explains the programming in terms I understand, without condescension, and occasionally asks questions that reveal he remembers my technical background.

"The visual recognition needs refinement." He frowns at the screen where the app has misidentified a pour-over as a Chemex brew. "It's struggling with similar preparation methods."

"The distinction is in the filter shape and extraction time." I reach across him to adjust the image, our fingers brushing. "If you added a time-lapse feature for the brewing process, the algorithm could better distinguish methods."

He looks at me with new appreciation. "That's brilliant. Simple but effective."

"Just because I left the tech world doesn't mean I stopped understanding it."

"Clearly." His gaze lingers on my face. "You could have founded your own tech company, you know. Your insight is exceptional."

The compliment lands differently than expected—not as a painful reminder of what might have been, but an acknowledgment of capabilities I still possess.

"I prefer being hands-on with my coffee." I gesture around the shop. "No board meetings or venture capitalists to please." No knives in my back.

"Fair point." He leans back, stretching slightly. "Though, for what it's worth, I think the tech world lost something significant when you left."

Before I can respond, the bell chimes. Hannah Lewis strides in, auburn hair gleaming against her emerald sweater, arms full of library books.

"Lily! Just the caffeine sorceress I needed." Her smile falters slightly when she spots Max. "Oh, hello there, handsome."

"Hannah." I move toward the counter. "Your usual?"

"Please." Her gaze lingers on Max with unmistakable interest. "Triple shot mocha might be the only thing that'll get me through cataloging these local history books." She sets her stack down with a theatrical sigh.

Max offers her a polite nod, stepping aside to let her approach the counter.

Hannah leans in conspiratorially as I start her drink. "So," she says, voice pitched just loud enough for Max to hear, "the whole town's talking about how you two were trapped here during the blizzard." Her eyes dance with mischief. "Sheriff Donovan mentioned checking in on you. Said it was quite the coincidence that Max happened to be here when the roads closed."

Heat crawls up my neck. "The sheriff needs to focus on actual emergencies."

"Oh, he did." Hannah's smile widens. "But you know how

news travels in Angel's Peak. Especially when it involves our mysterious newcomer and our favorite coffee shop owner."

Max chuckles behind her. "Small towns."

"The smallest," Hannah agrees cheerfully. "Thirty minutes after that storm hit, everyone knew exactly who was trapped where." She turns to face him fully. "And being stuck with Lily? You lucked out. She's the best company in town."

"I couldn't agree more." The warmth in his voice makes my hands fumble the milk pitcher.

Hannah's gaze bounces between us, clearly delighted by my discomfort. "You know," she says, tapping her manicured nails against the counter, "in all the years I've known Lily, I've never seen her blush quite this shade of crimson."

"Hannah," I warn, sliding her drink across the counter.

"What?" She blinks innocently. "I'm just making conversation with your... unexpected overnight companion."

Max's smile grows, a glint of something possessive flickering in his eyes. "I was more of a stranded traveler," he says smoothly, "though I can't say I minded the company."

The look he gives me sends my pulse racing again. Hannah catches it and practically vibrates with glee.

"Well!" She collects her books and her drink with surprising grace. "I should get back to the library before Meredith sends out a search party." She pauses at the door, unable to resist one final comment. "You two have quite the chemistry. Very... electric."

And with that, she's gone in a flurry of books, copper hair, and knowing smiles, leaving an awkward silence in her wake.

I busy myself wiping down the espresso machine, painfully aware of Max watching me. When I finally look up, he's leaning against the counter, amusement playing at the corners of his mouth.

"Electric," he repeats thoughtfully. "Accurate assessment."

"Hannah has an overactive imagination." I fold the cloth with more precision than necessary.

"Does she?" He steps closer, voice dropping to that low register that seems to vibrate through my bones. "Because I remember very real electricity between us last night."

The memory of his mouth on mine, his hands in my hair, floods back with vivid clarity. "Max—"

"Have dinner with me tonight." His tone is soft but intent, eyes holding mine with quiet certainty. "Not here. Somewhere we can talk without the whole town providing commentary."

"Dinner?" The invitation catches me off guard. "I don't know if that's a good idea." Even as I say it, I know I'm going to say yes.

"Yes, that evening meal people often share." His eyes crinkle at the corners. "At Timberline, in The Haven. I've heard it's the best restaurant in town."

"It's the only *actual* restaurant in town."

"Then my research is accurate." He leans against the counter, close enough that I catch the citrus notes of his cologne. "Say yes." It's not a question but a command, echoing the same authority that had sent shivers down my spine last night. "After all the coffee sampling, we should try something different. Let me take you on a proper date."

A proper date. The words hang between us, transforming what happened on the couch from an isolated incident into something with potential—something real. Somehow, the idea of sitting across from him at a candlelit table, fully clothed and in public, seems more intimate than the heat of his body pressed against mine during the blizzard.

"I don't think—" I begin, but he reaches across the counter, his fingers brushing a strand of hair from my face. The casual touch sends sparks racing across my skin.

"Seven o'clock," he says, his tone brooking no argument. "I'll pick you up here."

A dozen reasons to refuse line up in my mind—most prominently Mabel's warning about tourist romances. But his eyes hold mine, steady and certain. I'm nodding before I can stop myself.

His smile could power the entire town through another blackout.

"This isn't a date," I clarify, needing the boundary for my own sanity.

He leans in closer, his voice dropping to a register that only I can hear. "Lily Brock, this is most definitely a *date*," he counters, my full name on his lips, sending an unexpected thrill through me. "With hand-holding, dinner conversation, and kissing." His eyes drop to my mouth for a brief, scorching moment. "And whatever else you're comfortable with."

The promise in his voice makes my skin flush hot, memories of his whispered intentions from last night flooding back. The café suddenly feels ten degrees warmer.

"Though perhaps wear that blue sweater you had on last Tuesday." His voice drops even lower, almost a caress. "It matches your eyes."

He noticed what I was wearing last Tuesday?

"I'll wear whatever's clean," I respond, fighting a smile despite the heat coiling in my stomach. "Now, don't you have work to do? That corner booth doesn't rent itself."

He returns to his station with poorly concealed satisfaction, and I turn away to hide my flustered pleasure, pressing my cool palms against my burning cheeks.

Definitely a date, his words echo in my mind. *Definitely a date.*

My body hums with anticipation at the thought of his hands on me again—this time without the restraint of "just sleeping."

Angel's Peak

Chapter 17

Timberline glows with understated elegance as we enter. Soft lighting from iron chandeliers, white table-cloths, and floor-to-ceiling windows showcase the snow-covered mountains. Despite my protests, I'm wearing the blue sweater, paired with my only decent black pants and boots that haven't seen use since I left San Francisco.

"Mr. Lawson, Ms. Brock." The host greets us with elegance and hospitality. "Your table is ready."

We're led to a corner table beside the windows—the best in the house, with views of moonlight on fresh snow. A single candle flickers between place settings, creating the unmistakable atmosphere of a romantic dinner.

Not a date, I remind myself, even as Max holds my chair, but my body remembers his promises from the night of the blizzard, the controlled hunger in his touch, the darkness he admitted to craving.

"This is lovely." I unfold the heavy linen napkin, suddenly aware of how special this evening feels compared to my usual routine. "I haven't been here since they renovated last year."

"First time for me." Max surveys the space appreciatively. "Lucas Reid clearly has an eye for design."

"Chef Morgan's food is the real star. His farm-to-table approach transformed the local culinary scene."

Conversation flows easily as we order—a shared charcuterie board featuring local ingredients, followed by rosemary lamb for Max and cedar-plank salmon for me. The wine—a rich red from Silverleaf Vineyards—complements both perfectly.

Between courses, Max tells me about his childhood in Detroit—son of an auto factory worker and a nurse, scholarship student who coded his first program at thirteen on a computer rescued from a dumpster. His path to tech success wasn't privileged or connected; it was built through innate talent and relentless work.

"My father thought I was wasting my time." He swirls wine in his glass, expression distant. "He wanted me to get a 'real job' at the plant. Couldn't understand why I'd spend hours debugging code instead of working on cars."

"Did he ever come around?"

"Eventually. When I sold my first app and paid off their mortgage." A smile touches his lips. "Though he still introduces me as 'my son who does something with computers.'"

I laugh, warmed by the glimpse of his roots. "My parents were the opposite. Both professors who expected me to pursue academia. Opening a coffee shop was my rebellion."

"And the tech career in between?"

"A detour that proved them right, then wrong, then right again." I take a sip of wine. "Though after the BrewTech disaster, I'm sure they'd agree I made the right choice leaving tech behind."

He nods, his expression thoughtful. "Even with your talent for algorithms? The work you showed me when we were testing my app was impressive."

"Even with that," I say firmly, though his acknowledgment of my skills warms me in a way I don't expect. Unlike Eric, who always took credit for my innovations, Max seems to genuinely value my expertise.

"Well. Angel's Peak's newest power couple." We look up to find Dominic Mercer—tall, ruggedly handsome in that specific way of men who work outdoors—standing beside our table. Beside him, Elena Santiago—elegant in a simple black dress—observes us with knowing eyes.

"Dominic." I recover first. "Elena. Lovely to see you both."

"We didn't mean to interrupt your evening." Elena's smile is warm but perceptive. "Just wanted to say hello. Max, how are you enjoying Angel's Peak?"

"More than expected." His gaze flickers briefly at me. "The local specialties have exceeded all expectations."

Dominic's laugh is knowing. "They have a way of doing that. Wait until you taste Hunter's chocolate soufflé. Life-changing."

Dominic extends his hand to Max. "How's the app testing coming along? Elena's been tracking our inventory with it all week."

I blink in surprise, looking between them. "You two know each other?"

"Max approached us about a week ago about beta testing his inventory app at the vineyard," Dominic explains. "Perfect timing since we needed a better system for tracking vintages and yields."

Max smiles, almost apologetically. "I've been working with several local businesses. Silverleaf Vineyards, The Haven, The PickAxe..."

"And me," I realize aloud, thinking of our afternoon spent photographing and cataloging coffee beans. "I didn't know there were other beta testers."

"Small businesses with complex and diverse inventory

needs," Max explains. "Angel's Peak has been the perfect testing ground."

"Keeping you quite busy, I imagine," Elena observes with a knowing smile.

"Some beta testers more than others," Max replies, his eyes meeting mine briefly.

Brief introductions transition to the discovery that Elena —now partnered with Dominic at Silverleaf Vineyards—was once one of San Francisco's top sommeliers. The conversation turns to mutual acquaintances and favorite Bay Area haunts until they tactfully excuse themselves.

"They seem nice," Max observes after they've gone. His fingers find mine under the table, intertwining with casual intimacy. "You realize by tomorrow morning, the entire town will know we're officially dating." A smile plays at the corner of his mouth.

The thought of becoming town gossip should alarm me more than it does. Instead, I find myself surprisingly unconcerned.

The intensity in his blue eyes reminds me of that night during the blizzard—his confession about control, about desires that would leave marks, about appetites darker than I'd known. *I'm a patient man, Lily," he told me then, his voice a rough caress. "Especially when it comes to something I want."* The memory sends heat coursing through me, despite my better judgment.

His understanding only makes the situation more dangerous. It would be much easier if he pushed, demanded, and acted as if he were entitled to more than I'm ready to give. Instead, his patience and respect dismantle my defenses more effectively than any persistence could.

Eric did that often enough—demanded, pressured, made me feel that my reluctance was unreasonable. He never had Max's restraint, never understood that patience could be more seductive than force. The contrast between them only makes Max more devastating to my resolve.

I want to give him everything he desires, but knowing there's no future complicates things. Part of me says, take the plunge already. Enjoy life. Live dangerously. The other part of me still aches after the disaster that was Eric Denton. I'm more careful now. Hesitant. Guarded even. Which I hate.

The rest of dinner passes in a pleasant blur of excellent food and increasingly personal conversation. By the time we step outside into the crisp night air, stars blazing overhead in the clear post-storm sky, something fundamental has shifted between us.

"Mind if we walk?" Max asks, breath forming clouds in the cold. "Too beautiful a night to rush back."

The path from The Haven to downtown is well-lit and recently plowed. We move side by side, close but not touching, until Max offers his arm at a particularly icy patch.

"For safety," he clarifies, eyes twinkling.

"Of course. Safety." I slip my hand through his arm, the contact sending warmth through me despite the cold.

Neither of us is willing to break the spell by mentioning the obvious—that I don't need his support to navigate familiar paths, that our linked arms have nothing to do with ice and everything to do with wanting connection.

Halfway down the path, my cottage comes into view—a tiny converted carriage house with the vibrant teal door I painted myself and windows glowing with the timer lights I set before leaving.

"That's your place?" Max asks, slowing our pace.

"Home sweet home. All nine hundred square feet of it."

"It suits you." There's no condescension in his tone, only appreciation. "Distinctive. Unapologetically individual."

We continue past without stopping, both aware that crossing that threshold would change everything. Instead, we walk to Mountain Brew, our breath synchronizing in the quiet night.

"Coffee?" I offer as I unlock the door. "I've been experimenting with a new nighttime blend."

"I'd love to try it."

The darkened shop feels intimate as I move through familiar motions—grinding beans, heating water, and preparing two mugs with a technique that falls somewhere between pour-over and French press.

"My own invention." I hand him a steaming mug. "Designed specifically for evening consumption. Lower acidity, subtle chocolate notes, a hint of cardamom."

Max tastes it thoughtfully. "It's remarkable. Complex but soothing."

"The cardamom is the secret." I lean against the counter. "Most people use cinnamon for sweetness, but cardamom adds dimension without the sugar rush."

He moves closer, setting his mug aside. "You are a sorceress."

"Just experienced."

"More than experienced." Another step closes the distance between us. "Brilliant. Innovative. Extraordinary."

Each word diminishes the space between us until we're breathing the same air, the coffee forgotten.

"Max..." The word emerges as barely more than a whisper.

His hand rises to cup my cheek, thumb tracing my lower lip. The touch is gentle, but his eyes are anything but—dark with hunger barely leashed, pupils dilated until only a thin ring of blue remains. Tension radiates from him, taut as a wire about to snap.

"Tell me to stop, and I will." His voice is rough, strained with the effort of control. The power in that restraint is intoxicating—knowing what he wants, what he could take, yet holding back for my permission.

His thumb continues its path across my lip, applying just enough pressure to part them slightly. My pulse hammers at my throat, drums in my ears, throbs between my thighs.

"I told you what I want," he murmurs, his breath warm against my skin. "Nothing's changed." The reminder of his whispered confessions sends heat flooding through me. His free hand moves to my waist, fingertips pressing just hard enough to hint at the strength he's holding in check.

The last threads of my resistance dissolve beneath his touch. Instead of answering, I close the final distance, my lips finding his with newfound certainty.

Unlike our previous kisses—frantic in the storm, tentative in the generator's glow—this one simmers before it sparks. His mouth claims mine, as if he's intent on tasting every part of me. The hand at my waist tightens, drawing me closer but still maintaining that exquisite control that speaks of darker promises to come.

When his tongue traces the seam of my lips, I open for him without hesitation. He makes a sound low in his throat— approval and hunger mingled—before deepening the kiss, each movement a demonstration of exactly how thoroughly he intends to claim every part of me.

My palms glide up the solid wall of his chest, over the breadth of his shoulders. He gathers me closer, arms tightening until there's no space left, until the hard press of his body pins mine to the counter. The edge digs into my hips, but I don't care—I want the weight, the possession.

Heat blooms where his hand slips under my sweater, calloused fingertips tracing the bare skin at my lower back. The contrast makes me shiver, arching into him, craving more. He swallows the gasp I can't contain, answering with a deeper sweep of his tongue, coaxing me open, leaving me dizzy with want.

He breaks away only to trail kisses along my jaw, his

stubble scraping in delicious friction down the column of my throat. My head tips back, surrendering. He finds the sensitive spot where my neck meets my shoulder and lingers, sucking lightly until pleasure sparks through me like electricity.

I tangle my fingers in his hair, anchoring him there, unwilling to let him go. His hands slide higher beneath my sweater, palms spreading wide against my ribcage, thumbs brushing the swell of my breasts. The involuntary gasp rips out of me, sharp and helpless.

That sound halts him. He lifts his head, breath ragged, eyes dark and unsteady as they lock on mine. Desire crackles between us, sharp as lightning. For a beat, neither of us moves. His question is unspoken, written in the tension of his body, the heat in his gaze—how far I'll let him take this, how much I want.

"I want you," I whisper, daring the words, daring him. "But..."

That single syllable stills him more effectively than if I'd pushed him away. His forehead drops to mine, both of us breathing hard, chests colliding with the force of restraint.

"That hesitation," he rasps, voice rough as gravel, taut with control. "That tiny pause tells me now isn't the time." His thumb traces across my lower lip, swollen and trembling from his kiss. "I don't want part of you, Lily. I want all of you. Not just the fire you give me when passion takes over. I want your thoughts. Your doubts. Your fears. I want to know what you crave—what terrifies you. Every part."

His words undo me more completely than the press of his body ever could. Desire knots tighter inside me, not less, because his restraint feels as dangerous as his hunger. My body screams to keep going, to let him take me against the counter, to surrender to the heat clawing through my veins.

But he's right. He's always right. Because what he wants isn't just a night stolen before he leaves in a few weeks. He wants something far more profound, something I don't know if I can give without shattering.

My breath catches, my fingers still tangled in his hair.

"That's what scares me," I whisper, raw and unguarded. "That you'll see it all. That you'll know too much."

His gaze burns into mine, steady and relentless, as if he's already peeling back every secret I've buried. "That's exactly what I want," he says, voice low and certain. "All of you. The parts you're proud of and the parts you hide. The achievements and the failures."

His thumb traces my jawline, a touch both tender and possessive. "Every flaw, every fear, every doubt—I want to savor them all." His eyes never leave mine, unflinching in their intensity. "Nothing you show me will change what I want. Nothing."

The conviction in his voice steals my breath. No one has ever looked at me like this—as if I'm both a mystery to solve and a prize already claimed.

"Let me in," he murmurs, the command wrapped in velvet steel. "Because I don't just want your body against mine. I want your surrender. Your trust. Freely given. Without hesitation."

The words hit harder than his kiss, harder than the press of his body pinning me to the counter. Because he could take me—right here, right now. Every muscle in him vibrates with the restraint it takes not to. His arousal throbs against me, undeniable proof of how much he wants. And yet, he holds back, framing my face with hands that could cage but instead caress.

"I could have sex with you right now," he admits, voice hoarse, eyes dark with hunger. "But I don't want your body if your mind isn't there with me. If your heart isn't begging me to take you. I want more than release. I want everything. Your desires. Your fears. Every corner of you that you've never let another man touch."

Heat floods my skin at his words, at the naked truth in them. His control is a leash he refuses to drop, even though my body is already his, trembling with need, silently pleading.

His thumb traces along my cheek with surprising tenderness. "This is about what you truly want. I'll wait until you're ready to stop doubting yourself. Until you know with absolute certainty that this is what you want. No reservations, no holding back."

The intensity in his gaze makes it difficult to breathe. "I'm patient enough to wait for that moment. When you come to me fully present, without fear. That's when we'll truly begin."

His mouth brushes mine again, a torment of what he's denying us both. "Until then," he whispers, breath hot against my lips, "I'll keep showing you exactly how much I want you... so that when you finally surrender, it's not just your body I take. It's everything."

The raw promise in his voice makes my knees buckle, makes me cling to him even as he gently, deliberately begins to pull back. His control sears deeper than any kiss—because real dominance isn't in taking what he wants. It's in waiting until I'm desperate enough to give it all.

And, I'm ready.

Almost.

Angel's Peak

CHAPTER 18

THE NEXT FEW DAYS MELT AWAY LIKE SNOW IN spring sunshine. The routines Max and I have established feel both new and oddly familiar—his morning arrival with that half-smile that's just for me, afternoons of work punctuated by stolen glances across the shop, occasional evenings that stretch later than either of us intend.

We've settled into a rhythm that's becoming dangerously... *comfortable*.

One thing that's new and exciting is that morning brings a parade of Angel's Peak business owners, all eager for their slice of Max's expertise. Hunter Morgan from Timberline Restaurant arrives first, tablet in hand, gesturing animatedly about inventory categories for his kitchen supplies. Before he's even finished, Mabel Wilson from the guesthouse slips into the opposite chair at Max's booth, spreadsheets and projections at the ready.

The seamless flow of entrepreneurs continues all day— Lucas Reid discussing operations at The Haven Resort, Dominic Mercer from Silverleaf Vineyards showcasing his implementation of Max's tracking system, and even Sheriff

Donovan stopping by to see if *this app* he's heard about might help manage equipment at the station.

Each visitor orbits around Max's booth like planets around a sun, drawn by his gravity, his expertise. I watch from behind the counter, struck by how he gives each person his complete focus, how his fingers occasionally brush their hands while pointing at screens, how his laughter fills the shop when someone makes a joke.

Yet somehow, no matter how engaged he seems, his eyes always find mine across the room at precisely the moment I'm looking at him, as though some invisible tether connects us.

The parade of beta testers only makes his professional appeal more potent. Watching him solve problems with the same focus and command he showed when his hands were on my body during the blizzard makes my skin warm with inappropriate thoughts.

Authority suits him, whether it's in coding or... other arenas.

Authority. Command. Purpose.

What have I opened myself up to?

An envelope sits unopened on my counter all morning, the return address—Kirkland Properties—promising nothing good. I finally tear it open during a quiet moment between customers, stomach sinking as I read the contents.

There will be a thirty percent rent increase when my lease renews next month.

Thirty percent.

I do the mental calculations three times, hoping the numbers will somehow rearrange themselves into something manageable. They don't. Between the shop's financial struggles and this new blow, my life in Angel's Peak suddenly feels built on shifting sand.

The rest of the day passes in a fog of worry. I serve customers on autopilot, smile without feeling it, move through familiar motions while my mind races through increasingly desperate scenarios. Even Max's presence in his usual corner booth fails to lift my spirits.

By closing time, I've worked myself into a complete spiral of anxiety. As the last customer leaves, I flip the sign to CLOSED and rest my forehead against the cool glass, eyes closed, breathing deeply.

"Lily?"

I startle slightly, having forgotten Max was still here.

"Sorry." I straighten, attempting normalcy. "Lost in thought."

"Troubling thoughts, from the look of it." He stands, concern evident in his expression, but there's something else too—a watchfulness, as if he's cataloging my reactions. He moves toward me with deliberate steps. "What's wrong?"

"Nothing major." The lie tastes bitter. "Just business stuff."

He studies me with those perceptive blue eyes that seem to see right through my defenses. His gaze holds me in place, commanding without words.

"I don't believe you."

Something about his quiet authority breaks through my resolve. I retrieve the letter from beneath the counter, wordlessly handing it to him.

"Thirty percent?" His expression darkens as he reads. "That's highway robbery."

"That's real estate in a growing tourist town." I take the letter back, folding it with precise movements. "People are discovering Angel's Peak. Demand increases, prices follow."

"What will you do?"

The simple question unravels me further. "I don't know. Business is already tight. The shop barely breaks even in the off-season, and now my rental costs..." I swallow hard against the tightness in my throat. "I'll figure something out. I always do."

Max is quiet for a moment, thinking. He moves closer, his hand reaching out to tilt my chin up, forcing me to meet his gaze. The gesture is gentle but brooks no resistance. "What if we increased your business revenue? Not just incrementally, but substantially?"

"By magic?" A hollow laugh escapes me. "I've tried everything. Loyalty programs, specialty items, and extended hours during peak seasons. There's only so much coffee one small town can drink."

"But it's not just about the town anymore." His fingers linger on my skin, a point of warmth that anchors me to the present. "It's about reach. Digital presence. Alternative revenue streams. What about a tech center?"

I recognize the look in his eyes—the same intensity he gets when solving coding problems. "What are you thinking?"

"Let me show you."

For the next three hours, we huddle over his laptop at the counter, exploring possibilities I previously dismissed as beyond my capabilities as a solo proprietor.

Not to mention the costs.

Max, however, guides me through creating a simple but effective website with online ordering functionality, setting up shipping logistics for my signature coffee beans, and developing subscription options for recurring customers.

I've considered everything he says, but something held me back. It's fear, but there's more to it. I hate to say this, but it's as if I believe I'm doomed to fail, and because of that, I'm afraid to try.

Eric destroyed many things when he trashed my career. My belief in myself is merely a tiny fragment of what he destroyed.

"The key is maintaining your brand identity while expanding your reach." Max's fingers fly across the keyboard, building a digital version of Mountain Brew that somehow captures the essence of the shop. "What if we combine it with a coworking space?"

I lean closer to see the screen, catching the scent of his cologne.

"A coworking space?" I repeat, considering the concept.

"Remote work is booming, even in small towns like Angel's Peak. People need somewhere besides their kitchen table to work, but many can't afford dedicated office space." His eyes remain on the screen as mockups take shape—my familiar coffee shop transformed with designated workstations, small meeting areas, and comfortable lounges.

"You already have the Wi-Fi, the coffee, and the atmosphere. Add power outlets at each table, maybe a few privacy booths, a small conference room in that storage space you never use..." His enthusiasm is contagious. "Monthly memberships for regular users, day passes for tourists or occasional visitors. You'd essentially double your revenue streams without doubling your overhead."

The possibilities unfold before me—Mountain Brew evolving beyond just a coffee shop into a community hub, a place where local entrepreneurs and remote workers could thrive.

"You'd be offering something this town doesn't have," Max continues, "while still keeping everything that makes your café special. The perfect blend of your coffee expertise and practical business needs."

Every time he pauses to ask my opinion, he shifts slightly closer, his shoulder pressing against mine, his hand occasionally covering mine to guide my movements on the trackpad. Each touch lingers a moment longer than necessary, sending ripples of awareness through my body.

"Your story is what sets you apart. The artisan attention to detail, the unique blends, the mountain location—these are marketable differentiators in the specialty coffee market."

His enthusiasm is contagious, slowly displacing my earlier despair. As the site takes shape, incorporating my existing logo and the copper-and-wood aesthetic of the physical shop, I feel something new unfurling—possibility.

"This could work," I murmur, watching as he integrates a secure payment system.

"It *will* work." His confidence leaves no room for doubt. When he reaches across me to type something, his breath brushes my neck, sending a shiver down my spine.

He notices.

His eyes darken momentarily before returning to the screen. "Here, try the user experience yourself."

I navigate through the site he's created, marveling at its intuitive design and authentic representation of my business. When I complete a test purchase of my signature cinnamon bean blend, the confirmation page includes options for brewing recommendations and complementary flavor pairings.

"That personal touch will drive customer loyalty and word-of-mouth marketing." Max's smile is triumphant as he leans in to observe my reaction, his chest pressing against my back, one hand resting possessively on my hip. The casual ownership in the gesture makes my breath catch. "No mass-market coffee company offers that level of customization."

"This is..." I struggle to find adequate words, distracted by his proximity. "Max, this is incredible."

"It's just the beginning." He turns me to face him fully, hands gripping my waist with gentle authority. "With targeted social media and strategic partnerships with local businesses for cross-promotion, you could double your current revenue within six months."

The technical side of me—the part I've kept suppressed since BrewTech—springs fully to life, engaging with his ideas and offering refinements. We lose track of time, deep in creative collaboration that feels both professionally stimulating and undeniably intimate. Each time our ideas align, his expression warms. It's the kind of approval that makes me inexplicably eager to please him.

When we finally pause, the clock reads nearly midnight.

"We should celebrate." Max closes his laptop with an air of satisfaction. "The official digital launch of Mountain Brew's expansion."

"With what? Everything's closed at this hour."

He glances toward the liquor shelf where I keep spirits for specialty coffee drinks. "Irish coffee?"

Ten minutes later, we sit side by side on the small couch in my office, sipping warm Irish coffees and admiring our work on his tablet. The whiskey adds a pleasant warmth to my veins, though I suspect my lightheaded feeling has more to do with Max's proximity than the alcohol.

"Thank you for this." I turn to face him, our knees touching in the small space. "Not just the technical help, but... believing it could work. I gave up before I even tried."

"Why?" His question is gentle but direct. He sets his mug down, giving me his full attention. His hand finds my knee, thumb tracing small circles that somehow make it harder to concentrate.

I stare into my coffee, gathering courage. "After BrewTech, I lost faith in myself and my business instincts. Figured I was better off keeping things small and manageable. I reinvented myself as a coffee shop owner. No algorithms, no innovation, nothing that could be stolen or twisted against me." I attempt a smile that feels brittle.

Max is quiet for a moment, processing. Then, unexpectedly, he shares in return. "My father lost his job. The factory closed; operations were moved overseas. Within six months, we were a week away from losing our house."

The admission comes without self-pity, stated as a simple fact.

"We were going to move into my uncle's basement. One room for three people." He rotates his mug slowly between his palms. "I watched my father—proudest man I've ever known —break down when he thought no one could see him. That's when I promised myself I'd never be financially vulnerable. It's why I worked so hard on that first app. I knew what I could do, and I wasn't going to let my family down. That week passed. And then another. The mortgage company was beating down the door, and then..."

"And then, you sold the app."

"I sold the app." He grins. "Seven-figures. Paid off the mortgage, and the rest is history."

"Is that why you work so much?" I ask softly.

"Partly. Success became my security blanket." His smile turns self-deprecating. "Though there's a certain irony in working so obsessively that you never actually enjoy the security you've created. There were failures along the way, but I never stopped believing in myself. Eric stole that from you, your belief in yourself. I aim to show you that you can do anything you set your mind to."

"Thanks."

We sit in companionable silence, each absorbing the other's confession. These aren't casual disclosures but foundational truths—the kind that shape a person's core motivations and fears.

Max shifts closer, his thigh pressing firmly against mine. He reaches out to tuck a strand of hair behind my ear, his fingers lingering against my cheek. The simple touch carries an electric current that makes my skin tingle. His eyes are darker now, focused on my lips with unmistakable intent.

"It's late." He finally breaks the silence, gesturing to the time, though the last thing I want is for him to leave. "I should get back to The Haven, but can I walk you home first?"

The offer shouldn't make my pulse quicken—it's a simple courtesy, especially given the late hour—yet something in his tone suggests this isn't merely about safety.

"I'd like that."

Outside, the night wraps around us in crisp mountain clarity. Stars punctuate the velvet sky, impossibly bright and numerous, away from city lights. Our breath forms matching clouds in the cold air as we walk the short distance to my cottage.

Instead of walking side by side, Max places his hand at the small of my back, a possessive gesture that makes me acutely aware of his strength, his height, his control. His fingers occasionally flex against my spine, guiding me around ice patches or adjusting our pace. Each small direction sends tremors of anticipation through me.

We don't speak much, both aware of a threshold approaching that has nothing to do with my physical doorstep. When my cottage comes into view, its teal door vibrant even in moonlight, a decision crystallizes within me—clarity emerging from too many days of uncertainty and self doubt.

I unlock the door with steady hands, then turn to face him. "Would you like to come in?"

His eyes search mine, understanding the invitation extends beyond beverages. "Are you sure?"

Instead of answering, I take his hand and lead him inside.

My cottage welcomes us with familiar simplicity—the mismatched furniture I've collected piece by piece, walls adorned with coffee-themed art and vintage café signs, the patchwork quilt draped over my small sofa. The space is tiny but intentional; every element is carefully selected and arranged to maximize comfort within the minimal square footage.

"It's perfect." Max takes in the details with genuine appreciation. "Exactly what I imagined."

"You imagined my cottage?"

"More than once." His admission comes with a slightly sheepish smile.

I move to the kitchenette, suddenly nervous despite my resolve. "Coffee?"

"Lily." He steps closer, gently taking the kettle from my hands and setting it aside. There's a shift in his demeanor—something more deliberate, more controlled. "You didn't ask me inside for coffee. All I need to know is, are you ready?"

His palm cups my cheek, thumb tracing the curve of my lower lip. The tenderness of the gesture nearly undoes me. I lean into his touch, eyes closing briefly as his forehead rests against mine.

"You can always say no," he says.

"I don't want to..."

His eyes darken at my words, something primal and possessive flaring in their depths. "Then say what you do want," he murmurs, his voice dropping to that commanding tone that makes my knees weak. "Be specific."

The request should embarrass me, but instead, it ignites something I've been suppressing since that night during the blizzard. The memory of his whispered confessions about control, about darker appetites, about leaving marks—they flood back with visceral clarity.

"I want you," I whisper, swallowing hard against the vulnerability of the admission. "I want... what you described during the storm. I want to know what it feels like to surrender to someone I trust."

The words hang between us, irrevocable once spoken. Part of me can't believe I've said them aloud, but the way Max's expression transforms—hunger and tenderness merging into something breathtakingly intense—tells me it was exactly what he needed to hear.

"Once we start," he says, his voice a rough caress against my skin, "it's complicated going back to who we were before. You understand that?"

"Yes." The single syllable carries the weight of consent, of trust, of desire too long denied.

His fingers tangle in my hair, tightening just enough to tilt my head back, exposing my throat to his gaze. "I've waited for this moment since I first saw you," he confesses, his lips hovering just above mine. "Imagined all the ways I would take you apart and put you back together again."

The promise in his words sends liquid heat pooling between my thighs, a visceral response I couldn't hide even if I wanted to. And I don't want to hide anything from him—not anymore.

"I don't know what to do. I need you to show me," I breathe, surrendering to the current that's been pulling us toward this moment since our first collision.

His answering smile is darkly triumphant, a predator finally claiming its prey. "With pleasure."

Angel's Peak

CHAPTER 19

MAX'S RESPONSE IS IMMEDIATE, BUT MEASURED—HIS arms encircling my waist and lifting me slightly as the kiss deepens. One hand slides up to cradle the back of my neck, controlling the angle with subtle pressure that makes my knees weak.

"I want you," he murmurs against my lips, his voice deeper than I've heard it before. "But I need you to understand something first."

I pull back slightly, breathless. "What?"

His eyes hold mine, intense and serious. "Remember what I told you?"

A flush of heat spreads through me. "Yes."

"Tonight won't be like anything you've experienced before. I'll take care of you, but I'll also push you." His thumb traces my lower lip, pressing slightly. "I need to know that you trust me. That you'll tell me if anything becomes too much."

"I trust you." The promise in his words sends a shiver down my spine—part anticipation, part nervousness.

"Good." The approval in his voice triggers something primal within me—a desire to please him that I've never felt before. "If anything becomes too much, tell me to stop, and I will. Immediately."

His eyes hold mine for one breathless moment before his mouth claims mine, possessive, commanding. His hand slides to the nape of my neck, fingers threading through my hair to grip gently, angling my head exactly how he wants it. The subtle display of control makes my knees weak.

I arch against him, my body responding to his unspoken demands as if we've done this dance a hundred times before. His other arm wraps around my waist, pulling me flush against him until I can feel every hard plane of his body pressed against mine. A soft moan escapes me as his tongue sweeps into my mouth, claiming, exploring with devastating precision.

The kiss deepens, growing more urgent, more demanding. My hands clutch at his shoulders, then slide beneath his sweater to find warm skin stretched over solid muscle. His sharp intake of breath encourages me further, my nails scraping lightly down his back. In response, his grip tightens in my hair, the slight edge of pain amplifying the pleasure coursing through me.

We stumble backward, locked together, unwilling to break apart even for the seconds it would take to navigate the room properly. My hip bumps the small table, sending something clattering to the floor—neither of us pauses to see what it was. Max's hands move restlessly over my body, as if he can't touch enough of me at once, each caress leaving trails of heat in its wake.

Somehow, we make it to the bedroom, though I couldn't trace the path if my life depended on it. All I know is the burn of his mouth on mine, the strength of his arms around me, the way his touch makes everything else fade into insignificance.

When my legs meet the edge of the bed, Max draws back slightly, his breathing uneven, but his control firmly in place.

"Last chance to change your mind," he murmurs, eyes searching mine for any hesitation.

In answer, I reach for the buttons of my blouse, but his hand stops mine.

"No." The single word carries unmistakable authority. "Tonight, I undress you. I decide what happens and when it happens. All you need to do is feel and experience."

The concept should make me bristle—I've always valued my independence, my control—but instead, a strange relief washes over me. The idea of not having to make decisions, of simply experiencing, resonates deeply within me.

Max's fingers move to my blouse, working each button free with deliberate, unhurried movements. His eyes never leave mine, gauging my reactions with careful attention. When the garment finally slides from my shoulders, he steps back slightly, his gaze traveling over me with such focused appreciation that I feel more exposed than if I were already naked.

"Beautiful," he whispers, circling behind me. His fingers trail along my collarbone, down my spine, mapping me with a precision that leaves goosebumps in their wake. "I've thought about this since that first day you spilled coffee on my laptop."

His hands find my hips, pulling me against him so I can feel his arousal pressing insistently against me. His lips brush the sensitive spot where my neck meets my shoulder, sending electricity coursing through me.

He kneels before me, his hands sliding up my calves, behind my knees, along my thighs—a deliberate journey that has me trembling with anticipation. When his fingers reach the button of my jeans, he pauses, looking up at me with a question in his eyes.

I nod, not trusting my voice.

He undoes the button and slowly slides the zipper down, his movements measured and deliberate. The denim is peeled away with agonizing slowness, his hands warming every inch of skin as it's revealed.

Standing again, he guides me to the edge of the bed. His thumbs knead into the arches of my feet, drawing a helpless moan from my lips. His eyes flicker at the sound, darkening like a storm, as though he's tucking the noise away for later.

In one smooth motion, he rises and pulls his sweater over his head. The movement ripples lean muscle across his chest and shoulders, every line carved in shadow and firelight. My breath stutters, my fingers twitch to reach for him—but he catches my wrist before I can touch.

"Not yet." His voice is a velvet command, quiet but absolute. "Tonight, I teach you patience."

The words curl through me, leaving me trembling even as he casually unbuttons his jeans. The denim loosens against his hips, sliding lower with every deliberate tug, but he leaves them hanging, a promise instead of a gift. His focus shifts back to me.

His fingers skim the lace edge of my bra, teasing under the fabric without touching where my body aches for him most. The soft drag of knuckles just beneath the curve of my breast is enough to have me arching toward him, silently begging. Still, he denies me.

Finally, he reaches behind me, unclasping the bra with expert ease. The straps fall down my arms before he slips it free, dropping it carelessly aside. Cool air kisses my exposed skin, making my nipples harden, but the real heat comes from his gaze—devouring me, stripping me bare long before his hands do.

"Lie back," he orders, softer this time, but no less commanding.

I obey, sliding across the sheets until I'm fully stretched out before him. He stands at the foot of the bed, tall, broad, carved in shadow and light. His chest is all lean muscle and sculpted strength, the kind of body born of discipline rather than vanity—shoulders wide, arms roped with power that looks capable of both tenderness and devastating control.

His jeans hang low on his hips, clinging to the deep lines that disappear beneath the waistband. With excruciating slowness, he pushes them lower. Denim slides down over strong thighs, revealing black briefs stretched tight across the thick outline of him. The sight alone makes my pulse trip into a frenzy.

He doesn't free himself right away. No—he prowls in his restraint, fingers lingering at the band, deliberately giving me time to take in every ridge of muscle, every shadowed line of masculinity. My breath hitches, anticipation spiraling tighter.

Only when my hips lift unconsciously toward him— silent begging—does he slide his briefs down, releasing himself fully. The sight steals my air. Hard, heavy, proud, he stands in the low light like temptation given form. Heat rushes through me so fast I'm dizzy, my thighs pressing together instinctively.

A small, satisfied smile flickers across his face, as though my reaction is the prize he's been waiting for. He climbs onto the bed, moving over me with a predatory grace. Every shift of muscle is deliberate, a reminder of his strength, of the weight I'm about to feel pinning me down.

He pauses at my hips, fingers slipping beneath the lace of my panties. Instead of rushing, he lowers his head, inhaling deeply against me. The intimate sound of his breath nearly undoes me, a raw, possessive note that leaves my skin tingling. Only then does he peel the fabric away slowly, leaving me bare beneath his gaze.

When he finally lowers his weight over me, the heat of his body sears against mine, chest to chest, thigh to thigh, his hardness pressed heavy between my legs. Not inside me—yet —but so close I can feel the steady throb of him. A promise. A torment. My body arches instinctively, begging for more, but he holds me pinned, dictating the pace.

"Tell me what you want," he murmurs against my throat, his teeth grazing the delicate skin there, just enough pressure to make me shiver.

"You," I manage, though my voice cracks with need. "Please."

"More specific." His hand drifts down, knuckles grazing my stomach, skimming the edge of my core without granting me the relief I crave. His restraint is unbearable. "Tell me exactly what you want me to do to you."

The command slices through the last shreds of inhibition. My pulse hammers, shame drowned by the sheer force of desire. "Touch me," I whisper, raw. "Inside. I need you inside me."

Approval flashes in his dark eyes, a flicker of satisfaction that makes my insides twist. "Good girl."

His fingers finally part me, sliding into slick heat with maddening precision. He doesn't rush—he maps me, learns me, finds the places that make my breath stutter and my hips buck helplessly against his hand. When one long finger pushes inside, I cry out, my body clutching around him as if even that isn't enough.

"So tight," he growls, adding a second finger, stretching me until the ache turns delicious. His thumb circles my clit with devastating accuracy, and when his fingers curl just right —oh God—I see stars, my back bowing off the bed.

"Max," I gasp, hands clutching the sheets, the tension inside me a coiled spring about to snap.

His mouth finds my ear, voice a dark caress. "Not yet."

He pulls back just as I teeter on the edge, leaving me trembling, wrecked, desperate. His restraint is ruthless, his control absolute.

"Not until I decide," he says, his lips brushing my jaw in a tormenting kiss. "Because when I let you fall, Lily—you're going to shatter for me."

The words curl through me like fire, leaving me trembling. I whimper at the loss when his hand leaves me, but he silences me with a kiss that steals the sound from my throat—deep, possessive, claiming. His hand tangles in my hair, tugging gently to expose my throat to his mouth. He works his way down my body, his lips and tongue and teeth leaving a trail of fire across my skin.

When he reaches my breasts, his mouth lingers, teasing until I'm writhing beneath him, shameless in my need. He lavishes attention on each tight peak, suckling until my back bows and desperate sounds tumble from me. His restraint is unbearable, his mastery infuriatingly perfect.

Lower, his mouth trails across my stomach, each kiss lower, closer, until his breath ghosts over the ache between my thighs. His hands grip my hips, holding me pinned when I lift toward him, begging without words.

"Please," I whisper, broken, beyond pride now.

"Since you asked so nicely." His smile is wicked, dark, but there's reverence in it, too.

When his mouth closes over me, I shatter into gasps, clutching at his hair as his tongue works me with the same devastating precision as his fingers. He teases, tastes, and learns me all over again, drawing me higher and higher—until he pulls away, leaving me teetering on the brink, my body a desperate, quaking mess.

"Not yet." His voice is both tender and unyielding. "Not until I claim every part of you." He pulls away again, his expression both tender and unyielding. "Not until I'm inside you."

He rises, reaches for protection from his discarded jeans. And then he's back, looming over me, sliding between my legs, eyes locked on mine with searing intensity.

The first press of him is deliberate—slow, inexorable. My breath catches as he pushes deeper, stretching me, filling me inch by exquisite inch. The sensation is overwhelming, every nerve alight, my body molding around his.

My breath catches at the sensation of fullness, of rightness that defies rational explanation.

"Perfect," he groans when he's fully seated, his thumb brushing my cheek with a gentleness that undoes me more than any command. "You're perfect."

He stays there, buried deep, holding me still while my body adjusts, his control absolute even as his muscles tremble with restraint. And when he finally begins to move—measured, deliberate thrusts—his rhythm is worship and possession both. He takes me with the kind of patience that feels like torture, every stroke drawing me closer, every shift reminding me who's in control.

And through it all, his eyes never leave mine, as though he's determined not just to take my body, but to own my surrender, my trust, my every unspoken need.

He studies every reaction, cataloging every gasp and shiver like he's memorizing a map of my pleasure. When he finds a spot that makes me clutch at his shoulders, he returns to it, adapting to my responses with the same focus he brings to everything else.

His movement speaks of mastery—not just of his own desire, but of mine. He seems to know exactly how to build the tension coiling inside me, alternating between deep, measured strokes and shallow ones that make me arch against him, seeking more. It's as though he's conducting an orchestra where my body is the only instrument, and he's determined to draw out every possible note.

His hand slides between us, fingers finding where we're joined, pressing against my slick heat in a way that makes my entire body jolt. He strokes with devastating precision, each touch synchronized with the thrust of his hips until I'm spiraling upward, climbing too fast, too hard.

"Not yet," he commands, voice low and rough with restraint. Somehow he knows—feels—the way I'm teetering on the edge. His tone brooks no argument. "Eyes on me."

It takes everything I have to obey, to wrench my gaze up to meet his. The force of his stare nearly undoes me; it's dark, consuming, intimate in a way that lays me bare.

"When you come," he growls, his rhythm never faltering, "it will be knowing exactly who you belong to in this moment."

The possessiveness in his words burns hotter than the fire in my veins. My body arches, straining toward him, desperate. He claims my mouth in a kiss that's all heat and teeth and hunger, stealing what little breath I have left.

His lips break away, dragging down my throat, finding the hollow of my neck. His teeth graze the tender skin there, not quite biting, but enough to make me cry out, enough to promise he could mark me if he chose. I tip my head back, offering myself up without even realizing it.

His mouth trails lower—over my collarbone, down to the swell of my breasts. He doesn't rush. His tongue circles one peaked nipple, then the other, lavishing each with attention until my cries fill the air. My fingers twist in his hair, holding him there, begging for more, though I no longer have words for what I need.

Then his eyes lift to mine, molten, unreadable, and his hand slides lower between us again. The calloused pad of his thumb finds my center, stroking firmly, ruthlessly, in perfect counterpoint to the deep, relentless thrust of his hips. My world narrows to the exquisite torment of his body and his will.

"Now," he commands at last, voice like gravel, like fire. "Come for me. Now, Lily."

The permission detonates inside me. My body shatters around him, muscles clenching, pleasure tearing through me in violent waves that border on agony. I scream his name, not caring who hears, not caring about anything except the way he owns me in this moment.

And through it all—my climax, my surrender—his gaze never leaves mine, holding me fast as though he's claimed something deeper than my body, something I can't take back even if I wanted to.

The second my body convulses around him, his control fractures. A raw sound tears from his throat as he drives deeper, harder, no longer measured or restrained but taking, claiming, chasing his own release with ruthless hunger.

His face buries in my neck, his breath ragged against my skin, and his arms lock around me with a strength that steals my breath. The careful rhythm is gone, replaced by a primal need, each thrust desperate, consuming, as though he's waited too long to finally let himself have me.

I cling to him, still trembling from my own unraveling, every nerve alive as he pounds into me with a force that borders on brutal—but never careless. His need pours into every movement, raw and unrestrained, and I can feel him giving over to it, surrendering to me as completely as he demanded my surrender.

He shudders violently, his release crashing through him as he holds me pinned beneath the weight of his body. His groan vibrates against my throat, a sound of possession and relief, as though in this moment he's emptied everything into me—every ounce of restraint, every ounce of need.

And when he collapses against me, still holding me so tightly I can barely breathe, it doesn't feel like too much. It feels like everything.

Afterward, we lie tangled together, heartbeats gradually slowing. His fingers trace idle patterns on my bare shoulder, while I rest my head on his chest—the steady drum of his heart pounds beneath my ear. Neither of us speaks, unwilling to break the spell with words that might prove inadequate.

Eventually, Max pulls the quilt over us against the night's chill, tucking me more securely against his side. The simple domesticity of the gesture creates a lump in my throat. This feels nothing like the calculated encounters with Eric, where intimacy was currency rather than connection.

This feels like...*home*.

The thought should terrify me. Instead, it settles inside my chest with surprising comfort. Max presses a kiss to my forehead, arm tightening around me protectively.

"Stay," I murmur, already half-dreaming.

"As long as you'll have me," he whispers in reply.

Morning arrives with soft golden light filtering through the curtains I forgot to close. I wake slowly, momentarily disoriented by the unfamiliar weight of an arm around my waist, the steady breathing against my neck.

Max.

The events of last night return in vivid detail, bringing a flush to my cheeks even as contentment spreads through me. I turn carefully in his embrace, not wanting to wake him yet.

This man—brilliant, driven, accomplished—chose to share not just his body but his fears with me. The past that shaped him, the insecurities beneath the confident exterior. In return, I've given him access to parts of myself I locked away after BrewTech—including a side of my sexuality I never knew existed.

The realization settles over me with both warmth and apprehension.

My cottage feels different with him in it. His presence fills spaces I hadn't realized were empty. His clothes draped over my reading chair, his watch on my bedside table, his scent mingled with mine on the sheets—all create an impression of belonging I never anticipated.

The rising sun gilds the mountains outside my window, painting the snow-capped peaks in shades of amber and rose. The beauty that first drew me to Angel's Peak now serves as a backdrop to a more immediate wonder—Max, sleeping peacefully in my bed, integrated into my world as if he has always been part of it.

I'm suddenly faced with a terrifying truth. What started as an attraction is becoming something far more dangerous. Something that won't end neatly when his time is up.

Angel's Peak

Chapter 20

Max stands at my tiny stove, spatula in hand, concentration evident in the slight furrow between his brows. The domesticity of the scene—him making breakfast in boxers and a t-shirt, coffee already brewing in my French press. It all creates a warmth in my chest that has nothing to do with the mountain sunshine streaming through the window.

"You don't have to cook every morning, you know." I wrap my arms around him from behind, pressing my cheek between his shoulder blades. "Cereal exists for a reason."

"Cereal isn't breakfast." He flips a perfectly golden pancake. "It's a sad approximation created by people who don't understand the importance of proper morning nutrition."

"Says the man who survived on caffeine and protein bars during coding marathons."

"Exactly." He turns in my embrace, dropping a quick kiss on my lips. "I'm speaking from hard-won wisdom. Besides, your pantry is begging for intervention."

Four days of this new routine—Max staying over, mornings together before opening the shop, evenings returning to my cottage—and already it feels like a natural extension of my life rather than a disruption. The ease of our togetherness should terrify me. Instead, it feels like discovering a puzzle piece I hadn't realized was missing.

I lean against the counter, watching him move through my kitchen with the ease of familiarity. His confidence is intoxicating—not just in how he navigates my space, but in how he has navigated me over the past four nights, each night revealing new depths to desires I barely knew I had.

The first night after we finally crossed that threshold, tangled in my sheets, breathless and sated, he traced patterns on my bare shoulder and whispered, *"That was just the beginning."* The promise in his voice sent shivers cascading through my already sensitized body.

He has been faithful to his word. Each night since has been an education in sensation and surrender. The second night, he blindfolded me with one of my silk scarves, his fingers alternating between the ticklish sweep of feathers and the firm stroke of leather against my skin. The contrast was maddening, building a sensitivity I never knew possible.

"What are you thinking about?" Max asks, his voice pulling me from my reverie. The knowing glint in his eyes suggests he's already guessed.

Heat rises to my cheeks. "Nothing."

"Liar." He sets a plate of pancakes on the counter, stepping closer until I'm trapped between his body and the kitchen island. "You're thinking about last night."

Last night.

My body flushes at the memory—the slow drip of hot wax across my stomach, my thighs, the exquisite edge between pleasure and pain as Max controlled each drop to land and sear exactly where he wanted. Each hiss of my breath seemed to please him, his mouth curving against my ear as if he planned every reaction.

The sting faded almost instantly, replaced by a flood of heat that spread low and insistent. I writhed, arching, begging for more without words, but he made me wait.

Every drop became its own torment, its own promise.

He wasn't just touching my body—he was unraveling my mind, teaching me how to crave the anticipation as much as the release.

And when he finally moved over me—skin against skin, heat sliding into heat—the sensation of him, the slickness of my arousal against the faint tack of cooling wax, sent me spiraling. My body was already on edge, primed and desperate from his control, and the rhythm he set tore me apart ruthlessly.

The wax made me his canvas.

The sex made me his possession.

And the way he whispered against my throat, voice rough with hunger, made me his completely.

I never imagined finding such freedom in surrender, such pleasure in the careful application of sensations that danced along the borders of comfort, but he has shown me the decadent delight hidden in ceding control.

"Maybe," I admit, my voice barely above a whisper.

His fingers brush my collarbone, tracing the exact spot where a drop of wax fell just hours before.

"I love watching you discover yourself," he murmurs. "Seeing you embrace each new sensation, pushing a little further each time." His thumb grazes my bottom lip. "The way you trust me with your pleasure..."

Four days ago, I would have flinched away from such intimate words. Now, I lean into them, into him, meeting his intensity with my own.

"I never knew it could be like this."

"Like what?" His eyes darken as his hand slides to cup my

neck, thumb resting against my pulse point, where he can feel my heart racing.

"So... consuming." I struggle to articulate the transformation happening within me. "It's like you're systematically dismantling every boundary I've built, every preconception I had about sex."

"And you're letting me." The pride in his voice is unmistakable. "Every time you surrender a little more, every time you say *'more'* instead of *'enough'*—" he presses his lips to the sensitive spot below my ear "—you become more magnificent."

I close my eyes, overwhelmed by the truth of it. Each night has built upon the last—from the gentle introduction of blindfolds and feathers to the more intense sensations of leather and wax. Each time, he's challenged me to reach beyond what I thought I could handle, and each time, I discovered new landscapes of pleasure I never knew existed.

"Pancakes are getting cold," I murmur, though neither of us moves.

His laughter vibrates against my skin. "I can make more." His hands settle on my hips, drawing me closer. "Besides, I have other ideas for breakfast."

The heat in his eyes sparks something primal in me. Four days of discovering new dimensions of pleasure have emboldened me in ways I never expected. I raise an eyebrow, challenging him.

"Is that so?"

Max's hands suddenly tighten around my waist. He lifts me with startling ease, my feet leaving the ground as he sets me firmly on the kitchen counter. Jars rattle, a spoon clatters to the floor, but neither of us cares. My back presses against the upper cabinets as he positions himself between my thighs.

"I've been thinking about this since the first day in your shop," he growls, his voice dropping to that commanding tone that makes my insides liquefy. "You, on your counter, completely at my mercy."

His mouth claims mine with fierce possession, nothing tentative in the way he takes what he wants. I meet his hunger with my own, fingers threading through his hair, pulling him closer. Four days of exploration have taught us each other's rhythms, the perfect pressure, the exact tilt of heads that deepens the connection between us.

His hands slide beneath my oversized sleep shirt, callused palms skimming up my sides. When his thumbs brush the undersides of my breasts, I gasp against his mouth. He takes advantage, his tongue sweeping inside, tasting of coffee and desire.

"Tell me what you want," he demands against my lips, echoing the command that's become a familiar refrain in our nights together.

"You," I breathe, no longer hesitant about voicing my needs. "All of you."

"Good." His smile turns predatory. "That's exactly what you'll get."

The praise sends a shiver down my spine, a reaction he has discovered and exploited over the past few nights. Max understands my body's responses better than I do—how I arch toward his touch when he praises me, how I tremble when he whispers explicit promises in my ear.

With decisive movements, he tugs my sleep shirt over my head, leaving me bare from the waist up on my own kitchen counter. The cool morning air pebbles my skin, but Max's hands are warm as they map every curve and hollow.

"Look at you," he murmurs, eyes darkening as he takes in my exposed flesh. "Perfect."

His mouth descends to my neck, leaving a trail of biting kisses along my throat, down to my collarbone. When he reaches my breast, he pauses, his breath hot against my sensitive skin.

"Remember what I showed you the other night?" he asks, glancing up through his lashes. "How anticipation makes everything more intense?"

I nod, remembering the exquisite torture of the feather, the leather, the hot wax—each sensation building upon the last until I was desperate for release.

"I want you to feel that now," he continues, "but without any tools. Just my hands and my mouth." His thumb traces my lower lip. "And, of course, your willing surrender."

The word 'surrender' no longer frightens me. With Max, I've learned that giving up control doesn't diminish me—it transforms me, opens doorways to pleasure I never knew existed.

His mouth closes over my nipple, the sudden heat making me cry out. My head falls back against the cabinets with a thud, but the slight pain only heightens the sensation of his tongue circling the sensitive peak. His hand drifts down my stomach, fingers slipping beneath the waistband of my sleep shorts.

"These need to go," he says, his voice rough with desire.

I lift my hips, allowing him to tug the shorts down my legs, leaving me completely naked on the counter. The way he looks at me—like I'm something precious and rare—banishes any thought of covering myself.

His hands spread my thighs wider, opening me fully to his view. The hunger in his eyes as he takes in the sight of me makes my breath catch.

"Beautiful," he murmurs, one finger tracing a teasing path up my inner thigh. "So responsive to my touch. So ready for me."

When his finger finally makes contact with my center, I jerk at the intensity, already slick and ready for him. He chuckles, the sound vibrating against my skin as he presses kisses along my stomach.

"Eager?" He circles the sensitive bundle of nerves with maddening restraint. "What happened to my cautious coffee shop owner? The woman who insisted on taking things slow?"

"You happened," I gasp as he slides one finger inside me, curling it expertly to hit the spot that makes me see stars. "Max, please—"

"Please what?" His thumb replaces his finger on my most sensitive point, maintaining the perfect pressure as he works a second finger inside me. "Tell me exactly what you want. Be specific."

This too has become part of our dance—his insistence that I articulate my desires, teaching me to voice what I need without shame.

"I want your mouth," I manage, the words coming easier now than they did the first night. "I want to feel your tongue—"

Before I can finish, he drops to his knees, his shoulders pushing my thighs further apart. His hot breath against my core is my only warning before his mouth replaces his fingers, tongue flat against me in a broad stroke that makes me cry out.

My hands fly to his hair, fingers tangling in the dark strands as he devours me with single-minded focus. The sight of him between my legs, fully clothed while I'm spread naked across my kitchen counter, adds another layer of erotic intensity to the sensation.

He works me with deliberate skill, alternating between broad strokes and precise flicks of his tongue, building a rhythm that has me teetering on the edge within seconds. When he adds his fingers back into the equation, curling them inside me as his tongue circles my most sensitive point, I'm lost.

"Max—I'm going to—"

"Come for me," he commands against my flesh, the vibration of his voice sending me over the edge.

The orgasm crashes through me with stunning force, my body arching off the counter as waves of pleasure radiate outward. Max doesn't relent, drawing out every aftershock with gentle suction and careful strokes of his tongue until I'm trembling, oversensitive.

When he finally pulls away, his chin is glistening with evidence of my release, his eyes dark with unfulfilled desire. He wipes his mouth with the back of his hand, a gesture that should be crude but somehow manages to be devastatingly sexy.

"That was just the appetizer," he says, voice rough as he stands. His hands make quick work of his pajama bottoms, pushing them down his hips along with his boxers. His erection springs free, thick and ready. "Ready for the main course?"

The playful question breaks through the intensity, making me laugh even as desire coils tight in my belly again. This is what I've discovered with Max—that passion can be punctuated with laughter, that surrender can coexist with joy.

"More than ready," I answer, reaching for him.

He steps between my legs again, positioning himself at my entrance. With one smooth thrust, he fills me completely, both of us groaning at the perfect friction. My legs wrap around his waist, drawing him deeper as his hands grip my hips.

"You feel incredible," he breathes against my neck, setting a punishing rhythm that has the cabinet doors rattling behind me. "So tight, so perfect for me."

Each thrust pushes me closer to another peak, my body still sensitive from the first orgasm. Max seems to sense this; his movements become more controlled and deliberate. One hand slides between us, his thumb finding my center again.

"That's it," he encourages as I tighten around him. "Let go for me again. I want to feel you come around my cock."

His words are my undoing. The second climax hits even harder than the first, my inner muscles clenching around him as pleasure spirals through me. Max follows moments later, his rhythm faltering as he buries himself deep, my name a reverent curse on his lips as he finds his release.

For several heartbeats, we remain locked together, his forehead pressed against mine, our breath mingling in the space between us. The kitchen is silent except for our ragged breathing and the distant ticking of the clock.

"Well," he says finally, a smile playing at the corners of his mouth. "I think we've thoroughly christened this counter."

I laugh, the sound bubbling up from somewhere light and free inside me. "I'll never be able to make coffee here again without thinking about this."

"Good." His possessive tone sends a pleasant shiver through me. "That was my plan all along."

He helps me down from the counter, my legs wobbly as they take my weight again. We clean up quickly, exchanging small touches and heated glances that promise more to come.

We've established a pattern—beginning and ending each day wrapped in each other, with the hours between spent casting longing glances across my coffee shop. It should feel rushed, this rapid acceleration from reluctant attraction to consuming passion. Instead, it feels like we're making up for lost time, like we've been circling each other for much longer than the few weeks he's been in Angel's Peak.

As he retrieves his discarded pajama bottoms from the floor, I'm struck by how naturally he fits into my space, how easily he's dismantled the barriers I spent two years constructing. The thought should terrify me, but as he turns and catches me watching him, the smile he gives me isn't the calculated grin of the tech executive I first met—it's something softer, more genuine, something that makes me believe that maybe, just maybe, this isn't as temporary as I feared.

"Tonight," he whispers, his breath hot against my ear, "I want to try something new."

My body responds instantly to the promise in his voice, heart racing with anticipation. "What did you have in mind?"

"That would ruin the surprise." He steps back, eyes glittering with mischief and desire. "Just know that I intend to push you a little further than we've gone before."

The thought both terrifies and thrills me. Four days ago, I would have retreated from such intensity. Now I lean toward it, curious and eager to discover what other secrets my body has been keeping from me all these years.

I'm addicted to the way he makes me feel—powerful in my surrender, free in my submission to his careful guidance.

Who would have thought that the tech executive who disrupted my quiet coffee shop would so thoroughly disrupt my understanding of pleasure? Or that I would welcome the disruption so eagerly?

Angel's Peak

Chapter 21

"Are you sure you don't mind the gossip?" I ask as we walk to the shop, hands linked between us. "Small towns have big mouths."

"I've dealt with worse than nosy neighbors." His thumb traces circles on my palm. "Though I did get thoroughly interrogated by Ruth at The PickAxe yesterday while picking up that bottle of wine."

"Ruth considers herself Angel's Peak's unofficial relationship counselor." I laugh, remembering her similar inquisition when Noah and Riley first reconnected. "Did she give you the 'intentions' talk?"

"Complete with thinly veiled threats about what happens to men who break hearts in her town." Max's smile is warm with amusement. "I think she was cleaning a shotgun behind the bar for dramatic effect."

"That's just for show. Her preferred weapon is social ostracism."

"Noted. I'll be on my best behavior."

"But Ruth is nothing compared to Eleanor." I pity any man who goes against Eleanor's meddling. They're doomed to lose, although Eleanor seems to have left Max alone. Almost as if she's ceded her elder duties to Ruth.

We separate at the shop door with a quick kiss that still sends butterflies through my stomach. Max heads to his usual corner while I begin opening procedures, both of us falling into comfortable patterns that somehow accommodate the other's presence.

By mid-morning, Max ventures out on errands, promising to return for the afternoon. The shop hums with steady business—a promising uptick since launching the online presence Max helped create. Three mail orders for my signature beans came in overnight, a small but significant expansion beyond local customers.

Max returns mid-afternoon, settling into his usual routine with a quick kiss over the counter that draws knowing smiles from the customers.

By closing time, contentment has replaced my earlier unease. Max helps me shut down the shop, working alongside me, which makes the tasks go faster.

"We could stop by Margie's for pastries on the way home."

Home. The casual way he refers to my cottage creates a flutter in my chest. "Sounds perfect."

The evening air is crisp, carrying the scent of pine and woodsmoke as we walk hand in hand down Main Street. The town is winding down for the night—Sheriff Donovan's cruiser passes with a friendly wave, the PickAxe's windows glow with warm light, and Margie's Bakery is just about to close.

Max holds the door for me, his hand resting lightly at the small of my back as we enter. The touch is casual yet deliberate, a subtle reminder of his constant awareness of my body, which sends a thrill down my spine.

"Lily! Max! I was just about to lock up." Margie's flour-dusted hands gesture to the nearly empty display case. "Not much left, I'm afraid."

"Whatever you have is fine," I say, unable to keep the impatience from my voice. The weight of Max's hand on my back, the memory of last night's explorations, and the promise of what's to come tonight have me unusually distracted.

Max seems to sense my restlessness. His thumb traces small circles against my lower back, the innocent gesture somehow intimate enough to make my breath catch.

"The almond croissants look wonderful," he says to Margie while his touch continues its maddening pattern.

"Fresh this afternoon." Margie begins boxing up the pastries, oblivious to the tension building between us. "Will these be for your breakfast tomorrow?"

"Yes," Max answers before I can speak. His voice drops slightly as he adds, "We have other plans for tonight."

The double meaning isn't lost on me. Heat rises to my cheeks as I fumble with my wallet, but Max is already handing Margie payment.

"You two enjoy your evening," Margie says with a knowing smile that makes me wonder how transparent our anticipation is.

Outside, the streetlights have come on, casting pools of golden light along our path. Max carries the pastry box in one hand, the other firmly entwined with mine. Our pace quickens by mutual, unspoken agreement.

"Eager to get home?" Max asks, his voice teasing but rough with desire.

"Just cold," I lie, though the flush on my skin has nothing to do with the temperature.

His low chuckle tells me he sees right through me. "Is that so? Because I could have sworn you've been watching the clock since we left the shop."

I've been caught. "Maybe I'm just curious about what you have planned."

"Curious?" He stops abruptly under a streetlight, turning me to face him. His eyes are dark with intent as they search mine. "Or impatient?"

"Both," I admit, past pretending. Our escalating intimacy has stripped away my defenses, leaving me raw and honest in ways I never expected.

His smile is slow and predatory. "Good. I like knowing you want this as much as I do."

We resume walking, but at a faster pace. My cottage comes into view, the teal door a welcome sight. My fingers tremble slightly as I fit the key into the lock, hyperaware of Max standing close behind me, his breath warm against my neck.

Once inside, he sets the pastry box on the kitchen counter before turning to me. The intensity in his gaze makes my knees weak.

"Hang up your coat," he says, his voice quiet but commanding. "Then come here."

The directive sends a shiver down my spine. I respond to this aspect of him—the controlled authority, the quiet confidence that expects obedience. I shrug out of my coat, hanging it on the hook by the door, my movements deliberately slow as his eyes track me.

"Now what?" I ask, though we both know I'm not really asking for instructions. I'm inviting him to take control, to guide me through whatever new territory he plans to explore tonight.

His phone chimes with an incoming email, breaking the moment. He glances down. His brow furrows. Only gradually, do I become aware of his prolonged silence.

When I look up, his expression has darkened, jaw tight as he stares at his screen.

"Everything okay?"

"Not exactly." He turns the phone toward me, revealing the headline: "Tech Genius Max Lawson's Secret Mountain Hideaway—Exclusive Photos Reveal Romantic Getaway with Mystery Woman."

My stomach drops as I scan the article. There are photos of us walking together in town, entering my cottage, and even one through my kitchen window of Max cooking breakfast. The invasion of privacy is shocking enough, but it's the final paragraphs that make my blood run cold:

"Sources close to the tech mogul suggest this mountain romance might be more than a casual fling. The mystery woman, identified as local coffee shop owner Lily Brock, appears to have her own tech background. Insiders are now questioning if there's a connection to Lawson's latest security project and Brock's controversial exit from BrewTech following allegations of corporate espionage..."

The room spins slightly as I hand the phone back to him. Two years of carefully constructed anonymity, destroyed in one tabloid article.

Angel's Peak

CHAPTER 22

"How did they—" My voice falters as I reread the article, my vision tunneling until all I can see is my name next to "BrewTech" and "corporate espionage" in stark black letters. The room tilts sickeningly, my stomach plummeting as if I've stepped off a cliff.

"This is going to ruin everything." Cold sweat breaks out across my skin as the full weight of exposure crashes down, my lungs constricting until each breath becomes a struggle.

Max's expression hardens. "I'll have my team issue a cease and desist immediately. This is a clear invasion of privacy."

"That won't matter." I sink onto a nearby stool, legs suddenly unsteady. "Once it's out there, it's out there. Everyone in Angel's Peak will see this. Everyone will know."

"Know what?" Max sets his phone down and moves closer. "That you were wrongfully accused? That you're the brilliant mind behind algorithms that revolutionized an industry?"

"They'll know I lied. That I've been hiding." My voice catches. "That I'm not Lily the coffee shop owner. I'm Lily Brock, the corporate spy who sold out her company."

"You're not a spy. You were framed." Max's voice is firm with conviction.

"Do you think that matters?" I gesture toward his phone. "They've already connected me to your security project. How long before someone suggests I'm trying to steal your work, too?"

Understanding dawns in his eyes. "Lily, no one who knows you would believe that."

"No one here knows me. Not really." The truth of this hits harder than expected. "I've spent two years carefully constructing this life, keeping everyone at arm's length so my past couldn't catch up. And now..."

"Now what? You'll run again?" There's an edge to his voice now.

"I don't know." The admission feels like giving up. "I just know I can't face everyone once this spreads. Ruth, Eleanor, Darlene... they'll all look at me differently."

Max runs a hand through his hair, frustration evident. "Or maybe they'll support you. Have you considered that possibility?"

"You don't understand what it's like to have your name dragged through the mud, to have everything you worked for taken from you." The words come out sharper than intended.

"You're right, I don't." His tone softens. "Talk to me." His voice is gentle but insistent. "Help me understand what you're afraid of."

"You know what I'm afraid of. Eric didn't just steal my work." The admission breaks from me like a dam giving way. "He systematically erased every contribution I made to Brew-Tech while positioning himself as the sole innovator."

Max remains quiet, letting me speak.

"When I confronted him, he was prepared." The memory still burns, humiliation fresh despite the passing years. "The next morning, the entire company received an email with doctored logs 'proving' I'd accessed protected files, copied proprietary algorithms, and attempted to sell them to competitors."

I pace the small space, needing to move as the story pours out. "It was meticulous, Max. Timestamps altered, access records manipulated—all pointing to me as the thief. Then came the internal investigation, the public statement about 'unfortunate corporate espionage,' the cease-and-desist letters threatening legal action if I spoke against the company."

"I can't imagine how difficult that must have been."

"Without actual evidence of his theft, it was his word against mine. And he was the charismatic founder with powerful connections, while I was just a developer who'd gotten 'too ambitious and slept with the boss.'" Bitterness colors my words. "Within weeks, I couldn't get an interview anywhere in the industry. Former colleagues stopped returning my calls. Industry publications ran thinly sourced stories about the 'scandal at BrewTech.'"

Max's expression darkens with each detail. "Why didn't you fight back? Take legal action?"

"With what resources? Eric had company lawyers, family money, industry connections." I laugh without humor. "I had depleted savings and a reputation in tatters. The legal consultation I scraped together money for told me it would be years of costly litigation with minimal chance of success."

"So you left." Understanding fills his voice.

"I left. Changed career focus. Found Angel's Peak. Built something small but mine, something no one could steal." I wrap my arms around myself, suddenly cold despite the warmth of the cottage. "And now your spotlight threatens to undo all of that."

Max steps closer, bridging the distance between us. "Lily, I had no idea the extent of what happened. I'm so sorry."

"It's not your fault." The fight drains from me, leaving

exhaustion in its wake. "But you need to understand why this publicity terrifies me."

"I do." He reaches for my hand, which I allow him to take. "But hiding isn't the solution."

Something in his tone shifts my defensive posture to one of alertness. "What does that mean?"

"It means you let Eric win." His words are gentle but direct. "You let his actions define your choices, limit your potential, and keep you small when you should be changing the industry that failed you."

The observation lands like a physical blow, too accurate to deflect but too painful to accept.

"That's not fair."

"Isn't it?" His thumb traces circles on my palm. "The woman who created those algorithms, who built that technology—she shouldn't be hiding in a mountain town, no matter how charming. She should be revolutionizing coffee science, patenting her innovations, forcing the industry to acknowledge her brilliance."

"You think I should just... what? March back to Silicon Valley and demand justice?" Anger flares, hot and protective. "It doesn't work that way."

"No, but letting fear of exposure dictate your choices isn't the answer either." Frustration edges into his voice. "You've built a fortress around yourself. I'm just suggesting that perhaps it's time to consider whether the walls are still protecting you or keeping you imprisoned."

"That's easy for you to say." I pull my hand away. "You've never had your entire identity stripped away, your credibility destroyed overnight."

"No, but I recognize someone running from their potential when I see it." His eyes hold mine, challenging rather than accusatory. "You're brilliant. Your technical knowledge, your coffee expertise, your business instincts—they're exceptional.

And you're burying them in this town because you're afraid of being seen."

"I'm not afraid of being seen." The denial rings hollow even to my ears. "I'm afraid of being destroyed again."

"There's a difference between caution and hiding." Max runs a hand through his hair, frustration evident in the gesture. "What happened to you was criminal, and Eric should face consequences. But you letting it define your future is exactly what he wanted."

The truth in his words cuts deep, exposing fears I've refused to acknowledge. "You don't understand what it's like to lose everything you've worked for."

"Don't I?" His voice rises slightly. "After I sold my first app, I felt invincible, that there was nothing I couldn't do, but my first company failed spectacularly. My initial investors lost everything. I know exactly what public failure feels like."

"That's not the same as betrayal."

"No, it's not, and I'm not sharing this to compare or suggest that what happened to me is the same as what happened to you. I understand the nuance, but rebuilding from ashes is still rebuilding, whatever caused the fire." He steps closer, intensity radiating from him. "You can't spend your life afraid of what might happen if your past catches up to you. That's not living. That's just existing."

The words strike too close to truths I've carefully avoided confronting. "You've known me for a few weeks. You don't get to judge the choices that kept me sane, that let me rebuild something from nothing."

"I'm not judging your choices. I'm questioning whether they're still serving you." His tone softens slightly. "The woman I've come to know is too extraordinary to spend her life hiding from what happened."

"The woman you've come to know exists because of those

choices." My voice breaks slightly on the words. "If I hadn't left, if I hadn't started over, I wouldn't be who I am now."

"And maybe that's exactly why you were meant to go through it." He reaches for me again, but I step back. "But at some point, healing means moving forward, defending yourself, not running away."

"You don't get to decide what healing looks like for me." The words emerge cold and final. "You don't get to waltz into my life and restructure my existence because it doesn't align with your vision of what I should be."

Hurt flashes in his eyes, quickly replaced by frustration. "That's not what I'm doing."

"Isn't it?" The fear transmutes to anger, protecting the vulnerable places his words have exposed. "You've been here for weeks. You're leaving soon. You get to go back to your life, and it goes on unchanged, while I'm left dealing with whatever the fallout might be."

Silence stretches between us, the space filled with words we can't take back and truths neither of us is ready to face fully.

"You talk as if I'm going to abandon you."

"Aren't you?" I take a step back, needing distance. "This is different for you. There's no way you can understand."

"I've upset you." Max's movements are stiff with suppressed emotion. "Eric stole more than your code—he stole your belief in your own resilience. I won't let him get away from it. What do you need from me?"

The accuracy of his assessment stings. Four days of intensity, of discovering parts of myself I'd buried long ago, and now this—reality crashing back in with brutal efficiency.

"I need time to process this." I wrap my arms around myself, suddenly cold despite the warmth of the cottage. "I need to think about what this means, what I'm going to do. I need *space*."

Instead of arguing, he nods. "I understand."

"It's not that I don't want—" I begin, unsure how to explain the storm of emotions churning inside me.

"Lily." He cuts me off gently. "You don't have to explain. This is a lot to take in, and you need time to process it. I get it."

"Thank you." Relief washes through me at his understanding.

He reaches for my face, cupping my cheek gently. "For what it's worth, you're stronger than you give yourself credit for, and the people here care about you more than you realize."

"Maybe." I don't sound convinced, even to my own ears. "We'll see what they think of me in the morning."

"I'll be at the lodge when you're ready to talk." He pauses at the door. "And Lily? I'm going to fight this. My legal team won't let them get away with this invasion of privacy or the implications about you."

The protectiveness in his voice both warms and terrifies me. Max Lawson has become entwined in my life in ways I never anticipated, and now our connection threatens the very anonymity I've fought to maintain.

"I know." I manage a weak smile. "That's who you are."

Part of me wants to stop him, to bridge the sudden chasm between us. Instead, I watch in silence as he gathers his things.

At the door, he pauses. "Whatever you decide to do, running doesn't solve the problem. It postpones facing it. You deserve better than a life spent looking over your shoulder, afraid of lies some asshole spread to make him look like the victim."

The door closes behind him with a quiet click, infinitely more devastating than a slam would have been.

Alone in my cottage, I sink onto the sofa, the absence of Max's presence a tangible ache. The article on his phone screen replays in my mind, words and images that will inevitably shatter the carefully constructed sanctuary I've built in Angel's Peak.

For two years, I've lived in the shadows, avoiding attention, keeping my history buried. Now it's all unraveling, thanks to a few photos and a journalist eager for clicks.

The thought of facing the town—of seeing realization dawn in Ruth's shrewd eyes, of watching Eleanor's warm smile fade to uncertainty, of enduring Darlene's inevitable questions—makes my chest tight with anxiety.

Yet beneath that fear, something else stirs. A whisper of the woman I used to be before Eric's betrayal—the one who fought for recognition, who stood behind her work with pride, who didn't shrink from challenges. The woman Max seems to see and believe in.

I wrap myself in a blanket that still smells faintly of his cologne, trying to sort through the tangle of emotions. Fear of exposure, of judgment, of being hurt again. But beneath those familiar anxieties, something new has taken root during these four days with Max—something that feels dangerously like hope.

The cottage feels too quiet without his presence, without his laughter rumbling through the rooms, his hands creating breakfast, his voice murmuring praise against my skin in the darkness.

Four days shouldn't be enough to create such dependency, such longing. Yet here I am, already missing him while simultaneously needing this solitude to find my footing.

Tomorrow, I'll have to decide whether to run again or finally stand my ground. Tonight, I'll let myself feel the ache of his absence, the fear of what's to come, and the faint, persistent hope that maybe—just maybe—Max is right about my strength and about the people of Angel's Peak.

Angel's Peak

CHAPTER 23

SLEEP ELUDES ME, MY BED TOO EMPTY, TOO COLD without Max's presence. The argument replays on an endless loop, his words cutting deeper with each mental repetition. By morning, exhaustion settles into my bones, making even routine tasks feel monumental.

Mountain Brew opens on schedule despite my leaden limbs and hollow chest. The morning rush—blessedly busy with the weekend crowd—provides a distraction from the ache of Max's absence. With each chime of the bell, my heart performs a traitorous leap of hope, only to crash when the entering customer isn't him.

It's my fault. I asked for space when I should've let him hold me, but my battles aren't his to fight.

The bell chimes again, and Ruth Fletcher strides in, her salt-and-pepper hair pulled back in its practical ponytail, expression uncharacteristically somber.

"Morning, Lily," she says, approaching the counter with deliberate casualness.

"Ruth." I manage a smile that feels brittle. "The usual?"

"Please." She settles onto a stool, watching me work. "Quiet morning?"

"Busy, actually." I focus on the familiar routine of preparing her double espresso. "Just a lull now."

Ruth accepts her drink, then sets it down without tasting it. "So. I saw the article."

My hands freeze on the espresso machine. Here it comes—the questions, the doubt, the subtle withdrawal that inevitably follows when people learn about my past.

"Terrible invasion of privacy," Ruth continues, her voice hardening. "Taking photos through your window? Disgusting. I've already called the editor and gave them a piece of my mind about journalistic ethics."

I blink, thrown by her response. "You... called the editor?"

"Of course I did. What kind of friend would I be if I let that stand?" Ruth takes a sip of her espresso, eyes never leaving mine. "And for what it's worth, whatever happened at that tech company—BrewTech, was it?—doesn't change a damn thing about who you are in Angel's Peak."

My throat tightens unexpectedly. "You don't think I'm a corporate spy?"

Ruth snorts, the sound so undignified it startles a laugh from me. "Please. I've known you for two years, Lily. You're the woman who stays late to help Margie repair her ancient refrigerator. Who delivers coffee to Eleanor when her arthritis is acting up. Who teaches those kids from the high school about running a business." She leans forward, expression fierce. "I don't need to know what happened in San Francisco. I know who you are here."

The unexpected acceptance leaves me momentarily speechless. "I... thank you."

"Nothing to thank me for." Ruth waves away my gratitude. "Though I will say, you could have told us. We're your community, Lily. That means something in Angel's Peak."

Before I can respond, the bell chimes again. Several customers enter at once—a family of tourists, Hannah from the library, and Sheriff Donovan.

Hannah catches my eye immediately, offering a warm smile as she approaches the counter. "Morning, Lily. Could I get a triple shot mocha?"

I prepare her drink, tension coiling in my stomach as I wait for her to mention the article. Instead, she chatters about the new books arriving at the library, asks about a coffee delivery for their upcoming book club, and departs with a friendly wave.

The pattern repeats throughout the morning. Customers come and go—some locals, some visitors—and while I catch occasional curious glances, no one mentions BrewTech or corporate espionage. Several regulars seem to make a point of being warmer than usual, leaving larger tips or lingering to chat about inconsequential town matters.

By mid-afternoon, the quiet acceptance has me more unsettled than outright confrontation would have. The bell chimes again, and Eleanor Morgan enters, silver braids crowned atop her head, keen eyes missing nothing as she surveys the shop.

"Your young man isn't here today." She settles onto a stool at the counter, observing rather than questioning.

"He's working from The Haven." I focus on preparing her usual, grateful for the familiar routine.

"Seems a shame, when he was so comfortable here." Eleanor accepts her mug with a thoughtful expression. "Especially with so little time remaining in his stay."

My hands falter slightly. "We had a disagreement."

"About that article, I presume." Eleanor's directness shouldn't surprise me after all this time, but it still catches me off guard.

I nod, unable to form words.

"Lily." Eleanor's weathered hand covers mine, stopping my nervous wiping of the already clean counter. "Did you think we'd believe some tabloid gossip over what we know of you?"

"I don't know what I thought," I admit. "I've spent two years hiding that part of my life. And now..."

"And now the sky hasn't fallen." Eleanor's eyes crinkle with gentle amusement. "Though I imagine it feels that way to you."

"Everyone's being so... normal."

"What did you expect? Pitchforks and torches?" She sips her coffee, studying me over the rim. "This morning at Margie's, we all agreed—whatever happened in your past is your business. Though I will say, if you'd trusted us sooner, you might have saved yourself a great deal of unnecessary worry."

"Ruth said something similar."

"Ruth Fletcher may be the most aggravating woman in three counties, but she's rarely wrong about people." Eleanor sets her cup down with a decisive click. "You know, when my Charles died, I sealed off his study. Kept it exactly as he left it for nearly two years. Couldn't bear to disturb a single paper or book."

The apparent non sequitur throws me. "I'm sorry for your loss, but I don't see—"

"Grief takes many forms, Lily." Her weathered hand covers mine briefly. "Some of us lose people. Some lose dreams, reputations, futures we thought were certain. The pain is different, but the protective instincts are the same."

Something loosens in my chest at the unexpected understanding.

"What changed? With the study?"

A smile touches her lips, gentle with memory. "My granddaughter needed a quiet place to study. I realized Charles would have hated knowing that room sat empty when it could be serving someone he loved." Her eyes hold mine steadily, wisdom accumulated over decades. "Sometimes our protective barriers outlive their usefulness. They harden from shelter to prison without us noticing the transformation."

"I built a life here." The defense emerges softer than intended. "A good life."

"Yes, you did." Eleanor nods approvingly. "The question is whether it's the full life you're capable of building." She stands, gathering her things. "Fear makes excellent armor but poor foundation material."

After she leaves, her words linger like the scent of fresh coffee, impossible to dismiss. The rest of the day passes in mechanical motions, muscle memory carrying me through tasks while my thoughts spiral around the uncomfortable truths Max and Eleanor have forced me to confront.

Darlene from the diner stops by late afternoon, ordering her usual double espresso to go.

"I've been meaning to tell you," she says, leaning casually against the counter, "that cinnamon maple latte you made for my son's birthday party was perfect. His friends are still talking about it."

I smile, grateful for the normal conversation. "I'm glad it was a hit."

"It was." She hesitates, then adds, "Look, I know everyone's probably tiptoeing around that stupid article, but I just wanted to say—we all have pasts, Lily. What matters is who you choose to be now." She accepts her espresso with a wink. "And you chose to be the person who makes the best damn coffee in Colorado, so as far as I'm concerned, you're golden."

The simple acceptance in her words nearly undoes me. "Thank you, Darlene."

"Nothing to thank me for." She echoes Ruth's earlier dismissal. "Though if you want to show your appreciation, maybe consider a discount on my next order?"

The joke breaks the tension, and I find myself laughing genuinely for the first time all day. "Nice try."

At four, the typical mid-afternoon lull settles over the shop. I take advantage of the quiet to begin preparations for closing, eager to retreat to my cottage despite knowing its emptiness will only amplify my loneliness.

The bell chimes. I look up automatically, prepared for disappointment.

Max stands in the doorway, holding a small potted cactus with a single vibrant pink bloom.

"Peace offering." His smile is hesitant, uncertainty shadowing his usually confident expression. "The florist said it's nearly impossible to kill, which seemed appropriate for someone who spends their life nurturing things."

Words desert me entirely, relief and lingering hurt creating a bottleneck in my throat.

"I was wrong to push so hard." He approaches the counter slowly, setting the cactus down as carefully as if it were made of glass. "Your boundaries exist for reasons I didn't fully understand, and I had no right to challenge them."

"You were right, though." The admission comes easier than expected. "About some of it, at least."

Surprise flickers across his face. "Can we talk? Properly?"

I glance around the empty shop, then flip the sign to CLOSED.

"Let's go home."

The walk to my cottage passes in silence, not an uncomfortable silence, but a weighted one. Inside, the space feels different somehow—as if our argument reshaped its contours, leaving nothing quite as it was before.

Max waits for me to take the lead, remaining near the door until I gesture toward the sofa. We sit facing each other, close enough to reach out but maintaining a small distance that feels symbolic of the gap between us.

"I need to tell you everything." The decision crystallizes as I speak. "The full story, not just the sanitized version."

He nods, giving me space to continue at my own pace.

"I should start by saying... I was wrong to panic about the article." I meet his eyes directly. "Everyone in town has been incredibly supportive. Ruth, Eleanor, even Darlene—they all made a point of letting me know they don't care about what happened in San Francisco. That they know who I am now, and that's what matters to them."

"I'm not surprised." Max's smile is gentle. "That's what community means in a place like this."

"I never gave them the chance to prove it until now." The realization sits heavy with regret. "I've spent two years afraid of something that never would have happened."

"Fear is rarely rational." His hand reaches for mine, a tentative bridge across the space between us. "Especially when it's rooted in trauma."

I squeeze his fingers, drawing strength from the connection. "I'm ready to tell you everything now. The full story, not just the highlights."

He nods, giving me space to continue at my own pace.

"Eric and I met at a tech conference. I was presenting early research on algorithmic predictions for coffee extraction variables." The memory rises with surprising clarity. "He approached afterward, full of questions about commercial applications. Within weeks, he offered me a position at Brew-Tech, which was then just a small startup with promising funding."

Max listens without interruption as I detail the next two years—the algorithms I developed, the growing recognition within specialty coffee circles, the romance with Eric that evolved alongside our professional partnership.

The words flow more freely than I would have believed possible, unwinding the tangled narrative of my time at Brew-

Tech, the betrayal, the accusations, and the aftermath that drove me to Angel's Peak.

"The coffee analytics platform was my creation, but Eric was the face of the company. He had the connections, the charm, the business acumen." I trace a pattern on the sofa cushion, focusing on the familiar texture. "When we secured Series B funding, the pressure intensified. Investors wanted results, scalability, market differentiation."

"That's when things changed?" Max prompts gently when I pause.

"That's when I discovered he'd been meeting privately with investors, taking sole credit for the technological innovations I developed." The old anger flares briefly. "When confronted, he apologized profusely, claimed it was a misunderstanding, that he'd correct the record."

My hands tighten around a throw pillow. "A week later, I found altered code in the repository—my algorithms, subtly modified and tagged with his credentials. When I checked the logs, they showed retrospective changes dating back months, creating a false history of his contributions."

Max's expression darkens. "Digital gaslighting."

"Precisely." The technical term for what happened feels validating in some way. "I gathered evidence—original notes, earlier versions stored on my personal drives, email exchanges discussing the development process. I planned to confront him privately first, then take everything to the board if necessary."

The most painful part of the story approaches, and I steel myself to share it. "The night before my planned confrontation, we had dinner at our usual place. Eric was unusually attentive, full of compliments about my work and our partnership."

"He knew." Max's intuition jumps ahead.

"He knew." I nod, swallowing against the tightness in my

throat. "While we were at dinner, someone accessed my apartment. My backup drives and paper notebooks containing my original work disappeared. By morning, the company's Slack channels, email server, and code repository had all been scrubbed of evidence showing my contributions."

"Then came the company-wide email." My voice hardens with remembered humiliation. "Eric claimed to have discovered 'disturbing evidence' that I had attempted to steal proprietary algorithms and sell them to competitors. Security escorted me from the building while colleagues I worked alongside for years watched in silence."

Max reaches for my hand, his touch grounding as I continue through the aftermath—the legal threats, the industry blacklisting, the financial devastation as legal consultations depleted my savings.

"The final blow was the press coverage. Tech blogs ran stories based entirely on BrewTech's version of events." I meet Max's eyes directly. "My name became toxic. No one would hire me, partner with me, or even hear my side."

"So you reinvented yourself." His thumb traces gentle circles on my palm. "Left the industry entirely."

"I retreated to the one thing no one could take away—my knowledge of coffee itself." I gesture around the cottage. "Angel's Peak was supposed to be temporary. Just a place to regroup while planning my next move."

"But it became home instead."

"It became a sanctuary." The distinction feels important. "A place where my past couldn't find me. Where I could build something small but entirely mine, and yes. It became a home to me. I love this town. I love the people. I love everything about it."

Silence stretches between us, but it's different now—cleared of shadows, open with shared understanding.

"I knew who you were." Max's quiet admission breaks the

silence. "Not immediately, but after our first few conversations about coffee technology. The details clicked into place."

Shock reverberates through me. "You recognized me from the BrewTech scandal?"

"I followed the case when it happened. It never made sense." He shifts closer, earnestness in his expression. "The timeline of events, the convenient disappearance of evidence, the aggressive legal posturing—classic misdirection tactics."

"You... believed my side?" The possibility that someone in the tech world had seen through Eric's deception feels momentous.

"The technical community wasn't as universally fooled as you might think. Several respected developers questioned the official narrative privately." His gaze holds mine steadily. "Eric had a reputation before BrewTech. Your situation fit a pattern of behavior he exhibited with previous collaborators, though never so dramatically."

The revelation that some doubted Eric's version—that Max doubted it—unleashes something tightly coiled within me. Tears break free after years of containment, not of sorrow but of vindication.

Max gathers me close, arms creating a safe harbor as emotions cascade through me. "You deserved better. From BrewTech, from the industry, from all of it."

When the storm passes, I remain in his embrace, face pressed against his shoulder. "Why didn't you tell me you knew?"

"I was waiting for you to trust me enough to share it yourself." His hand strokes gently down my spine. "Some stories need to be offered, not extracted."

The wisdom in his patience humbles me. "I'm sorry about yesterday. I panicked at the thought of being exposed, of having to face it all again."

"Thank you for trusting me with this," Max says simply

when I fall silent. "All of it. I understand better now." He pulls back slightly to meet my eyes. "And I'm sorry I pushed when you weren't ready. It wasn't my place to dictate how you should handle your past."

In that moment, surrounded by the warmth of my cottage and the acceptance in his eyes, I recognize the truth that Ruth and Eleanor tried to show me: the walls I built to protect myself became limitations without my noticing.

"Maybe I needed the push." The admission comes more easily in the aftermath of emotional release, and Eleanor's words. "The walls I built to protect myself became limitations without my noticing. I think I'm ready," I say, the words surprising me even as they emerge.

"Ready for what?"

"To stop hiding. To reclaim my name, my expertise, my past—all of it." My voice strengthens with each word. "Whatever happens next, I don't want to live in fear anymore.""

His smile warms his entire face. "So where does that leave us?"

"Healing, I think." I reach up to trace the line of his jaw. "And moving forward, if that's what you want."

Max's eyes darken, his expression shifting from cautious hope to raw vulnerability. "It took everything in my power not to show up this morning," he confesses, voice rough with emotion. "I kept staring at my phone, drafting messages I never sent. Spending the day without you..." His hand covers mine where it rests against his face. "It was the worst pain I've felt in a long time."

"For me too," I whisper, the admission easier now that my walls have crumbled.

He reaches for me then, strong hands gently pulling me toward him until I'm cradled against his chest, the steady rhythm of his heartbeat beneath my ear. His arms encircle me completely, creating a sanctuary of warmth and acceptance that feels both foreign and achingly familiar. We stay like that for several breaths, neither speaking, both absorbing the simple comfort of reconnection.

"Lily," he murmurs into my hair, the sound of my name on his lips sending a shiver down my spine. One hand slides up to cup the back of my neck, fingers threading through my hair as he guides me to look up at him. His gaze travels over my face with deliberate tenderness, memorizing each feature as if seeing me anew. "I don't just want to move forward," he says, thumb tracing the curve of my cheek. "I want to build something with you. Something real."

The conviction in his voice steals my breath. Before I can respond, he dips his head, his other hand tipping my chin upward as his lips meet mine.

His kiss tastes of forgiveness and new beginnings, sealing our reconciliation with tenderness that gradually transforms to passion. We find our way to the bed, reconnecting physically with the same openness we achieved emotionally. Afterward, lying tangled together in the fading light, the future seems suddenly less frightening, despite its uncertainties.

Angel's Peak

Chapter 24

"Are you sure about this?" I survey Mountain Brew's interior, transformed overnight with a mockup of workstations and tech setups occupying what was once my quiet seating area. Laptops hum on sleek desks, power strips snake discreetly along baseboards, and a temporary high-speed internet hub blinks in the corner—a vision of what my coffee shop could become if I embraced Max's idea.

The flutter of nerves in my stomach hasn't subsided since he first proposed it. Mountain Brew reimagined as a haven for remote workers, digital nomads, and local professionals seeking both premium coffee and a functional workspace. My cozy shop would maintain its artisanal soul while expanding into territory I'd deliberately avoided since fleeing BrewTech.

"Absolutely sure." Max's confidence is infectious as he adjusts one of the demonstration laptops, ensuring the screen is visible from all angles.

His hand brushes mine as he reaches past me, and the casual contact still sends electricity shimmering through my veins. Since our reconciliation, his words echo in my mind constantly: *I want to build something with you. Something real.*

This morning, he arrived before dawn with a small team, transforming half of my shop into this prototype remote workspace while preserving the rustic charm of the original café area. Now Mountain Brew feels like a physical manifestation of my divided self—the coffee artisan and the tech innovator, no longer at war but working in harmony.

"Angel's Peak has no dedicated workspace for remote professionals," Max continues, surveying his handiwork with pride. "With more companies embracing flexible work policies, there's a growing market of people who need more than their kitchen table but less than a formal office."

I run my fingers along one of the desks, imagining a coder typing away while enjoying a pour-over, or a graphic designer sketching concepts beside a steaming latte.

"And you think my coffee shop is the right place for this?"

"I think it's the perfect place. It's been a haven for me these past few weeks." His eyes meet mine, warm with an unspoken question: *Do you see it now? The possibility?* "Mountain Brew already has the atmosphere people crave—authentic, comfortable, with exceptional coffee. All it needs is the infrastructure to support digital work."

Three days after our reconciliation, what began as a casual conversation has evolved into this tangible demonstration. The mockup workspace occupies the back half of my café—five elegant workstations with ergonomic chairs, charging ports, and small privacy dividers, all designed to complement rather than overshadow the coffee shop's aesthetic.

Local business owners begin arriving for our private preview, curiosity evident in their expressions—Ruth from The PickAxe, Margie from the bakery, Hannah from the library, even Dominic and Elena representing Silverleaf Vineyards. Each arrival sends a fresh wave of nervous anticipation through me. These people—my people—are about to witness the merging of my carefully separated worlds.

"Welcome, everyone!" Max addresses the small gathering, standing confidently beside one of the workstations. The pride blooming in my chest takes me by surprise. This brilliant man, who could have anyone, anywhere, wants to build something with me.

In Angel's Peak.

The thought still feels surreal, like a dream I might wake from at any moment.

"Thank you for joining us this morning to experience a glimpse of what Mountain Brew could become—not just Angel's Peak's premier coffee destination, but also its first dedicated remote work space."

As Max continues explaining the concept, I watch realization dawn across the faces of Angel's Peak's business owners. This isn't just about my coffee shop—it's about transforming our entire town's economy.

"The beauty of this model," Max explains, moving through the mockup workstations, "is how it creates a ripple effect throughout the community. Digital nomads and remote workers don't just need coffee and Wi-Fi—they need places to stay, restaurants to eat at, and activities to enjoy after work hours."

Ruth's eyes light up with understanding. "Like my bar. Remote workers finishing their day might want to unwind at The PickAxe."

"Exactly," Max confirms, gesturing toward her. "And they'd need accommodations—"

"Mabel's Guesthouse could offer weekly rates for longer stays," Margie suggests, excitement building in her voice. "Or The Haven for those wanting more luxury."

Dominic Mercer, typically reserved, leans forward with interest. "Wine enthusiasts working remotely could schedule tasting events at Silverleaf after their workday. We could even create special 'digital nomad' vineyard tours."

The conversation explodes with possibilities, everyone suddenly seeing how their business could benefit from this new demographic. Hannah from the library suggests digital literacy workshops. Sheriff Donovan mentions enhanced safety protocols for solo travelers. Even Pete from the General Store chimes in about expanding his inventory to include tech accessories and travel essentials.

I stand back, watching my community embrace a vision I would have run from just weeks ago. The irony isn't lost on me—that my past in tech, the very thing I've hidden for so long, might become the catalyst for Angel's Peak's economic revival. Not through corporate exploitation, but through thoughtful integration of technology with our mountain town values.

"This could put Angel's Peak on the map for an entirely different kind of tourist," Eleanor Morgan observes, her shrewd eyes assessing the mockup. "Not just those seeking outdoor adventure, but professionals looking to combine work with mountain living."

"Seasonal businesses could become year-round," Ruth adds, calculations clearly running behind her eyes. "Winter months when tourism typically drops—"

"Would be filled with remote workers escaping city winters," Max finishes, nodding. "Exactly. The beauty of digital nomads is they often travel counter-cyclically to traditional tourists, filling in your slow seasons."

The energy in the room builds, everyone contributing ideas, seeing connections I hadn't even considered. This isn't just about expanding my coffee shop—it's about creating an ecosystem where technology enhances rather than replaces our community's character.

I catch Max watching me, his expression a mixture of pride and question. *Do you see it now?* his eyes seem to ask. And I do—I see how my two worlds, tech and coffee, could merge to create something greater than either alone. How my past doesn't have to be buried to build my future.

For the first time since fleeing San Francisco, I allow myself to imagine a life that doesn't require hiding half of who I am. A life where Mountain Brew becomes a bridge between worlds—my worlds—creating something entirely new in the process.

Throughout the morning, I observe Max in his element—explaining how secure network protocols protect user data, demonstrating the scheduling app that would enable remote workers to reserve space, and outlining potential revenue models that could double Mountain Brew's income without compromising its core values.

Yet something has shifted in his approach since I met him. The driven intensity remains, but it's now tempered with patience and a genuine connection to the people who would use this space.

"Now for the centerpiece of our digital nomad vision," Max announces, gathering everyone around one of the central workstations. "This is Nexus Local—our small business security and management platform, specifically designed to protect the kind of data that remote workers handle daily."

The screen displays an elegant interface with multiple modules—secure file sharing, encrypted communication, virtual private network controls, and a suite of collaborative tools.

"Every workstation would come equipped with this security suite," Max explains, navigating through the various features. "Remote workers often handle sensitive company information. Our platform ensures that even in a public setting like a coffee shop, their data remains protected by military-grade encryption."

Ruth leans forward, clearly intrigued. "And this would protect my business records, too? The PickAxe's inventory and sales data?"

"Exactly," Max confirms, switching to a demonstration module tailored for local businesses. "Nexus Local isn't just for the digital nomads—it's designed to protect Angel's Peak businesses as well."

I watch with quiet pride as Max demonstrates the very technology that could have prevented what happened to me at BrewTech—secure access controls, audit trails that can't be altered retroactively, versioning systems that preserve original authorship of digital assets. He's created not just a product but a shield against the kind of betrayal I experienced.

"We'd like your help testing these systems," Max tells the group, gesturing to tablets set up at each workstation. "Try to break in, find flaws, tell us what's confusing or difficult to use. Real-world feedback is invaluable in refining the platform."

The business owners dive in with unexpected enthusiasm, Hannah from the library immediately testing the document sharing features, Dominic exploring the customer database encryption, Sheriff Donovan examining the emergency alert integration. Even Eleanor Morgan, who often claims to be "allergic to computers," gamely attempts to navigate the user-friendly interface.

"This feels different from other tech I've tried," Margie comments, successfully setting up a secure inventory tracking system for her bakery in minutes. "It's like it was designed for actual humans, not computer scientists."

"That's the whole point," Max says, catching my eye with a warm smile. "Technology should adapt to people, not the other way around."

The demonstration evolves organically into an impromptu testing session. Everyone takes turns exploring different aspects of the platform, offering suggestions, identifying improvements, and imagining applications specific to Angel's Peak. No one mentions BrewTech or the article about Max.

Not one person looks at me differently. The revelation of my history with BrewTech, rather than creating distance, has given them context for understanding this new direction. They see the fullness of who I am—not just Lily the coffee shop owner, but Lily the innovator, the creator, the woman with both technical knowledge and artisanal skill.

Darlene from the diner arrives late, apologetic as she juggles her tablet and attempts to corral her two young children. "Babysitter canceled last minute. I can come back another time—"

"Nonsense." Max intercepts the more rambunctious child —six-year-old Jake—with ease. "How about you test the app, and I'll test whether Jake here can beat me at thumb wrestling?"

"You're good with them." I join Max on the floor when Jake races off to get pizza, Emma now contentedly drawing on his tablet with a design app he opened for her.

"I volunteered at a community center during college." He helps Emma select colors for her digital masterpiece. "Free coding classes for kids from the neighborhood. Turned out I liked the teaching as much as the coding."

This glimpse of Max—patient, playful, at ease with children—reveals yet another layer of the man behind the tech genius facade. My heart performs dangerous acrobatics in my chest as I watch him praise Emma's artistic efforts with the same focused attention he gives to coding problems.

Later, walking home under a sky dusted with emerging stars, Max's hand warm in mine, we discuss the day's success.

"The app's almost ready for launch." Pride colors his voice. "The feedback today was invaluable—issues we never would have identified in controlled testing."

"The community loved being involved." I bump his shoulder playfully. "You might have created a new Angel's Peak tradition. Annual tech testing day."

"I'd like that." Something in his tone catches my attention —a wistfulness that suggests thoughts of future possibilities.

"They've adopted you," I observe as we claim a spot near the lake for the upcoming fireworks. "The Angel's Peak assimilation is nearly complete."

"Is that a good thing?" Max's arm slides around my waist, drawing me against his warmth.

"It's unprecedented." I lean into him, savoring his solid presence. "This town usually takes years to embrace newcomers."

"Maybe I'm just exceptionally charming." His smug expression earns him a playful elbow to the ribs. "Or maybe they recognize how I feel about a certain coffee shop owner."

The casual reference to his feelings creates a flutter in my chest that I'm increasingly unable to suppress.

I'm falling in love with Max Lawson. The realization should terrify me, given his imminent departure and our different worlds. Instead, it feels like the most natural evolution imaginable.

"You'll be gone next week, though." The reminder emerges more vulnerable than intended. "Back to Silicon Valley and Nexus Systems headquarters."

Max slows our pace, expression thoughtful in the moonlight. "Actually, I've been considering alternatives."

My heart stutters. "What kind of alternatives?"

"Remote work, primarily. At least part-time." His thumb traces circles on my palm. "The pandemic normalized remote work. There's no technical reason I need to be in Palo Alto full-time."

Hope flutters dangerous wings in my chest. "You'd consider working from... elsewhere?"

"I'd consider working from wherever I felt most creative and focused." His eyes meet mine, his meaning clear without being explicit. "Silicon Valley has advantages, but also significant drawbacks. Constant competitive pressure and a lack of work-life balance."

"And Angel's Peak?" The question emerges barely above a whisper.

Angel's Peak

Chapter 25

The calendar on the wall behind the counter has become my enemy. Each morning, I resist the urge to tear off the page, as if destroying the physical reminder might stop time's relentless march.

Days remain until Max's departure, and the knowledge colors everything with bittersweet urgency.

"Order up for table four!" Max calls from behind the espresso machine, his movements confident after weeks of informal training. The sight of him there—sleeves rolled up, concentration evident in the slight furrow between his brows as he creates perfect microfoam—feels simultaneously right and heartbreaking.

"Since when do you take orders?" I tease, collecting the cappuccino he's prepared. The rosetta pattern on top is nearly perfect, a testament to how quickly he absorbs new skills.

"Since your online orders doubled after the website launch." His smile carries pride untainted by the smugness I initially expected from a tech CEO. "Someone has to keep the caffeine flowing while you handle shipping logistics."

The changes at Mountain Brew border on miraculous.

The online store Max created has attracted customers from Denver to Salt Lake City, specialty coffee enthusiasts willing to pay premium prices for my unique blends. The automated inventory system has streamlined ordering, reducing waste and increasing margins. Even the in-store experience has evolved, with a tablet-based loyalty program replacing the old punch cards.

Throughout it all, Max has integrated himself into daily operations with surprising humility—learning coffee basics, greeting regular customers by name, and troubleshooting technical issues without making me feel incompetent. The shop feels as much his as mine now, a transformation I never anticipated.

"The website analytics look promising." Max joins me during the mid-afternoon lull, tablet in hand displaying colorful graphs of customer engagement. "You've got returning customers already, and the subscription feature is gaining traction."

I study the data, pride mingling with melancholy. "It's more successful than I imagined possible for Mountain Brew."

"Just the beginning." His confidence is infectious. "The foundation is solid. You could expand into wholesale, develop signature brewing equipment, maybe even franchise eventually."

The future he envisions stretches beyond anything I've allowed myself to consider since BrewTech—ambitious but achievable with the systems we've built together. A future that necessarily continues without him managing it alongside me.

"One step at a time." I cover my conflicted emotions with practicality. "Let's see if I can handle shipping orders without you double-checking my packing slips."

His expression softens as he understands the unspoken concern. "You were running this place brilliantly before I showed up. You'll continue to do so after..." He doesn't finish the sentence, the word "leave" hovering unspoken between us.

We've developed an unspoken agreement to avoid direct discussion of his departure, dancing around the topic with euphemisms. "When you're back in California," or "After your trip ends," or "When things return to normal"—as if his absence will be temporary, a brief interruption rather than a fundamental reshaping of my daily reality.

"Close up early with me today?" I change the subject, unwilling to dwell on the inevitable separation. "There's somewhere I want to take you while the weather's perfect."

Curiosity brightens his expression. "Mystery location?"

"Somewhere special." A place I've shared with no one else since moving to Angel's Peak. "Bring a jacket. The evenings still get cool."

We close the shop at four, leaving a note for any disappointed customers. The spring afternoon bathes Angel's Peak in golden light, softening the mountain's rugged edges. Max follows my lead as I drive us to the Lookout Point trailhead, understanding this is something significant without needing explanation.

"Moderate hike, about thirty minutes." I shoulder a small backpack containing water and a blanket. "Not too strenuous, but the payoff is worth every step."

The trail winds through pine forest before gradually ascending toward exposed granite outcroppings. Spring wildflowers dot the path—purple lupine, bright yellow balsamroot, and delicate white phlox —creating natural gardens amid the rocks. We walk in comfortable silence, occasionally pointing out particularly striking views or unusual plants.

As we climb higher, Angel's Peak reveals itself from new angles—the town appears smaller with each elevation gain, and the surrounding mountains become more majestic. Finally, the trail curves around a massive boulder to reveal my destination—a small natural plateau jutting out from the mountainside, providing unobstructed views across the entire valley.

"Here we are." I spread the blanket on the smooth stone warmed by the afternoon sun. "My thinking spot."

Max stands at the edge, taking in the panorama with wonder. The town lies below us like a miniature model, the lake reflecting the sky, mountains stretching to the horizon in layered blue ridges.

"This is incredible." He turns to me, expression softened with appreciation. "How did you find it?"

"Accident, actually." I join him at the edge, our shoulders touching. "Got lost hiking my first month here. Sat down to check the map and realized I stumbled on the perfect view."

"Perfect is right." His arm slides around my waist, drawing me closer as we watch the sun begin its gradual descent toward the western peaks. "Thank you for sharing it with me."

The simple gratitude carries a more profound meaning we both recognize. This place represents more than a scenic viewpoint—it's a sanctuary I've kept private until now, a place of personal significance deliberately opened to include him.

We settle on the blanket, backs against sun-warmed stone, as the sky shifts from golden to amber. Below us, lights twinkle as early evening transforms Angel's Peak into a constellation of tiny stars against the darkening landscape.

"I come here when I need perspective." My voice sounds different in this space, more vulnerable and authentic. "When problems seem overwhelming in town, seeing everything from up here reminds me how small they really are in the grand scheme."

"Does it help?" His question feels weighted with more than casual curiosity.

"Usually." I draw my knees to my chest, wrapping my arms

around them. "Though some problems follow you no matter how high you climb."

His hand finds mine, fingers interlacing. "Like what we do about next week."

The direct acknowledgment of his departure catches me off guard. We've been so careful to avoid the topic, as if not discussing it might prevent it from happening.

"Yes. Like that." My throat tightens around the words. "Though I'm not sure there's anything to do about it. Your life is in California. Mine is here."

"It doesn't have to be that simple." His thumb traces patterns on my palm, a soothing gesture that's become familiar. "Technology makes distance more manageable than ever. Remote work, video calls, regular visits..."

The possibility hangs between us—not a solution but a potential bridge across the gulf that's about to separate our daily lives.

"Long distance." The concept feels both hopeful and inadequate simultaneously. "That's what you're suggesting?"

"I'm suggesting we don't give up on this—on us—just because of geography." His expression in the fading light holds determination and something softer, more vulnerable. "What we've found together in these few weeks is rare. I'm not ready to walk away from it."

The sentiment mirrors my own unspoken feelings, hope blooming cautiously in my chest. "It won't be easy."

"Few things worth having are." His smile carries certainty I wish I could fully share. "I can come back regularly. Every other weekend, at minimum. More when projects allow."

"And what happens when that becomes too difficult? When the novelty wears off and the travel becomes exhausting?" The practical questions emerge from a deep-seated fear of future disappointment. "When your board demands more in-person time, or I'm overwhelmed with running the shop and the online business?"

"Then we adapt. Find new solutions." He turns toward me, eyes holding mine with intensity that makes my breath catch. "I'm not suggesting this would be simple or perfect. I'm saying what we've built is worth the effort to maintain."

The conviction in his voice nearly undoes me.

"I want to believe that's possible."

"It is." He gathers both my hands in his. "These past weeks have changed something fundamental for me. The man who arrived in Angel's Peak was hollow—successful but empty, driven but directionless in any way that actually mattered."

His vulnerability strips away my remaining defenses.

"And now?"

"Now I understand what I've been missing. Connection. Purpose beyond profit. The feeling of contributing to something sustainable rather than just scalable." His forehead touches mine, voice dropping to near-whisper. "You've shown me what matters. I'm not willing to lose that lesson—or lose you."

The mountain falls silent around us, even the breeze pausing as if respecting the gravity of the moment. Neither of us speaks the word "love," yet it saturates every syllable, every touch, every shared glance as sunset paints the sky in impossible colors.

"Six hundred miles." I voice the distance that will soon separate us. "That's a lot of space between coffee and good-night kisses."

"Just enough room for anticipation to build." His attempt at lightness carries an undercurrent of determination. "Think of it as extended foreplay."

The unexpected description startles a laugh from me, breaking the emotional tension. "That's one way to frame long-distance romance."

"I prefer to see possibilities rather than obstacles." He pulls me closer, arm secure around my shoulders as the first stars appear overhead. "One day at a time. That's how we'll navigate this."

As darkness envelops the mountain, we remain huddled together, watching lights spread across the valley below—each representing lives being lived, stories unfolding, connections forming and breaking in endless cycles. The perspective shifts something inside me, softening the sharp edges of my anxiety about the future.

"Ready to head back?" Max asks when the temperature drops further, his breath visible in the mountain air.

"Not quite yet." I nestle closer, unwilling to end this perfect moment. "Just a few more minutes."

We stay until the cold becomes impossible to ignore, then make our way down the trail by flashlight, hands linked, conversation flowing easily. The drive back to town passes in similar quiet companionship, both of us processing the unspoken commitments we've made on the mountainside.

At my cottage, warmth welcomes us—both physical and emotional as we move through the familiar space together. Max builds a fire in the small woodstove while I prepare hot chocolate.

"Thank you for today." He accepts the steaming mug, drawing me down beside him on the sofa. "For sharing your special place with me."

"Thank you for wanting to make this work." The vulnerability in my voice surprises me. "For believing it's possible."

His eyes soften in the firelight, reflecting amber flames and something deeper—a certainty I've never seen there before. His hand reaches up, fingers tracing the curve of my cheek with reverence that makes my breath catch.

The hot chocolate sits forgotten as he sets his mug on the

side table, taking mine and placing it safely aside. His eyes hold mine with an intensity that makes my breath catch, something raw and vulnerable breaking through his usual composed exterior.

"Lily," he says, my name low and reverent on his lips, a caress that makes my pulse trip. His hand cradles my face, thumb stroking across my cheekbone as if he's memorizing me. "I've never been more certain of anything in my life." He leans closer, the space between us charged, humming with something electric. "These past weeks with you... It's like finding something I didn't know I was missing. Something I'll never be able to let go."

His voice drops lower, rough with emotion. "I need you to understand what you are to me. Not just desire—though I ache for you every second. I need your strength, your brilliance, that fire in you that refuses to break." His fingers weave into my hair, anchoring me gently. "I want you, Miss Lily Brock. All of you. In ways I can't even put into words."

The kiss that follows tastes of chocolate and conviction, soft at first, deepening as mugs are forgotten and pulled aside. My fingers tangle in his hair, dragging him closer, desperate to feel him pressed against me. His hands map my waist with warm, steady possession, guiding me with a control that feels natural now, an extension of his dominance that makes me shiver with anticipation.

Clothes fall away piece by piece, each removal slow and intentional. He doesn't just undress me—he unveils me. His hands and lips follow each new inch of exposed skin, claiming me with featherlight touches and teasing bites that have me trembling. My bra falls away, and his breath ghosts across my breasts, lips hovering but not touching.

"Lie back," he murmurs, voice dark silk, his words both command and promise.

I lie back as instructed, the sheets cool against my heated skin. He reaches for the blindfold—soft silk he's used before—and ties it gently over my eyes.

Darkness sharpens everything: his scent, the brush of his fingers, the anticipation coiling tight in my belly. He trails his mouth from my collarbone down my stomach, lips teasing every sensitive spot he knows by heart. My breath hitches when his fingers trace the edges of my panties, slipping beneath the fabric but withdrawing before I can whimper a plea.

"Every sound you make tonight," he whispers, lips near my ear, "is mine."

The words ripple through me as he slowly removes the last of my clothes, leaving me bare under his intense gaze. He pauses, breathing deeply as if memorizing my scent, my vulnerability, my trust. When he crawls up the bed, it's with heat and intention, his body a shadow of heat and restrained power above me.

His hands skim down my arms, over my ribs, staking claim in every inch they touch. Sensation builds unbearably as he plays my body like an instrument, alternating between featherlight teasing and firmer touches that draw gasps from my lips. My back arches as his mouth closes over one nipple, teasing it with his tongue before moving to lavish the same attention on the other, his free hand exploring lower, circling, pressing, withdrawing before I can shatter.

"Not yet," he murmurs again, his restraint almost as intoxicating as the sensations he gives.

When he finally sheds his own clothing, I feel him pause, letting me sense the weight of his gaze. His arousal brushes against my thigh, thick and heavy, and the blindfold makes the moment sharper, more intimate. My breath catches as he aligns himself, pressing slowly into me, inch by inch, filling me with exquisite care.

"You're perfect," he groans, his voice strained. He presses his lips against my temple and stills, letting me adjust, his dominance now tempered with tenderness.

He moves slowly at first, setting a deliberate rhythm that has me clinging to him, every thrust perfectly angled to make me gasp his name. His hand slides between us, finding my pleasure point, circling it in rhythm with his body.

"Not yet," he commands again, sensing my nearness. "When I let you, you'll come apart completely."

The blindfold heightens everything—the drag of his lips against my throat, the bite of his teeth at my shoulder, the intoxicating sensation of surrender.

When he finally gives permission, his voice is dark velvet. "Now. Come for me."

I shatter at his words, convulsing around him as he takes me higher than I've ever been, his dominance and tenderness wrapping around me like a cocoon. He follows moments later, losing his iron control as he buries himself deep, groaning my name as his body trembles against mine.

Afterward, he removes the blindfold gently, his hands cradling my face like I'm the most precious thing he's ever touched. His lips press against my forehead, a tender, lingering kiss that makes my chest ache. He trails lower, brushing a kiss to my temple, then another just beneath my ear.

"Beautiful," he murmurs, his breath warm against my skin as his lips ghost along my jawline, slow and deliberate. Each kiss feels like a vow, a reminder of the restraint he just showed, of the control he holds even now.

He pauses at the corner of my mouth, teasing me with the faintest brush of lips before claiming me fully. The kiss is soft, unhurried, but it carries all the intensity of what just passed between us, deepening until I melt beneath him again.

We lie tangled together, his arm heavy around me, his body still thrumming with heat against mine. There's no going back—I'm his as much as he is mine, and that thought both terrifies and thrills me, leaving me breathless beneath the weight of everything unsaid.

Angel's Peak

Chapter 26

The day I've been dreading has arrived with cruel inevitability. Max leaves today.

We stand in his rented cabin, surrounded by the sparse evidence of his stay. One suitcase packed, his laptop bag ready by the door. The space already feels empty, as if preparing for his absence while he's still here.

"I think that's everything," Max says, surveying the room with his hands on his hips.

I pick up a charging cable he missed, coiling it neatly before offering it to him. Our fingers brush during the exchange, and the simple contact sends a current of longing through me.

"What time's your flight?" My voice sounds too bright, too normal for the storm raging inside me.

"Four." Max checks his watch.

Mere hours separate us from the start of an uncertain experiment of long-distance love. Video calls and weekend visits. Planning our lives around snatched moments together. My throat tightens at the thought.

Max's hands come to rest on my shoulders, his gaze serious as it meets mine. "We'll make this work."

"I know." I manage a smile that feels fragile. "It's just harder than I expected."

"Come here." He pulls me against his chest, arms encircling me completely. I breathe him in—bergamot cologne, coffee, the indefinable scent that's uniquely Max. His heartbeat beneath my ear is steady, reassuring. "This isn't an ending."

"It feels like one." The admission escapes before I can contain it.

He draws back enough to cup my face between his palms. "It's a beginning. A beginning that requires some logistics we haven't quite figured out yet." His thumb traces my lower lip. "I meant what I said about the remote workspace at Mountain Brew. That project alone will have me back here at least monthly."

"Monthly," I echo, trying to imagine the spaces between visits, the hollow days of waiting.

"For now." His voice softens. "While we navigate these early stages. But Lily—" He hesitates, unusual uncertainty flickering across his features. "I've spent my career building infrastructure that lets people work from anywhere. Maybe it's time I followed my own vision."

Hope blooms dangerous and bright in my chest. "What are you saying?"

"I'm saying that my life doesn't have to be in Silicon Valley forever. That there might be a future where Angel's Peak becomes more than just a place I visit." His gaze holds mine, serious and intent. "I'm not making promises I can't keep. This needs to unfold naturally, but I want you to know the possibility exists."

The revelation leaves me momentarily speechless. I've been so focused on managing the inevitable pain of separation that I hadn't allowed myself to consider a future where it might not be permanent.

"For now, though," he continues, "we have a three-hour drive to the airport and a goodbye to get through."

The drive passes too quickly, conversation flowing easily between comfortable silences. We avoid the subject of separation, instead discussing Mountain Brew's expansion plans, the community's response to the workspace concept, and the details of implementing his security platform. Professional topics provide safer ground than the emotions threatening to overflow.

At the airport departure area, time suddenly seems to compress. We stand beside the car, the moment of parting impossible to postpone any longer.

"This is ridiculous," I say, attempting to laugh through the thickness in my throat. "It's not forever. It's just—"

"Two weeks," Max finishes. "Sixteen days until I'm back for the official launch of the workspace."

"I'll have everything ready." I focus on practicalities, clinging to them like a lifeline. "The contractors start tomorrow on the renovations."

"Lily." Max steps closer, one hand settling warm against the side of my neck. "Stop planning and be here with me. Right now."

The gentle admonishment breaks something loose inside me. I surge forward, arms wrapping around his neck as I press myself against him. His response is immediate, arms encircling my waist, lifting me slightly as his mouth finds mine with fierce possession.

The kiss holds everything we haven't said—fear, hope, promise, need. My fingers thread through his hair, committing its texture to memory. His hands press against my lower back, eliminating any space between us. When we finally break apart, we're both breathing hard, foreheads pressed together.

"I love you," he says, the words dropping into the space between us like stones into still water. "I wasn't planning to say that yet, but it's true, and I need you to know before I leave."

Joy and terror collide inside me with equal force. "Max—"

"You don't have to say it back," he interrupts, thumb brushing my cheek. "That's not why I told you. I couldn't get on that plane without you knowing."

I swallow hard, searching for words that could possibly contain the magnitude of what I feel. "I'm falling in love with you, too," I finally whisper. "It terrifies me how quickly this happened, but it's real. More real than anything I've felt in years."

His smile transforms his entire face, relief and joy replacing the tension that had lined his features. He kisses me again, briefer but no less intense, before reluctantly releasing me.

"Sixteen days," he reminds me, picking up his bags.

"I'll be counting," I promise, forcing myself to step back, to let him go.

I watch him walk away, shoulders straight, confidence in every step despite the occasional glance back. Only when he disappears into the terminal do I allow myself to acknowledge the hollow ache spreading beneath my ribs.

The empty space of Max's absence follows me through the next week like a shadow. I throw myself into Mountain Brew, experimenting with new blends, deep-cleaning equipment, reorganizing storage—anything to keep my hands busy and my mind from wandering to the question of *us*.

True to his word, Max calls that first night from his San Francisco apartment. Our conversation is careful, focusing on his flight and the weather, avoiding the looming decision he faces. The second night is much the same. By the third, I'm beginning to accept that maybe this is our future—polite distance and gradual fading, the inevitable cooling of what burned so bright in Angel's Peak.

When Max doesn't call on the fourth night, I tell myself it's for the best. A clean break. The beginning of the end I knew was coming from the start.

Day five brings a downpour that matches my mood. The late winter rain washes away the last of the snow, turning Angel's Peak into a landscape of mud and slush. Business is slow, customers unwilling to venture out in the deluge.

I'm preparing to close early when the bell chimes, sending a spray of raindrops across the floor as Eleanor Morgan hobbles in, her silver braids darkened with water.

"Land's sake, it's coming down out there." She shakes her umbrella, sending another shower of droplets across the entryway. "You got any of that cinnamon concoction left? Need something to warm these old bones."

"Of course." I move to prepare her latte, grateful for the distraction. "Didn't expect to see you braving the storm."

Eleanor settles at the counter, her shrewd eyes tracking my movements. "Had to check on a delivery. Special order coming in for Mountain Brew."

I frown, setting her mug before her. "I didn't order anything."

"Didn't say you did." Her eyes twinkle with the mischief that's made her Angel's Peak's most notorious matchmaker. "Said it was coming in for Mountain Brew."

As if on cue, the bell chimes again. This time it's Jason from The Haven, soaked to the skin and grunting with effort as he maneuvers a large crate through the door.

"Where'd you want this, Ms. Morgan?" Jason calls, not seeming to notice me gaping at the wooden crate. "It's heavy as sin."

"Right there by the counter is fine." Eleanor sips her latte calmly, as if mysterious crates appear in my shop every day. "Careful with it, boy. That's high-end equipment."

"What is going on?" I demand, looking between them. "I didn't order any equipment."

Jason shrugs, producing a clipboard from his jacket. "Just delivering what came off the truck. Need your signature."

I sign automatically, still bewildered as Jason departs with a cheerful wave, leaving puddles in his wake. The crate sits imposingly in my shop, its top stamped with a logo I recognize immediately—La Marzocco, makers of the world's finest espresso machines. The kind I've dreamed of owning but could never afford.

"Eleanor," I begin slowly, "what is this?"

"Open it and see." She finishes her latte with a satisfied smack of lips. "Don't worry about the mess. That's why we brought it in the rain. Hard to tell what's water and what's coffee when it's all wet, eh?"

My heart thuds painfully as I locate a crowbar behind the counter. With trembling hands, I pry open the top of the crate. Inside, nestled in protective padding, gleams the copper and steel body of a custom La Marzocco—the most beautiful machine I've ever seen. A small envelope rests atop it, my name written in familiar handwriting.

I open it with unsteady fingers, aware of Eleanor watching with barely contained excitement.

For the perfect blend. Sorry, I'm late—had some business to arrange. Turn around. -M

The bell chimes a third time. I whirl to find Max standing in the doorway, rainwater dripping from his hair, his smile tentative but unmistakably hopeful.

"Special delivery," he says softly.

The crowbar clatters to the floor as I launch myself across the room and into his arms, not caring about the water soaking into my clothes. He catches me easily, lifting me off my feet in an embrace that feels like coming home.

"What are you doing here?" I ask when he finally sets me down, my hands framing his face as if to confirm he's real.

Max's smile widens. "I found a third option."

Before he can elaborate, the door swings open again, admitting the entire morning coffee crew—Ruth from The PickAxe, Darlene from Maggie's, Riley and Noah, Sheriff Donovan, and half a dozen other regulars, all mysteriously arriving at once despite the weather.

"Did we miss it?" Ruth demands, shaking her umbrella at Eleanor. "You were supposed to text when he got here."

"Just arrived," Eleanor assures her, producing a bottle of champagne from her enormous purse. "Perfect timing."

"What is happening right now?" I look around at the gathering crowd, bewildered.

Max takes my hands in his, drawing my attention back. "I'm taking a new role—Creative Director and Chief Innovation Officer—with full remote work capabilities."

Hope blooms in my chest, dangerous and sweet. "You can work from anywhere?"

"From anywhere with decent internet." His eyes never leave mine. "More importantly, I'm opening a satellite office focusing on rural tech initiatives. Turns out there's a perfect location in a small mountain town with excellent coffee."

The assembled crowd breaks into knowing chuckles.

"You're staying in Angel's Peak?" My voice comes out as a whisper.

"If that's okay with the local coffee shop owner." His smile turns suddenly uncertain. "I'm hoping she might be interested in a partnership. Professional and...otherwise."

Eleanor clears her throat loudly. "Boy, you're doing this all wrong. Show her the other thing."

Max shakes his head, a flush creeping up his neck. "I was getting to that part."

To my astonishment, he drops to one knee on the wet

floor of Mountain Brew, pulling a small box from his pocket. The coffee shop erupts in gasps and murmurs.

"Lily Brock," he begins, voice steady despite the vulnerability in his eyes, "I know this is fast. I know we've only known each other for a few weeks, but I've never been more certain of anything in my life."

He opens the box to reveal a ring unlike any I've seen—a coffee bean design in rose gold, tiny diamonds creating the impression of morning dew on the bean's surface.

"Marianne helped design it," he explains, nodding toward the town jeweler who's appeared in the growing crowd. "Said it had to be as unique as you are."

"Max," I breathe, my heart hammering against my ribs.

"I'm not asking you to marry me today." His smile is gentle, understanding. "This is a promise. A commitment that I'm all in—whenever you're ready."

The coffee shop has gone silent, every face turned toward us expectantly.

"I've spent my life coding perfect systems," Max continues, "creating order from chaos, but falling in love with you has taught me that the most beautiful things in life can't be planned or programmed. They happen in unexpected collisions, in messy, imperfect moments. Like when a distracted tech CEO crashes into a coffee shop owner and changes both their lives forever. I want to build something permanent with you, to grow together, to create our own perfect blend."

Tears blur my vision as I stare down at this man who has upended my carefully constructed world in the most wonderful way.

"Yes," I whisper, then louder, "Yes. To all of it. The partnership, the promise, the future—everything."

Max slides the ring onto my finger, then rises to capture my lips in a kiss that tastes of rain and coffee and infinite possibility. The coffee shop erupts in cheers and applause, the sound nearly drowning out my hammering heart.

When we part, breathless, Max rests his forehead against mine. "I've never been a believer in love at first sight," he murmurs for my ears alone. "But I fell for you the moment you yelled at me for spilling your lattes."

I laugh, dizzy with joy. "I distinctly recall thinking you were the most infuriating man I'd ever met."

"I'm still infuriating," he promises with a grin. "But now I'm all yours."

Eleanor clears her throat, holding up the champagne bottle. "If you two are quite finished, we have a toast to make. To new beginnings, perfect blends, and the best damn collision Angel's Peak has ever seen!"

One week later, snow falls gently outside the windows of my cottage—our cottage—as Max carries the last of his boxes through the door. The space that once felt so small now seems exactly right, filled with the mingled scents of coffee and his cologne, our possessions finding their places together as naturally as we found each other.

"That's the last of it," Max announces, setting down a box of tech equipment. "Though we might need to think about a bigger place eventually. Your coffee book collection alone could fill a library."

"You're the one with three monitors and enough cables to circle the mountain," I retort, helping him unpack. "Besides, I love this cottage."

"I know you do." He pulls me into his arms, pushing a strand of hair behind my ear. "We can make it work for now. And when we're ready for more space..."

"We'll find the perfect blend," I finish, echoing what has become our private motto.

Max smiles, his eyes crinkling at the corners. And as the

familiar fire ignites between us, I know that some combinations, once discovered, change everything forever.

Angel's Peak

Epilogue

Six Month Later

"Is the banner straight?" I squint at the hand-painted sign stretching across Mountain Brew's newly expanded storefront. The spring sunshine illuminates the fresh lettering: *Grand Reopening: Mountain Brew & Tech Lounge*.

"Perfect." Max steps back to admire our handiwork, slipping an arm around my waist. His wedding band catches the light as he gestures toward the renovated space. "Hard to believe this was just a dream six months ago."

I lean into his embrace, surveying what we've built together. The original coffee shop now flows seamlessly into the adjacent storefront, where sleek workstations and comfortable seating create Angel's Peak's first co-working space. The exposed brick walls and reclaimed wood tables maintain Mountain Brew's rustic charm while Max's technological touches—charging stations disguised as vintage fixtures, state-of-the-art WiFi boosters hidden in antique coffee canisters—blend old and new in perfect harmony.

Much like us.

"You've created something special here," Chef Hunter

Morgan approaches, champagne flute in hand. The expansion celebration has drawn nearly the entire town, the sidewalk outside overflowing with well-wishers. "Though I'm still waiting for you to implement that bean-to-cup tracking system at Timberline."

"Beta testing starts next month," Max promises. "Just need to finalize the blockchain verification component."

Hunter's wife, Audrey, joins us, her critic's eye appraising the space. "The integration is seamless. You can hardly tell where the coffee shop ends and the tech lounge begins."

"That was the point," I explain, accepting a congratulatory hug from her. "We wanted it to feel like one cohesive experience."

Max's app, now known as LocalLink, has become the gold standard for small business operations nationwide, its success surpassing even his optimistic projections. His Angel's Peak satellite office has grown from a one-man operation to a team of six, with two local high school graduates interning under Max's mentorship.

"There's the happy couple!" Eleanor Morgan's voice carries across the crowded shop as she makes her way toward us, Noah and Riley in tow. At eighty-four, she still commands every room she enters, silver braids now accented with turquoise beads that match her elaborate earrings.

"Congratulations on the expansion," Riley offers, notepad tucked under her arm even at a social event. Old habits die hard for journalists, even ones who've found their home. "Any comment for the Gazette piece?"

"Just that we're grateful to the community for making this possible," I say, squeezing Max's hand. "Mountain Brew was always about connection. The tech lounge extends that mission into the digital realm."

"Speaking of connections," Eleanor interjects with the conspiratorial tone that signals matchmaking, "have you met

Jason's new assistant? Lovely girl. Just moved from Denver. Engineering background."

Noah rolls his eyes affectionately at his grandmother. "Give it a rest, Gram. Not everyone needs your romantic intervention."

"Worked for you two, didn't it?" Eleanor retorts, nodding toward Noah and Riley. "And these two." She gestures to Max and me with a self-satisfied smile.

"You had nothing to do with us," I laugh. "We literally collided into each other's lives."

"Who do you think told Max about the cabin rental near The Haven?" Eleanor's eyes twinkle mischievously. "Coincidences take planning, my dear."

Max chuckles. "I knew it. When I called about accommodations, the reservation office suddenly had a cancellation for that specific cabin."

"I neither confirm nor deny," Eleanor sniffs primly before her attention is captured by Caleb and Harper entering with their rescue dog. "Excuse me, I need to introduce Harper to Margie's niece who just opened that wildlife photography gallery..."

As she bustles away, Max shakes his head in wonder. "That woman is terrifying and impressive in equal measure."

"She's Angel's Peak's greatest natural resource," Riley agrees fondly.

The party continues around us, the shop filled with laughter and conversation. I slip away to check on supplies, making my way to the new storage room behind the expanded counter.

Inside, I take a moment to breathe, overwhelmed by how perfectly the day is unfolding. Six months ago, I was a woman guarding her heart behind coffee machines, certain that happiness came with expiration dates. Now I'm married to the man who taught me otherwise; our business is thriving, and the collision of our lives has transformed our little corner of Angel's Peak.

"Hiding from your own party?" Max's voice startles me as he slips into the storage room, closing the door behind him.

"Just taking it all in." I gesture to the shelves stocked with beans from around the world, each variety carefully labeled with origin information—part of our new bean-to-cup tracking system that lets customers trace their coffee from farm to mug.

"Too much?" He steps closer, concern creasing his brow. "We can ask people to leave if you're overwhelmed."

"No, it's perfect." I reach up to smooth the worry from his forehead. "I'm just... happy. Sometimes it still catches me off guard."

His smile is tender as he pulls me into his arms. "I know the feeling." His lips find mine in a kiss that, even after all this time, still makes my heart race. "Have I mentioned today how much I love you?"

"Only twice. You're slacking."

"I love you, Lily Lawson," he murmurs against my hair. "More than excellent WiFi and perfectly extracted espresso combined."

"High praise indeed from a tech CEO turned mountain man." I laugh, then hesitate, suddenly nervous. "I have something for you. A gift to mark the expansion."

"You already gave me the custom router enclosure." Max raises an eyebrow, curious.

"This is... something else." I reach into my apron pocket, withdrawing a small package wrapped in coffee-bean-patterned paper.

Max unwraps it carefully, revealing a white coffee mug with black lettering. He reads the text aloud: "*Developer in Beta: Loading... 30% Complete.*" Confusion flickers across his face before understanding dawns, his eyes widening as they snap to mine.

"Lily," he breathes, "are you...?"

I nod, tears springing to my eyes. "Twelve weeks. Dr. Blake confirmed it yesterday."

The mug trembles in his hand as he sets it carefully on a shelf before gathering me in an embrace so fierce it lifts me off my feet. When he sets me down, his eyes shine with unshed tears.

"A baby," he whispers, one hand moving reverently to rest against my still-flat stomach. "We're having a baby."

"In about six months," I confirm, covering his hand with mine. "Right around Thanksgiving."

Max laughs, the sound thick with emotion. "Best launch day ever." He kisses me again, pouring all his joy and wonder into the connection between us.

A knock at the storage room door breaks the moment. "You two better not be making out in there," Riley calls teasingly. "Dominic's about to do the champagne toast."

"Be right there," Max calls back, never taking his eyes from mine. "Just one minute."

When Riley's footsteps fade, he presses his forehead to mine. "I never thought I'd have this," he confesses softly. "A home. A family. Someone to build a life with. I always thought I'd be married to my work."

"And now?"

"Now I'm living the best dream ever." His smile is brilliant.

We rejoin the party hand in hand, our secret joy a current running between us.

Dominic Mercer raises his glass in a toast.

"To Lily and Max," he begins, the gathered crowd echoing his words. "Who remind us that sometimes the best things in life begin with unexpected collisions."

As the sun sets over Angel's Peak, painting the mountains in shades of amber and gold, Max's arm encircles my waist, his hand resting protectively over our growing secret. The coffee shop and tech lounge—our first shared creation—hums with life behind us, while the future stretches before us, full of possibilities we're only beginning to imagine.

The perfect blend, indeed.

LOVE THE HEAT IN ANGEL'S PEAK?

If you're enjoying all the steamy, small-town instalove stories this mountain town has to offer, you're going to fall hard for Falling for the Firefighter

This next swoon-worthy romance serves up spice, sweetness, and a hero who knows exactly what he wants—*her*.

➡ Dive into Falling for the Firefighter

🔥 **Falling for the Firefighter**

An Angel's Peak Romance

SHE SWORE SHE'D NEVER LEAD ANYONE INTO danger again.

He swore he'd never forgive himself for the ones he couldn't save.

JOLINE "JO" MACKENZIE HIDES BEHIND HER HAND-drawn maps and a carefully guarded heart. Once a wilderness guide, one tragic wildfire changed everything—now she keeps people at arm's length, safe on paper but never in the field.

Captain Marcus "Mac" Sullivan doesn't run from fire—he commands it. Until a split-second decision cost him his best friend and half his crew. Sent to Angel's Peak on a "low-risk" assignment, Mac is here to rebuild his reputation...not fall headlong into a collision with the town's fiercest, most elusive cartographer.

Their meet-cute is anything but cute—coffee spills, maps scatter, and sparks fly hotter than any blaze. From the first touch, Jo feels the ground shift beneath her feet, while Mac knows he's found the one woman who makes him want to risk his heart again.

But when early-season wildfires threaten Angel's Peak, they'll have to face their deepest fears together. She must step back into the fire she swore to avoid. He must trust himself to lead without hesitation. And if they fail, the mountain isn't the only thing that will burn.

🤍 ONE INSTANT CONNECTION
    🤍 One sizzling, no-escape attraction
    🤍 One chance to trust love in the line of fire

IN ANGEL'S PEAK, THE ONLY THING MORE dangerous than wildfire is falling fast and falling hard.
    Dive into Falling for the Firefighter

Catch up on the Angel's Peak Small Town Instalove Romance Series Featuring the TROPES you LOVE

FORCED PROXIMITY - STRANDED TOGETHER during mountain storms
    Grumpy/Sunshine - Brooding ranger meets spirited photographer

💔 Wounded Hero - Haunted by tragic past, rebuilt by love

⚡ Instalove - Instant attraction that deepens into forever love

🌲 Wilderness Romance - Passion ignites in pristine mountain setting

🎯 Opposites Attract - Nomadic adventurer vs. rooted protector

🔥 Alpha Hero - Dominant, protective, utterly devoted

🔥 Steamy Romance - Explosive chemistry and passionate encounters

💕 Found Family - Building home together in the wilderness

📷 Career vs Love - Choosing between dreams and destiny

🦅 Shared Purpose - Wildlife conservation brings them together

🏠 Home is Where the Heart Is - Finding belonging in unexpected places

Keep current with Ellie Masters.
CLICK HERE
Receive news of her writing and new releases.

Angel's Peak

Please consider leaving a review

I HOPE YOU ENJOYED THIS BOOK AS MUCH AS I enjoyed writing it. If you like this book, please leave a review. I love reviews. I love reading your reviews, and they help other readers decide if this book is worth their time and money. I hope you think it is and decide to share this story with others. A sentence is all it takes. Thank you in advance!

Angel's Peak

ELLZ BELLZ

Ellie's Facebook Reader Group

If you are interested in joining the ELLZ BELLZ, Ellie's Facebook reader group, we'd love to have you.

Join Ellie's ELLZ BELLZ.
The ELLZ BELLZ Facebook Reader Group

Sign up for Ellie's Newsletter.
Elliemasters.com/newslettersignup

ALSO BY ELLIE MASTERS

The LIGHTER SIDE

Ellie Masters is the lighter side of the Jet & Ellie Masters writing duo!
You will find Contemporary Romance, Military Romance,
Romantic Suspense, Billionaire Romance, and Rock Star Romance
in Ellie's Works.

YOU CAN FIND ELLIE'S BOOKS HERE:

ELLIEMASTERS.COM/BOOKS

**Shop Ellie Masters Romantic Suspense and Steamy
Contemporary Romance by series.**

Angel Fire Rock Romance

Guardian HRS: Alpha Team

Guardian HRS: Bravo Team

Guardian HRS: Charlie Team

Guardian HRS: Delta Team

Cerberus Personal Security

The LaRouge Triplets

The One I Want Series

Angel's Peak Series

Billionaire Boy's Club

The Lovers

Changing Roles

Rescuing Jinx

Rescuing Maria

Bravo Team

Rescuing Angie

Rescuing Isabelle

Rescuing Carmen

Rescuing Rosalie

Rescuing Kaye

Cara's Protector

Rescuing Barbi

Charlie Team

Rescuing Rebel

Rescuing Stitch

Rescuing Mia

Jenna's Protector

Rescuing Sophia

Rescuing Malia

Rescuing Ally (Part 1)

Rescuing Ally (Part 2)

Delta Team

Rescuing Ember

Rescuing Aria

STANDALONES IN THE GUARDIAN HOSTAGE RESCUE SERIES YOU CAN READ ANYTIME

Military Romance

Guardian Personal Protection Specialists

Sybil's Protector

Lyra's Protector

Angel's Peak Series

Steamy Instalove Small Town

EACH BOOK IN THIS SERIES CAN BE READ AS A STANDALONE AND IS ABOUT A DIFFERENT COUPLE WITH AN HEA.

SNOWED IN WITH THE MOUNTAIN DOCTOR

Rescued by the Mountain Guide

Stranded with the Resort Owner

Matched with the Small-Town Chef

Trapped with the Forest Ranger

Snowbound with the Vineyard Owner

Reunited with the Hometown Hero

Colliding with the Coffee Shop Owner

Falling for the Firefighter

Wrecked with the Reclusive Author

Tangled with the Single Dad

Whirlwinded by the Helicopter Pilot

Sheltered by the Veterinarian

Bound by the Sheriff

The One I Want Series

(Small Town, Military Heroes)

By Jet & Ellie Masters

EACH BOOK IN THIS SERIES CAN BE READ AS A STANDALONE AND IS ABOUT A DIFFERENT COUPLE WITH AN HEA.

Saving Abby

Saving Ariel

Saving Brie

Saving Cate

Saving Dani

Saving Jen

The LaRouge Triplets

Asher

Brody

Cage

Billionaire Romance

Billionaire Boys Club

Hawke

Richard

Contemporary Romance

Cocky Captain

Romantic Suspense

EACH BOOK IS A STANDALONE NOVEL.

The Starling

The Swan

~AND~

Science Fiction

Ellie Masters writing as L.A. Warren

Vendel Rising: a Science Fiction Serialized Novel

If you enjoyed this book by Ellie Masters, the LIGHTER SIDE of the Jet & Ellie writing duo, and aren't afraid of edgier writing, you might enjoy reading BDSM themed books written by Jet, the DARKER SIDE of the Masters' Writing Team.

The DARKER SIDE

Jet Masters is the darker side of the Jet & Ellie writing duo!

Romantic Suspense

Changing Roles Series:

THIS SERIES MUST BE READ IN ORDER.

Command Me

Control Me

Collar Me

Embracing FATE

Seizing FATE

Accepting FATE

HOT READS

A STANDALONE NOVEL.

Down the Rabbit Hole

Light BDSM Romance

The Ties that Bind

EACH BOOK IN THIS SERIES CAN BE READ AS A STANDALONE AND IS ABOUT A DIFFERENT COUPLE WITH AN HEA.

Alexa

Penny

Michelle

Ivy

About the Author

Ellie Masters is a USA Today Bestselling author and Amazon Top 15 Author who writes Angsty, Steamy, Heart-Stopping, Pulse-Pounding, Can't-Stop-Reading Romantic Suspense. In addition, she's a wife, military mom, doctor, and retired Colonel. She writes romantic suspense filled with all your sexy, swoon-worthy alpha men. Her writing will tug at your heartstrings and leave your heart racing.

Born in the South, raised under the Hawaiian sun, Ellie has traveled the globe while in service to her country. The love of her life, her amazing husband, is her number one fan and biggest supporter. And yes! He's read every word she's written.

She has lived all over the United States—east, west, north, south and central—but grew up under the Hawaiian sun. She's also been privileged to have lived overseas, experiencing other cultures and making lifelong friends. Now, Ellie is proud to call herself a Southern transplant, learning to say y'all and "bless her heart" with the best of them.

Ellie's favorite way to spend an evening is curled up on a couch, laptop in place, watching a fire, drinking a good wine, and bringing forth all the characters from her mind to the page and hopefully into the hearts of her readers.

FOR MORE INFORMATION
elliemasters.com

facebook.com/elliemastersromance

x.com/Ellie__Masters

instagram.com/ellie_masters

bookbub.com/authors/ellie-masters

goodreads.com/Ellie_Masters

Connect with Ellie Masters

Website:
elliemasters.com
Purchase Direct:
elliemasters.com/shopify
Amazon Author Page:
elliemasters.com/amazon
Facebook:
elliemasters.com/Facebook
Goodreads:
elliemasters.com/Goodreads
Bookbub:
elliemasters.com/Bookbub
Instagram:
elliemasters.com/Instagram

Final Thoughts

I hope you enjoyed this book as much as I enjoyed writing it. If you enjoyed reading this story, please consider leaving a review on Amazon and Goodreads, and please let other people know. A sentence is all it takes. Friend recommendations are the strongest catalyst for readers' purchase decisions! And I'd love to be able to continue bringing the characters and stories from My-Mind-to-the-Page.

Second, call or e-mail a friend and tell them about this book. If you really want them to read it, gift it to them. If you prefer digital friends, please use the "Recommend" feature of Goodreads to spread the word.

Or visit my blog https://elliemasters.com, where you can find out more about my writing process and personal life.

Come visit The EDGE: Dark Discussions where we'll have a chance to talk about my works, their creation, and maybe what the future has in store for my writing.

Facebook Reader Group: Ellz Bellz

Thank you so much for your support!

Love,

Ellie

Dedication

This book is dedicated to you, my reader. Thank you for spending a few hours of your time with me. I wouldn't be able to write without you to cheer me on. Your wonderful words, your support, and your willingness to join me on this journey is a gift beyond measure.

Whether this is the first book of mine you've read, or if you've been with me since the very beginning, thank you for believing in me as I bring these characters 'from my mind to the page and into your hearts.'

Love,
Ellie

THE END

www.ingramcontent.com/pod-product-compliance
Lightning Source LLC
Chambersburg PA
CBHW021218310726

48971CB00006B/1606